D0942735

Praise for the novels of Seraphi

"A writer to watch."

—*Publishers Weekly*

"Welcome to the 'burbs...except you won't find much peace and quiet here. Brighton Hills is packed with secrets, lies, grief, and deceit, all of which make *On a Quiet Street* a brilliant and twisty tale. You'll be wondering who did what and to whom, who's telling the truth or feeding you lies, and you'll shift your allegiances faster than a tennis match. A fast-paced, highly-enjoyable and compulsive read that may well make you look at your entire neighborhood a little differently..."

—**Hannah Mary McKinnon, internationally bestselling author of** *Never Coming Home*

"A twisty thriller in the vein of *The Girl on the Train*."

—*Bustle* on *On a Quiet Street*

"Seraphina Nova Glass's twisty new thriller plunges the reader into a dark, compelling world of lies, adultery and murder. Bold, racy and masterfully plotted, *Such a Good Wife* kept me guessing from the very first page to the scorching, jaw-dropping conclusion."

—**Rose Carlyle, #1 internationally bestselling author of** *The Girl in the Mirror*

"*Such a Good Wife* hooked me from page one and didn't let go... The big reveal was both shocking and satisfying at the same time. And that ending—wow—dark in the most delicious way. Clear your calendar because once you open this book you won't want to close it until after you've read the last page!"

—**Amber Garza, author of** *When I Was You*

"In *Such a Good Wife*, Seraphina Nova Glass weaves a deliciously dark tale starring Melanie, a loving and overworked mother and wife having an affair with the handsome Luke...until he turns up dead. If you think you've figured out the culprit, think again. A sly and pulse-pounding murder mystery set in steamy Louisiana."

—**Kimberly Belle, internationally bestselling author of** *Stranger in the Lake*

Also by Seraphina Nova Glass

Someone's Listening
Such a Good Wife
On a Quiet Street

To learn more about Seraphina Nova Glass,
visit her website, www.seraphinanovaglass.com.

THE VANISHING HOUR

SERAPHINA NOVA GLASS

GRAYDON
HOUSE

If you purchased this book without a cover you should be aware
that this book is stolen property. It was reported as "unsold and
destroyed" to the publisher, and neither the author nor the
publisher has received any payment for this "stripped book."

**GRAYDON
HOUSE®**

Recycling programs
for this product may
not exist in your area.

ISBN-13: 978-1-525-81958-2

The Vanishing Hour

Copyright © 2023 by Seraphina Nova Glass

All rights reserved. No part of this book may be used or reproduced in any manner
whatsoever without written permission except in the case of brief quotations embodied
in critical articles and reviews.

This is a work of fiction. Names, characters, places and incidents are either the product
of the author's imagination or are used fictitiously. Any resemblance to actual persons,
living or dead, businesses, companies, events or locales is entirely coincidental.

Graydon House
22 Adelaide St. West, 41st Floor
Toronto, Ontario M5H 4E3, Canada
www.GraydonHouseBooks.com
www.BookClubbish.com

Printed in U.S.A.

For Sharon Bowers, my incredible agent and a pretty remarkable and kind human being.

THE
VANISHING
HOUR

1

A fist-sized lump of sour meat sits in a plastic bowl on the second-to-top stair. It must be midday because that's when, for a short space of time, thin fingers of light steal through the slits around the root cellar door and cut through the darkness like razor-thin laser beams. I open my eyes to take in the light while it's here. I can make out the shape of mops and a cleaning bucket in the corner, some old paint cans on a rotted wooden shelf, the bowl on the stairs.

I know that after nightfall, a gloved hand will replace the meat with something else; apples, or cheese, or stale pastries. Sometimes I eat. Most of the time I can't force myself up to the top of the stairs to retrieve whatever it is.

I make myself sit up, pushing my aching body from the dirt floor and onto an overturned milk crate. I blink, trying to adjust my eyes to the bit of light. I catch movement across the floor. Not human movement, but the twitch and vibration of tiny bodies moving together in one mass. There is a scratching, skittering of feet, and they disappear into the walls. A group of rats is called "mischief," I remember. It was a question at pub trivia one night. The memory of it—of life outside of this place—makes me retch. I hang my head between my knees, but nothing comes out—only a dry heave and the sound of my breath in the silence.

When the light is gone, I lay back down and wait for night when the doors will open, and the bowl of food is replaced, and I'll scream and beg to be let out, I'll plead and wail and ask "why?" until my voice is hoarse and weak, but I won't see a face or hear a voice. Sometimes I see the shadow of the hooded figure who comes, a silhouette against a moonlit backdrop crouching down to place the bottle of water and food on the stair, but never a face. My screaming does no good, and they are gone.

2

KIRA

It feels wrong to be here. The house is so silent that my ears ring. It's getting cold, and all I think about—all I have thought about in days is whether she is somewhere warm. A soft rain taps at the window, and at 10:09 a.m. it feels like dusk; the sky dark, the house lit only by the gas fireplace. I pull on an oversize cardigan and pour myself a cup of coffee before sitting in front of my laptop at the kitchen table.

I click on her Facebook page and see her face bloom onto the screen. It's the profile photo she updated the very night she disappeared—the same one that looks back at me from the stacks of missing persons fliers that fill the back seat of my car. I want to say she looks happy because I want to think of her happy on that last night. It's a selfie taken in her car. Her eyeliner is dark and dramatic, like she was mimicking a YouTube makeup tutorial but didn't get it quite right. She makes a peace sign with her fingers, her head tilted to the right. She's smiling in the photo but it doesn't reach her eyes. The caption above the post reads *About to do something wild.* What does that mean? If I knew the wild thing she was going to do, would it lead me to her? I bite at my cuticle and look around the dim room. A wineglass sits on the coffee table, a red circle congealed at the bottom where the last untouched sip evaporated over the almost five weeks I've been gone. I was drinking it the night we got the call, and then with shaky hands and forced calmness, we went into the bedroom and stuffed toothbrushes and sweaters, underwear and whatever we could remember was a necessity before rushing out the door and driving the three hours to Rock Harbor. The roads were wet, but we sped through red lights and sleepy residential streets until there were no more streetlights glistening off the rain-washed roads and we were on the black two-lane highway, on our way to her.

I reasoned all the way there. I wasn't hysterical yet. Not then. Even though my stomach felt hollow and my knees buzzed with something electric, the feeling of missing a stair, a weakness like I might collapse even though I was sitting down, I had calmed myself with reason.

Her boyfriend reported her missing, but that could mean a lot of things. Ryan is a good kid and maybe he was just being overly cautious by reporting it. Maybe they fought and she was with a friend. Maybe she lost her phone and was headed back to Boston but couldn't reach us. There were so many possibilities then. But all these weeks later, finding hope is like holding onto water. And then there—just sitting there is the glass I held when the world was still the right way round, and things made sense, and my baby girl was just staying with her boyfriend and working for the summer on the seaside. It seems impossible that the goddamn world has come to an end, and that glass still sits there like nothing happened.

I resist the urge to smash it. I take a deep breath and blow it out my cheeks, then look back to the laptop and click on the many now-familiar blog posts and missing persons sites I can update. Matt may have talked me into leaving Rock Harbor and coming back home, citing that we have done everything we can do there, but it doesn't feel right, and I don't know what else to do. "Try to get some rest" is all I am told, by Matt, the police, my father, but the notion of rest is absurd.

When I arrived home last night, I turned on the game show network to fill the silence, poured a glass of pinot, then thought better of it and dumped it down the sink, because what if she called from somewhere and needed me? I needed to stay alert and sober and near my phone at all times. I opted for ginger tea and flopped down sideways over the arm of the love seat, still with a coat and shoes on, my legs dangling over the side, and I stayed like that for a very long time.

In an attempt to keep my thoughts from going to dark places, I squeezed my eyes tight and remembered anything about her that came to mind. When she was seven and cut her Barbie's hair off so it would look like Ellen DeGeneres; the one-eyed cat named Noodle that roamed the neighborhood, and how she got up early every morning to set out food and milk for it; her Beetlejuice Halloween costume when all her friends went as slutty cats; her chipping pink nail polish, and watermelon lip gloss, and impossibly glossy hair—anything I can capture when I reach out into the dark, grasping for bits of memory or images.

Last fall when I came home and she had the kitchen covered in egg shells and white flour. I asked her why she was baking at 10:00 p.m., and she said it was because Chelsea Mulligan took her to a meditation course.

"Oh, I see," I said, eyeing the scattering of mixing bowls and rolling pins.

"Yeah, and I'm, like, super bad at it, my mind was just wandering, but not like normal stuff. There was a poster with a monkey on it, which made me think of chimps, which made me think of Jane Goodall, which made me think that although I like her, I hate the name Jane, and that made me think of the name Jane Doe, which sounds kind of stupid, and doe reminded me of dough, which made me think of pizza, and then I couldn't get pizza out of my head for the rest of the day." She smiled like this was a perfectly normal thing to say.

"And here we are," I said, dropping my bag onto a kitchen stool and shrugging off my coat. I pulled cans of stewed tomatoes out of the pantry to show her how to make sauce from scratch. We talked about meditation and Jane Goodall and nothing in particular while we chopped garlic and rolled out dough side by side, and at some point, no matter how hard I tried to stay with her, suspended in another time, a dreamless sleep took hold.

I woke up with an ache in my back from the odd position on the love seat. When I managed to get myself into a sitting position, it happened like it does every morning. Fresh, raw pain. I remember where I am, and what's happened, and a guttural howl escaped my mouth, then I realized I was here, and it was worse—the crying until my gut ached and my face swelled.

Now, two hours later, I'm trying to pull myself together and be useful. As useful as I can be from so far away. Matt's trying to be helpful, I know that—all the cups of tea and one-armed hugs around the shoulder and recited clichés filled with hopeful sentiments, but he can't possibly understand. He was a thirty-eight-year-old bachelor when I met him—a construction foreman making good money but living like a college student, still playing beer pong at house parties and doing shots of Jäger, still living in an apartment with a futon for a bed and a room dedicated to video games—the toilet paper in its original package next to the toilet instead of on a holder, no decor on the beige walls. No pots or pans in the kitchen. My father said any man over thirty-five with no divorce or kids under his belt is a commitment-phobe or some sort of pervert who probably prefers little boys to middle-aged women. Of course, he was trying to be funny, but maybe I let the words fester because I feared a grain of truth behind them. Or maybe I didn't like being referred to as a middle-aged woman. Regardless, I never forgot it.

There haven't been red flags though, and he really is trying to be a calming presence right now, which is irritating for some reason. I guess because he doesn't have kids of his own, so his well-meaning comments are often just infuriating. Things will not *be okay*, and she will not just *turn up soon*. I had to tell him to just stay in Rock Harbor a few days, pack up our stuff, clean my dad's cabin we've been staying in, whatever you need to do, just anything to give me some time alone. Now I'm regretting it. Not the time alone, the leaving the last place she was seen—like I've abandoned her.

I look at her face on her Facebook page again, and I see something new. The night she disappeared I wrote a desperate post explaining what we knew at that point, which wasn't much. I hoped one of her fifteen-hundred-odd friends, a few of whom I imagine she actually knew in real life, might be able to help. Since then, I update the post with all the facts, hoping they might trigger a friend to come forward with new information.

I explained that my father, Leo Everett, has a cabin on the lake in Rock Harbor and maybe folks know him. The rest of us frequent the cabin, and Brooke had been up there many weekends growing up, so even though she's only lived there a couple of months this summer, full-time, folks might recognize her. I don't add that she met Ryan Lambros on a family holiday a couple years ago because he spends his summers working at the docks and that's why she begged us to let her spend the summer because I'm not supposed to talk about Ryan publicly anymore because he's reported that I'm harassing him.

I also didn't say that my response to her living with him her last summer before college, instead of at home with us, was *over my dead body*, and this was followed by weeks of slammed doors, silent treatments, and screaming matches. But in the end, she was eighteen and there was nothing I could do.

I messaged each and every one of the 1,536 Facebook friends directly, cut and paste, cut and paste over and over, the same anguished words: Can you help? Brooke is missing. This is her mother writing. After sending the first few dozen I learned that I needed to add, This is not a joke. This is really her mother, Kira Everett. She was last seen on Hemlock Lane in Rock Harbor around 10:00 p.m. Any information you have might help. Please let me know the last time you spoke to her.

Almost none of them even lived in Rock Harbor. They were school friends from Boston or friends of friends who just add one another to look popular for whatever reason I don't understand. But I did it anyway in case there was a thread of a chance that it could help. Most people responded with promises of thoughts and prayers and no they haven't seen her. It's hard to tell if anyone besides Ryan is actually living in Rock Harbor. Many don't have a current city listed on their page. There were only two girls I knew for sure lived there, Emmy Katz and Melinda Harris, and they were beside themselves at the news, but said Brooke was always working and they only hung out for drinks once or twice over the summer. They knew nothing.

There were close to six hundred responses to my post on Brooke's page. Mostly the stupid little "I care" emoji, and a few dozen we love you, Brooke and come back, Brooke, but nothing now for weeks. An entire human being can just be forgotten by everyone she knew it seems once the shock wears off and the news of her missing is old and new tragedies have taken her place.

But today there is a new reaction to my post. A "sad face" emoji and then... I watch the bubbles pop up as I read the words *someone is typing a message*. Celie Hewitt writes, Omg. I can't believe this. So sad. I saw her that night too, crazy. We love you, Brooke! Please come back. I quickly click on messenger and scroll to find her name—see if she is one of the people who responded to my direct message weeks back. It shows that she never saw it. I write again now. Celie, Hi. Please respond. It says you saw Brooke the night she went missing!? Can we talk?

A ping sound as the little dot drops down showing she's read my message. My heart leaps. Then nothing. The glowing green circle showing she's online goes dark and there is radio silence on the other end. My hands tremble so violently I can barely hold the mouse to click on her profile. Shakily, I tap on her name and look through her profile page, not sure what I'm looking for. There's not much to find. Her last post was almost two months ago. It's a compilation of cat videos. One squashed into a tissue box, another purring under a running sink faucet, a few pawing unsuspecting dogs in the face. No caption. The more I scroll the more futile my search for something meaningful becomes. Just a handful of selfies, weeks apart, some motivational quote memes. A fit woman standing on a mountain at sunset with the word *if it doesn't challenge you, it won't change you* written across the crackly orange sky in the background. Some quotes about Jesus and forgiveness. Nothing very telling, nothing with Brooke. I look through her photos. Although they are sparse and relatively useless on the surface, I see clues—the sandwich board for Morty's diner boasting butternut squash soup as a special peeks out of the corner of a photo with Celie holding a paper cup of hot chocolate in mittened hands with flushed cheeks. Avery Hill Lighthouse stands by itself in a photo taken at dusk, and the unmistakable fishing docks appear in many photos—a man, probably her father, poses alongside her, wearing waders and holding up a Northern Pike. She is in Rock Harbor. She knows something. I have to go.

I choke back a sob as I run past Brooke's bedroom door and hurry down the hall. I kneel on my closet floor and shove the spilled contents of my suitcase back inside. I push my feet into red Wellies, and grab a parka on my way out the door. I should have never left. She's there somewhere—I know she is.

At stoplights, I watch the windshield wipers push autumn leaves and drizzle across the glass. I ignore two calls from Matt, but I pick up on the third, working to keep the irritation at his intrusion of my thoughts out of my voice.

"Hey, you okay?" he starts before I can say anything.

"Yeah," I start to say but the word gets stuck and I clear my throat and try again. "Fine. What's up—what's wrong?"

"Nothing. I just called to tell you I'm about to head back to Boston. I packed up the rest of the clothes and stuff you left in the bathroom, and…" He sounds almost cheerful about this.

"Why would you do that?" I snap.

"Uh…"

"Just—sorry, did you leave yet?"

"No, I was just about…"

"Leave my stuff, I'm on my way back."

"But, Kir, I have to go back to work tomorrow, I can't take

any more time—wait, why are you coming back? You've been home one night. I thought we agreed…"

"I'm not asking you to stay. I know you have work, but I need to be there. I don't wanna—I don't need a big discussion about it right now, okay. I just need to be there. I shouldn't need to explain it." I feel my bottom lip quiver and my lower lids fill with tears.

"Okay," he says softly, but I can hear the annoyance just under the surface.

"Just go home, and go to work, and I'll call when I can," I say and hang up before the gulping sobs can start, and before the argument about what's best for me and my health and safety and all the rest of it starts again too.

Rock Harbor is not a big city like Boston of course, but it's also not a small town where everyone knows one another either. It's somewhere in the middle where the Celie Hewitts of the world might get lost in police questioning if nobody knew they were in contact. I mean, I've never heard of her. She never came forward and said she talked to Brooke that night—maybe offer a clue into her mood or frame of mind, something. Did the police talk to her? Did they know she saw Brooke that night?

Asking them will get me nowhere. I need to find her myself. They are careful with what they tell me—*you'll be the first to know when we know more* is their go-to phrase now for every question I ask. Detectives Hendricks and Monohan glance at one another quite often in my presence—with a look that's a mix of genuine empathy and something else…exasperation, I think. They don't know what to do with my grief; they don't want to be burdened with it, but I suppose that's human nature even in their line of work.

I know Hendricks. Wesley. Wes, from back in high school. We shared a seat in the back of the school bus on a three-day field trip to Niagara Falls our senior year, and shared a kiss under a Mexican blanket on the long ride home. And here he is, a local detective. Never moved away, never married from what I can tell, and I wonder if he remembers our short time together, how we spent the early summer months after graduation under the sycamore tree near Bear Creek making out, telling one another we'd never leave until I packed my car for BU only weeks later for fall semester.

I wanted to wait a year before college to stay with Wes. I would have if my parents hadn't forced me to go. Should I have made her go straight to college instead of taking the year off? I was younger than Brooke is now back then, and I thought I was so in love.

It was a lifetime ago though, so maybe he's forgotten. I wonder what he must think of me now, standing here in my position. All I know is that he is the only one who can help me.

I'm told I'm the only mother who has gone door-to-door for miles around, questioning friends and acquaintances, and even strangers like a door-to-door salesman rather than letting the police "do their job." I can't sit at home wringing my hands and waiting for phone calls that don't come. I have to put fliers under every windshield and jam a foot into doors closing in my face, explaining that I'm not selling anything; I need to call Ryan over and over until the idiot tells me something useful; and I need to verbally abuse the useless detectives until they hang up on me. That is what I need to do because I just need answers. I need an answer for why she was last seen on Hemlock Lane. She promised she'd never go there. It was part of the agreement. I promised not to move into our family cabin three miles away from her and follow her everywhere she went, and show up at the apartment she was renting with Ryan every night with Scattergories and kettle corn. I would not sit in a back booth at the café where she was working and tell customers embarrassing anecdotes about her childhood until she was exhausted and mortified and forced to give up and come home. She, in turn, would follow a few simple rules: no booze, no drugs, no Hemlock Lane. Girls go missing from Hemlock Lane, especially after dark. Everyone knows that.

Her phone records are the only reason I even know she was there. Her car was not there, so she got a ride. Ryan doesn't seem to know anything, somehow. And now his parents have threatened a restraining order if I don't stop calling their son, citing that he has said everything he knows and that I am just upsetting him further in his already delicate state.

I guess it's not extremely suspect that he happened to leave town and go home, back to Maryland, at the close of the summer fishing season…just two weeks after Brooke went missing? Cops don't seem to be too concerned. He's been cleared. He was at Woody's pub with friends. Lots of eye witnesses. Leaving in the fall was always his plan apparently, but I think he's dodging my questions. There's something he's not saying, and I will keep calling him until they actually arrest me for it. Which could happen.

An hour outside of Rock Harbor, I pull off to pee at a greasy spoon called Margie's. Inside, red vinyl stools line the counter where a crumpled man sits hunched over a slice of blueberry pie. A couple of truckers share a booth and stare out the window while they poke at what's left of their breakfast samplers. An oily-faced waitress eyes me as I return from the bathroom with a look that tells me it's for customers only. I sit at the counter that appears to be made out of yellow linoleum and order a black coffee. A Journey song plays over the speakers and the utter sadness of the place is overwhelming—all green carpet and wood paneling and a mirrored wall like it's a Pilates studio. Who wants to watch themselves eat?

The waitress's name tag reads *Linda*. She sets the coffee in front of me on a saucerful of overspill. I can smell how weak and stale it is without tasting it. She hefts her considerable girth onto a stool at the end of the bar and lights a cigarette.

The sad chorus of a Journey ballad plays. The music is forcing my chest to tighten, and the stale coffee is making me nauseous. I push it away and take out my phone. I left the house in a hurry, with no plan on how to actually find Celie Hewitt, so I try and search for her further. Once Brooke went missing, I downloaded all the silly apps: Instagram, Twitter, and whatever the hell TikTok is. She was on a few of them, but no recent activity. I made the same appeal for help finding her across all these platforms and tried to learn how to use the ones I wasn't familiar with.

I google Celie Hewitt because there's nothing on Twitter or TikTok. When I search her name plus Rock Harbor, I find a few unhelpful things. She went on a mission trip to Guatemala with her church last month, her team won second place in a lacrosse game, and then a link to her Instagram page. I scroll through the images. In her most recent photo, she's wearing a T-shirt that says Daughter of the King.

"Okay, we get it already. You're all about Jesus," I muttered. "What else do ya got?" A cappuccino with the foam made into the shape of a flower. Celie with a barista apron on, smiling for the camera and pointing at the espresso she's pouring. Celie in front of… Coffee Corner, with the same apron on. My stomach flips. I leave a five-dollar bill on the counter and run to my car.

Social media is astounding. I had no idea how I'd start my search for this girl. I was just gonna start asking people and calling Ryan again until they arrested me, and… I don't even know what, but there it is. She works at Coffee Corner with Brooke. And a clue. Brooke didn't work the day she vanished.

So there was a reason for Celie to be with her besides a work shift. Maybe nothing of consequence on the surface—a party they went to, or no, maybe youth group for all I know, after seeing the girl's accounts, but since nobody knows where Brooke was and Celie Hewitt's name was never brought to my attention, it's something. It's something.

I drive the hour trip in just forty-five minutes and go straight to Coffee Corner. An uninspired name for an equally uninspired place. Not one of the cozy spots that dot the coastal towns—the ones with their walls of books, beanbag chairs by the fireplace, and mismatched tables and chairs. This place is simply a square room with a sterile feel. A glass case of pastries and a depressing dining area with art on the wall that looks like it belongs in a *Three's Company* episode or an 80s motel room.

I'd been here once to pick up Brooke after work one afternoon months ago, and then at least a half a dozen times since she went missing, asking questions and posting fliers. Of course, no one knows anything, but I'd never seen Celie. I guess she was on the mission trip last month. When I walk through the front door, a little Christmas bell hanging off the handle rings and the droopy acne-faced teen behind the counter turns and sees me. He looks around, probably searching for backup because he certainly knows who I am. I don't recall his name, but I recall asking all of her coworkers the same questions in those dizzying few days after.

"Is Celie working?" I ask.

"Uh… Hi, Mrs. Everett. Uh…" He looks around again, unsure what he's allowed to say to me, probably. "No. She only works a couple mornings before school."

"School? How old is she?"

"What do you…? I don't know. She's a senior at Edison?" he says like he's asking me the question.

"So she lives here. With her parents probably then?"

"I don't…" The boy has a monotone voice that makes me want to slap him. "Do you want to talk to Jeff…? I…" he trails off. Jeff is the manager, and no I do not want to talk to unhelpful fucking Jeff. I look at the kid's apron for his embroidered name. *Hunter.* Of course, that's his name.

"Hunter," I say with forced calmness. "It's a very simple question. If she's not working, do you know where she is? You look like you're probably a senior. Do you go to Edison?"

"Junior," he mumbles, "yeah." His eyes dart to the door when the Christmas bell rings again and he's saved by a customer. I wait. He looks at me out of the corner of his eye while the espresso machine hisses and sputters and he tries to make swirly shapes in the foam just like in the photo on Instagram, but his looks like someone spit on top rather than the signature flower I suppose it was intended to be.

When the customer leaves, he starts to wipe down the counter. I take the cloth from his hand and smile.

"Do you know where she lives?"

"I can't—I'm not supposed to give out personal…" Before I know what I'm doing, I pull a fifty out of my bag and lay it on the counter. His eyes widen. He looks from the bill to me, and back to the bill.

"I just need to ask her a few questions. You obviously know I'm not out to harm anyone, so just… Do you know where she lives?"

"Sorta, but I mean…" I pull out another fifty. I don't even know who I am right now, I feel like I'm in a mob movie all of a sudden, but I just don't have time for this. I don't want fucking Jeff coming out here and shutting the conversation down either. His mouth drops open, then…

"She's going to the bonfire on the beach with everyone else tonight, like at dusk. I don't know exactly where her house

24

is, but you should be able to find her at Castle Beach. If she's not there, her friends will know where she lives. That's all I can really tell you." I push the bills across the counter and give him a curt nod, then rush out to my car. I'm not sure why I'm rushing. I have a couple hours until dusk, but I head to Castle Beach anyway to wait.

Just a little while later around, 5:00 p.m., a few of the kids are setting up camping chairs and firewood down on the beach. The sky is still threatening more rain and it's gray and misty out. I lean against a wooden post at the top of the dunes within sight of the sandy trail leading down to the cold beach, but not close enough to alarm any of them or looking like I'm spying. It gets dark by six o'clock-ish this time of year, and teenagers are late for everything, so I don't know how long I'll be waiting. I wished I'd bought a to-go cup of coffee from the coffee shop now as I pull the hood on my parka over my ears and ignore my rumbling stomach. All I care about is answers, clues, anything.

I watch a kid with sandy bangs and ripped up jeans carry a cooler of beers down the path to the fireside, take a beer out, and sit on top of the cooler. A girl in leggings and fuzzy boots runs over and hugs him overdramatically, squealing in the way that young people do that embarrasses older people to watch. Was I ever like that?

I wonder if these kids know Brooke. She wouldn't be here right now at this bonfire party, she would have left for freshman year at BU already. These kids must still be in high school or locals at the community college. I watch a few more arrive, keeping my distance, and then I see her. I have memorized her face. Heart-shaped, prone to flushing, blond bobbed hair, little to no makeup. Always smiling. She's with a short curvy girl and they walk arm in arm, practically skipping toward the dunes. She touches her head; I hear something about forgetting her hat. She waves her friend to go ahead and starts back to her car.

When the friend is running down the dunes to the beach, I call Celie's name. She turns, a smile, her hair blowing across her face, she pushes the strands back against her head with one hand and looks to see where her name is coming from. I start to go to her. Her face falls when she sees me. She looks panicked and then…she runs.

She actually *runs* away from me.

3

GRACE

The Windmill Inn rests atop a seaside cliff on the eastern side of Rock Harbor. The curved drive in front of the inn is only steps away from the drop-off that descends to the jagged water's edge below, and behind the inn is a dense forest of pines and witch elders that are often described as eerily beautiful by guests, but scare the shit out of Grace Holloway.

Grace carries her piece of lemon meringue pie on a napkin with Hobbes close behind, supervising, making sure no crumbs are dropped. She stops at the wall of glass windows overlooking the black trees and pulls the fleece hood of her robe over her head, feeling exposed. Anyone could be watching her, except that she's safe. She reminds herself that she's safe. The inn is closed for the season, and she gets to be blissfully alone, just the way she prefers until April. No one is here.

A couple of nights earlier, there was a figure out there. She knows there was. Where did they go when they vanished from her view? She can't think about the what-ifs. She shuts down these thoughts and picks up her cup of tea. The only reason she took this job managing the inn is because it came with so much isolation and a free room. In the summer months, she suffered through checking guests in, and saying forced hellos when she passed them in the hall, but she mostly kept herself to the kitchen and let her small staff do the interacting. But now this longed-for seclusion comes with jumps and yelps with every creak of the old building. It comes with panic attacks in the night and racing thoughts—it comes with the unwelcome memories. Mostly tireless flashes about the unspeakable thing that happened in the dark.

"You're okay," she mutters under her breath, then makes a clicking noise at Hobbes, who follows her, up the echoey wooden staircase to her room on the second floor. She deadbolts the lock behind her and climbs into the crinkly down comforter. She opens her laptop and feeds Hobbes bits of buttery crust as she scrolls through Netflix to find a baking show she hasn't seen.

She wouldn't have the internet if it weren't for the inn supplying it. She doesn't want to know about kids decapitated on an amusement park ride, or school shooters, or missing girls. She can't know. She doesn't allow herself to know. It's only Netflix and Pinterest. This is the extent of her reach to the outside world. It's all she allows. She feels a little silly loving Pinterest so much. She learned of it last year when a guest named Babs, who called herself an influencer, whatever that was, showed Grace her cupcake business on the site.

She watched with delight as beautiful images bloomed on the screen, a screen full of colorful squares—a cannoli cake with ricotta filling and chocolate chips pressed around the sides, a yellow sundress with pockets, cinnamon lattes and succulent plants, DIY mittens you can make from cutting up an old wooly sweater. She immediately longed for the comfort of the happy, friendly, clickable squares, so she made an exception to her no-media rule.

Now, she cradles her sweet Jack Russell under one arm and flicks through a gallery of Moon Milk, quinoa bread, and snowball cookies. It's everything safe and soft and it's far, far away from those days in that basement. It's the only time she's not back there in her mind.

Hobbes whimpers and she kisses his nose, "You're fine," she whispers to him, or maybe to herself. Apple muffins, pumpkin seed butter, blue glitter nail polish. And then…

A hard rap on the front door. She screams, then covers her mouth with both hands as her eyes dart around the room. Hobbes leaps off the bed and barks at the bedroom door.

No one should be here. Grace grabs the hunting knife she keeps under her pillow with trembling hands and shoves it in her pocket, then she picks up the bat she keeps next to the door. It's the off-season. Nobody ever knocks after the weather turns except Vinny the delivery guy, but that's usually between 9:00 and 11:00 a.m., twice a week. Something is not right.

She clicks open her bedroom lock and peers down the empty, drafty hallway. Hobbes bounds ahead of her and runs to the front door, barking wildly at it. Grace pauses at the hall railing that looks down over the main foyer. She can't see who it is despite the slits of vertical window on either side of the grand front door. She wants to go back to her locked room and call the police, but she's even more afraid to be locked away without knowing what's happening outside. That was worse—the not knowing.

She feels in her pocket for the shape of her phone, ready to dial 911. Shakily, she tiptoes down the stairs, gripping the railing, keeping her eye on the door. Then, the doorknob starts to twist—to jiggle violently. That sound steals her breath—takes her back to that basement—what it meant when the doorknob jerked and twitched...then opened. She grips the bat and holds it out in front of her.

"Who's there!?"

4

ADEN

When he got the call, Aden was sitting in an armchair in front of his fireplace sipping sauvignon blanc that was too bitter for his taste and listening to a Vivaldi. Not the stuff used as generic classical music for a hundred movies, but the lesser known works he prides himself on introducing to people.

He wasn't relaxed though; he was angry-scrolling through his daughter's Instagram page and wondering if he needed to take her phone away again, or if this was normal fifteen-year-old stuff, and how the hell could he gauge that? Every single top she tried on at the mall last time they'd gone was a half shirt. It's as if they didn't make the bottom part of the shirt anymore. Maybe this was normal—maybe all teenage girls wear half shirts and high-rise mom jeans and caterpillar-thick eyebrows. He didn't understand it.

Just as he put down his phone and was deciding if he wanted to make it an early night, or meet Andy and Seth at The Grove for a pint, his phone rings.

"Ma?" he answers, confused because she's usually in a robe and house slippers by 8:00 p.m. watching *Sister Wives* or *The Long Island Medium* or whatever the hell happened to be on her favorite channel, and she didn't like interruptions.

"Oh, honey," she whimpers into the phone. Aden sits up, sharply, his heart speeding up.

"What? What's wrong?"

"It's your dad," she says, as if she's trying to torture him with half sentences and partial information instead of telling him what's actually happened.

"It's fine. She's overreacting," another voice says. His brother. His parents' place is the only house on the planet that still has a landline, and not just one, but multiple, still with the long, stretched-out cord. He knows his mom will be standing in the kitchen, twisting the mustard-colored coil in her fingers and pacing, and his brother—his grown-ass thirty-two-year-old moochy brother—will be in his own childhood bedroom, smoking a Lucky Strike on his twin bed and listening in on the phone call because he has nothing else to do with his life. The thought of this is at once comforting and nostalgic and also infuriating because he can't get a straight answer.

"Overreacting about what?" Aden asks.

"He's missing," she says.

"What?" Aden answers with a hint of a laugh in his voice because it's absurd.

"Listen," Brady says, and Aden hears the telltale inhale of smoke, then the sharp exhale. "Old men don't go missin'. Teenagers go missin'."

"He's been playing cribbage at the Eagle and gin rummy nights with the guys," his mom interrupts. "What if he had too many scotches and passed out in a ditch or got hit by a car. What if he had a heart attack and is in a hospital somewhere? You know he can't really drink very much… What if—" She stops to try to gather herself, and he hears her hiccupped sobs muffled by a handkerchief, no doubt the one she keeps in her cardigan pocket with the letter *P* embroidered on it for her name, Penny. Aden is suddenly relieved because it *is* absurd and it's very unlikely there is cause for real alarm here.

"Well, did you call the hospitals?" he asks.

"Yes!"

"And he wasn't there."

"No! But that's even worse, 'cause he could have been kidnapped or mugged."

"Ma," Brady's voice chimes in again. "He wasn't kidnapped."

"He could be. Oh, God. He—anything could have…"

"There's no ransom, Ma. You kidnap an old man, you don't sex traffic him, right? What do you want? Ya want money. That's what ya want."

"Oh, my God," Aden mumbles under his breath and looks at the ceiling, shaking his head. He tries to have patience with Brady. He's proud of him for kicking the meth and all the rest of it. But he's turned into a cliché, coffee-guzzling, chain-smoking thirty-something full of conspiracy theories and living in his mother's basement, and it's a struggle to get along.

"Don't oh-my-God me, it's logical, ain't it? You ain't here, so how do you know anything?"

"Really?" Aden says. "You're gonna start this right now?"

"Boys. That's enough," their mother says in that tone that communicates simultaneous firmness and disappointment without a raised voice.

"He probably went fishin', and you forgot he told you. Again. C'mon—" Brady says.

"Then why won't he answer his phone?"

"Tell me exactly what happened," Aden says.

"Well," his mother begins, "he said he was going to get a beer with Levi after their ministry last night, and he never came home. That's it. It's been almost twenty-four hours now." Aden knows Levi. He's a deacon at the church with his father. Every Friday some of the church leaders get together for Bible study and then volunteer as part of the church outreach program. They'd spend a few hours at a nursing home or even a prison sometimes, or go door-to-door handing out tracts, inviting people to church. Although Aden finds it presumptuous and heavy-handed and considers himself an atheist these days, he respects the selflessness of it, sort of. Martin Coleman was not a man who had too many drinks or passed out in a ditch or got himself into trouble. He was a man who invited people to church and called home if he was gonna be late. Penny Coleman *was,* however, a woman who tended to… worry. He's sure Brady's right and she simply forgot that he told her he was off to go fishing or to Lenny's cabin for the weekend. Something.

"Get off the phone, sweetheart. I'm talking to your brother," Penny says.

"Ma. Aden doesn't need to come home for this. That's all I'm saying. C'mon."

"What did the police say? Did you call them?" Aden asks.

"Of course, but they said it wasn't twenty-four hours yet and I said but it's not like him, and they asked what happened, and I says he went to hand out church fliers and then for a drink with Levi… The officer says *a drink?* all judgy, and I told him we were Lutherans, not Quakers, and yeah, they got a beer and then he never came home and that's all I know. They took down the information, but didn't sound like they took it seriously. Oh, honey." Penny starts to cry. "Something's very wrong here."

"Ma, it's okay. Don't cry, I'll—" Aden starts to say softly, but she interrupts.

"Nobody's seen Harry Flynn in days either. What if there's a serial killer?"

"Ma, Ma..." Brady says, letting out a long exhale of smoke. "Harry Flynn has a zillion dollars and disappears all the time, right? Right. And why? Because he's getting college girl ass on his yacht anytime he wants. I'd disappear for a couple weeks too. Duggy Spencer was on it once. Says it has a fuckin' margarita machine. Excuse my French, Ma. Sorry."

"Brady, that's inappropriate," she says.

"I know. Sorry, just sayin' though."

"Honey, please come home. We need you to help us find him," Penny says, stifling a sob. Aden bites his cheek and looks at the ceiling.

"Leah's coming home for the weekend, and I..."

"Oh, bring her. She should be here too. This is a family problem. We should all be here." This is not a family problem though. The whole reason he sent Leah to private boarding school is to get her away from the cruel and shitty real world for a while and make sure she's somewhere safe with rules and dress codes—with limited access to social media and curfews enforced by a large semi-armed guard named Martha. The last thing he plans to do is drag her into this.

It's only been two years since her mother's accident, and then over the summer, all the shit she got herself into. She's finally where she needs to be, and what it took to get her there...to literally drag her there? He's not exposing her to Brady's Armageddon theories and pervy friends and certainly not whatever shit show news about his father could turn into.

"Mom, why don't we give it…" But despite all of that and before he can make the excuse, he already knows he'll go.

"Please, honey. We need you home," she says, and he takes a deep breath and blows it out, away from the phone, through pursed lips.

"Okay," he says. He won't mention Leah not coming until he shows up and then lies about her wanting to stay at school with her friends, but he knows she won't be happy to stay and dreads the call to tell her.

Aden dumps his glass of wine down the sink, then goes into the bedroom and turns on the bedside lamp. He tosses a suitcase on the bed, then opens drawers and starts to pull out clothes mindlessly. Should he be worried? How many times has his mother forgotten that his father was at the cabin or on a fishing weekend? Of course, those times he answered his phone. Then again, rural Maine is spotty with reception so it's understandable he might not. Shit, he could have dropped his phone in a lake, bent over to reel in a bass for all anyone knows. This is a bit ridiculous. There is probably a 90 percent chance this is nothing. But still, something prickles underneath the surface of Aden's skin—a feeling like something bad is going to happen…again.

He thinks about his father—his Old Spice and bad haircut, his khaki trousers with the elastic band, his love for cribbage and college football, his comb-over and kind eyes. His sweet father. What if something really did happen?

He throws his clothes in with greater speed. He'll go right away, but he'll be damned if he's staying on a pull-out sofa bed in Brady's bedroom though. His own childhood room was converted into a storage area (because you can't call it a hoarder room) years ago, and he refuses to be kept awake from the background sounds of men being shot and slaughtered in Brady's *Call of Duty* video game until 4:00 a.m. Aden sits on the bed. He turns off Vivaldi and the silence rings in his ears. He second-guesses himself for a few minutes, then pulls on a coat and wheels his bag to his car. He has to go.

The night is still, and the air has a sharp edge, almost winter but not quite. A campfire is burning somewhere and Aden cracks the window to take in the smoky scent. Should he text Leah, or call? Of course, he knows the answer. He tells his car's Bluetooth to call her, and waits, hoping he can leave a message and then when she calls back, she'll have had time to absorb that he's not bringing her home this weekend—for the first time since he forced her into this school in the fall. She answers with the usual tone in her voice—like she's already bored of the conversation before it's even started.

"Hey," she says.

"Hey there, sweetie, how are you?"

"Oh, God, what's wrong now?" she says.

"What do you mean? Nothing. I..."

"You have that weird high-pitched thing you do when something is wrong," she says.

"No. I'm just calling to see how things are—how classes are."

"Stupid, but you already know that," she says, and he wonders if he should be honest about his father or lie. Would she hear it another way and be even more upset? Rock Harbor is not a big place. It's not a small town by any means, it's not like everyone knows each other, but word does tend to get around. Although he's in Hartford and she's at school in Westford, not Rock Harbor, she has friends and Twitter and all the rest of it and if this is actually a real thing—a serious thing—he should probably tell her.

"So, I'm headed to your grandparents' house, and it looks like I won't be able to bring you home for the weekend. I'm sorry... I..."

"What?"

"I know…"

"What the fuck, Dad? You promised. This is so typical. It's like you just left me here to rot, like you actually hate me or something."

"Lee, that's—look, your grandpa…he's—they can't find him," he says and there is a moment of silence on the other end.

"What does that mean?"

"They're reporting him…well…missing."

"They who?"

"Your grandma and Uncle Brady. But look, I'm sure it will be—"

She interrupts him. "Oh. My. God. Like that *48 Hours* show missing? Like *Forensic Files* real-life shit missing? Like he's actually missing-missing?" Aden can't tell if there is amusement or panic in her voice.

"You know, he probably just lost his phone and went fishing for the weekend like he does a lot. It's nothing to worry about right now, but I need to go be with Grandma and just make sure…"

"So, I should go too. He's my grandfather."

"I know. I know that, but listen. It was an immediate thing. You have classes tomorrow still, and I'm already on my way." There is a long silence and Aden can hear something like a sharp intake of breath—like she's probably crying. He feels sick about this. For a moment, he wants to tell her he'll come and get her, but it will just be more trauma—a hysterical grandmother, and what if police come to the house, and…no.

"That's really shitty," she says and now he knows she's crying but trying to hide it.

"I will make it up to you and sign you out the whole Thanksgiving week next month, a ten-day weekend."

"Yeah, sure," she says and then she's gone. He looks at the phone, confirming she's hung up, and then throws it hard on the floor of the passenger's seat.

"Fuck!"

He drives the next forty minutes in silence, going over every possible scenario that could explain his father's absence. He's not going to call it disappearance. He didn't even ask about his car—was his car missing? Could the phone company look at his location—his phone records or does that take a police order? Does it take a long time to do like he's heard? Has his mother called all his friends, their wives? What if he's in a ditch or went off a cliff on his way home? He doesn't see well at night. Aden feels panic begin to rise in his chest. He takes a deep breath and tells himself to be reasonable. There is very likely a reasonable explanation.

As he arrives in Rock Harbor, he drives around, contemplating going to his mother's house, trying to tell himself it won't be that bad, but between the cat litter smell lingering in the air, the mess, and the haze of cigarette smoke, he just cannot. He's going over the motel options in his mind when he sees his phone light up from the floor. He pulls over and stares down at the bright screen flashing a silver alert. Martin Coleman's face fills the frame. His mother was wrong; the police did take it seriously. And now this is really happening.

5

KIRA

"Celie!" I call after her and start to run to catch up with her before she can get to her car. Why the fuck is she running from me?

"Stop. I just want to—what the hell? I'm just trying to ask you a question!" I scream into the wind, but she doesn't turn around. When we reach the sand parking lot, she beeps her door locks open and rushes inside, slamming the door behind her. I leap onto her hood and she screams. She cracks the window.

"This is a Land Rover! You can't sit on the hood. What the hell is wrong with you?" She starts the engine.

"Okay," I say, hopping off, pulling my phone from my pocket and snapping photos of her and her license plate.

"What are you doing, you psycho?" she screams.

"You answer a couple of simple questions and I don't call the police and tell them about the underage drinking going on. I'm sure your unsuspecting friends down there would be very unhappy with you if the cops showed up. And your parents…if they knew you were drinking and driving." I nod to the red solo cup in the console, taking the chance it was some fruity vodka drink. She folds her arms across her chest and looks away from me.

"What?"

"First of all, why are you running from me? You obviously know who I am then?"

"Because I don't want to get involved. Nobody does."

"Nobody? What the fuck does that mean?" Her eyes widen. I forgot she was all Jesus-y, probably not used to adults swearing. I appeal to this. "You don't want to get involved in helping find your missing friend? Really?"

"She wasn't my friend," she says with a snotty edge to her voice.

"On Facebook she is, and you made a comment *we love you, Brooke.*"

"That's what you say when someone is dead or missing, right? You don't wanna look like the only asshole who doesn't care."

"That post about her missing has been up for weeks. Why now? Why comment all of a sudden?"

"No offense," she says, picking up the solo cup and taking a drink, "but Facebook is for old people. I never check it. I don't even know why I have it. I was bored at Coffee Corner and was on my phone, I just saw it." She looks at me, defiantly "Is that all?"

"No."

"You said a couple questions. I answered a couple. I need to get back to my friends." She doesn't make an attempt to start the car to leave or open the door to go back to her group. I know I have her.

"Why don't you want to be involved? Even if she wasn't your friend, why wouldn't you want to help if you could?" I say, trying to keep my voice steady, resisting the compulsion to grab a handful of her hair and smack her head into the steering wheel to wipe the self-righteous smirk off her face and fix the flippant way she is talking about *my daughter.*

"Because they're not the sort of people I want to be associated with, okay? I don't want anyone to think I was like them, her and her…ugh…her boyfriend, or hung out with them, I didn't. Eew."

"Like them? Like what? What does that mean—what do you mean?"

"Uhh. Like meth heads," she says, her head cocked to the side, a curl in her lip. I can't escape the involuntary laugh that escapes my lips.

"You know I'm Brooke's mother, right?"

"Uh. Yeah. So, you really don't know that Brooke and Ryan are total junkies? I guess she's like a stripper now too. We used to be friends but none of us—" she gestures vaguely to the direction of the beach where her friends are "—are into that, so nobody wants to get involved, like I said. Like if some pimp took her or something, why would we want our names anywhere near that? He could come for us next."

"What?" I gasp.

"Plus, I don't know anything. They already asked all of us. The police I mean." I can feel my mouth hanging open, and I am somehow paralyzed by the words coming out of her mouth. Out of the corner of my eye, I see her friend climbing back up the sand dune.

"Brooke would never touch a drug. You're out of your mind."

"Okay. Yeah, I'm sure you're right." she says, opening her driver-side door. I back up, still in shock. She slams it and pushes past me, running to her friend, then past her.

"Come on, Jenna!" she demands, then she's down the dune and out of sight. Jenna stares at me a minute, confused. I walk toward her. She looks behind her, instinctively for Celie, looking for an explanation probably—why is this grown-up here, and is she going to turn us in? She's ready to run, with panic in her eyes.

"Wait! It's okay. I'm Brooke's mom. I just came to ask Celie a question, see if she might help me find her."

"Oh. Oh, my God. I'm so sorry about what happened. I heard."

"You know Brooke...and Ryan?"

"No, I've like seen her. I mean Ryan is Celie's ex, so I just know about Brooke through her, but still. I mean I feel so bad for her. So scary. It could happen to any of us, right? Crazy."

"Jenna!" a voice comes from the beach. She gives a tiny apologetic wave and runs down the dunes.

I feel more lost than I did before I came here. Ryan is her ex. That explains something. So, is that motive to lie about Brooke to make her look bad? It has to be. But if she can spew that venom about Brooke and her instinct is to *run* from me, what if there's more to this?

I think of the *Dateline* episode where a teenager's two best friends lure her to the woods to brutally murder her over... what? I don't even remember, that's how insignificant it was— nothing—petty jealousy, a boy? I rush to my car, shaking away the dark thoughts. I need to stay levelheaded. I need to find Ryan.

I start driving around Rock Harbor. Ryan has ignored my calls for days. I have called at least two hundred times and it goes to voice mail. I've left a dozen messages. I'd leave more but don't want him to file some sort of harassment claim. He was cleared. I mean, he was essentially patted on the back and given a free pass by the police. I can't force him to talk to me. Unless I physically force him somehow or blackmail him, which I sort of just did to Celie, so maybe there is a way to do it again, and I'm not above trying but I need to find him first.

I drive the familiar narrow two-lane roads along the cliff-side and down into the main street of shops and bakeries and bars—all the restaurants we have been to a dozen times—Keen's Steak House, City Vineyard, The Eggsnest. It all looks the same as it always has. I don't know what I'm even looking for anymore—a miracle maybe. Someone has to know god-damn something though.

I drive to Hemlock Lane where she was last seen. Locals call it the Seedy Strip, or Stripper Street, or just The Strip. Brooke called it Hooker Highway once and laughed at her own clever wordplay. We were driving on an August night from our cabin to Easy Sweets to get a red velvet cake for Matt's birthday. A girl with booty shorts showing half her ass came into the shop and on the way home she made the comment. I don't remember exactly what it was—something about the girl though, and "Hooker Highway."

I wish I'd paid attention. Did she say she'd seen her before? Was she giving me a clue that she knew that area, or just being a catty teenager and making a jealous comment about the girl because she could pull off the shorts? I don't remember.

My girlfriends and I went to the strip clubs in our twenties for fun. There was nothing wrong with that, but that was a long time ago when it felt benign and careless—before it turned into a sex-trafficking meth hub. So, it's been very hard for me to reconcile what I know of my daughter and how it's possible that this was the last place she was seen.

I pull into a convenience store called Lucky's. I've been

here a dozen times in the last month. Because what was she doing here? What earthly reason would she have for being on this shit side of town with nothing but hookers and strip clubs and liquor stores?

The clerk that night sold her a Diet Dr. Pepper and a bag of Chex Mix. Her entrance and exit were caught in a grainy video from the camera outside the front door, and that was the last time anyone reported seeing her. It was just before 10:00 p.m. Of course, the clerk was seen on the surveillance camera until his shift ended at 5:00 a.m., so he wasn't a suspect. Ryan said he was out with friends until two o'clock, passed out when he got home, and reported her when he woke up the next morning—his alibi was supposedly tight because the friends vouched for him. That's not an alibi unless you live in Rock Harbor and your dad's a retired police sergeant. What if they were all involved?

It's dark now, and a cold drizzle taps at my windshield. I stare down the street which I am now, against my will, familiar with. Two women stand outside the strip club a few doors down, lighting cigarettes and hopping up and down from the cold. A pink neon sign blinks The Landing. One woman has a puffer coat draped over her shoulders and the other wears cat ears and white knee socks that match her kitty themed G-string and pasties. She yells something, impatiently, to the bouncer inside the door who hands her a man's suit coat that she covers up with.

I don't recognize these two—I feel like I've talked to everyone on this strip by now, but on the other hand, it's an endless stream of strangers with no information all at the same time. I jump out of the car and rush over to them, desperate for new information. The kitty-themed dancer clutches her borrowed coat and takes a step back. The other one with ponytails and blue eyeliner puts her hand on her hip and squares off in front of me, as if she's inviting a fight and isn't afraid to take the first swing.

"Uh-uh!" she says, waving her index finger with a pink, clawlike nail attached to the end of it.

"I'm sorry?" I stutter.

"Ain't nobody seen your husband, ain't nobody fucked your husband, and ain't nobody stole your pervy-ass husband, so just—"

"No, please." I hold up a photo of Brooke. "My daughter. She's missing. She was last seen just there." I point to where my car is still running with the driver's door open in Lucky's parking lot. "It was just over a month ago. Do you recognize her? Did she...come here?"

"Oh, honey," the cat-eared one says. She takes the photo and looks. "Oh."

"What? Oh, what?" I ask desperately. The ponytail woman speaks.

"It's just that there are posters up all over the block about her. Sorry. No, I would have called the number if I'd seen her."

"Right. Okay, thanks."

"Girls come down here after dark and they ain't seen again. Can't keep track of them," Cat-ears says, and I tense and turn to go.

"Sorry, hun. That's just awful," one of them calls after me as I walk numbly to my car. When I near the parking lot, I see a box truck with puffs of smoke pluming out of the exhaust pipe across the street at Coastal Grocery. The place has a little eat-in area in the front of the store, but mostly they deliver food and beer to a lot of the local hotels and restaurants. Every time I've been here I've only been able to speak to Giovanni, who runs the deli counter and speaks little English, but I understand that whoever else works there is always out on deliveries.

I watch a tall scrawny figure close the door on the back of the running box truck. He seems to freeze when he senses me looking at him. He turns his head my way and I hold up my hand to get his attention. He looks down, shoves his hands in his pockets and walks quickly around the trailer toward the driver's door.

"Hey!" I yell, waving my hands at him. He doesn't look back; he just jumps into the truck and shifts it into gear.

"Hey!" I scream now, but he starts to pull out of the lot. I jump in my car and tear out of the Lucky's lot to follow him. He turns left and drives off too fast for the busy two-lane street, but I keep up. *He didn't see me*, I tell myself because the idea that everyone seems to be literally running from me instead of helping is too overwhelming to absorb.

He runs a red light. He did see me. He's running. I plow through the light right behind him, determined to catch him. Why the hell is he running?

6

GRACE

Grace watches the doorknob jiggle, paralyzed in fear. Hobbes scratches at the door and growls. Someone is trying to get in.

"Who's there!? I'm calling the police!" Her heart pounds in her throat and her hands tremble.

"Whoa," a man's voice says. "My name's Aden. I'm just looking for a room. Why are you calling the police, exactly?" She feels a surge of relief. The man doesn't sound like someone trying to kill her or abduct her. The noise she heard in those woods the other night—the figure she saw—it's not a threat. She's safe, she reminds herself. She's overreacting.

"We're closed," she says firmly.

"You're not closed until November."

"I'm sorry?" she snaps.

"November first. I know, I'm from here." He's technically

right. She puts up the closed sign after Labor Day because all the tourists are gone by then, and she gets the glorious winter months all to herself. No one has ever challenged this before, but she needs to keep this job. She desperately needs to keep the only job that offers her this solitude. She can't be overtly rude or combative with this guy. She's been talked to about this by the owner before. Still, she tries to get rid of him.

"Why do you need a room if you live here?"

"I don't—I said I'm from here, I don't… It's pouring rain. Could we possibly discuss this inside?" She peeks out the side window and he gives a curt nod hello, holding his coat tightly around himself. She swallows, feels her palms sweat at the sight of this tall sandy-haired man on her doorstep. Then she shakes it off. He forces a tight smile as she reluctantly clicks open two deadbolts and a chain lock and opens the door to him. He steps inside and Hobbes nips at his legs.

"Stop. It's okay. Sorry." She picks him up and strokes his head. "So…? Sorry, why exactly *were* you trying to break in like a psychopath?" she asks him, taking a few steps back, still uncertain and ready to use the knife shoved in her waistband if she needs to. But he only smiles at this.

"Break in? You're a public establishment. I was trying to enter your lobby? To book a room?" She feels a little bit stupid, caught up in the shock of it all. It was a ridiculous thing to ask—of course, he wasn't breaking in. Still, she tries to hold her ground.

"You don't have a reservation, so…" she says, intent on being rid of him. He looks around the empty dark lobby.

"Oh. I didn't realize. I guess you're booked." She just stares at him, arms folded.

"What's the problem, exactly?" he continues.

"The problem is that nobody stays here after Labor Day. Why are you here?"

"Is it normal for you to ask your customers why they need a room? Ethical? Seems a little weird. Maybe I should be the one asking you why you wouldn't just let a paying customer get a room without the third degree... I mean, since you're open until the first and all," he says, and she chews her bottom lip and places Hobbes on the floor. She walks behind the front desk in the corner of the lobby and she can feel him watching her—her pronounced limp with every step. She turns to look at him, and he looks down at the floor. She wakes up the computer and taps at it, the clicking sounds she makes with her fingertips echo in the empty room.

"Aden what?" she asks.

"What?"

"What?"

"I don't know, what are you asking?"

"Your last name."

"Oh. Coleman."

"And you're from here, Aden Coleman?"

"I live in Hartford now," he says and gives his address and credit card. She plugs in the information and notices him taking in the room—the midnight blue crushed velvet couches in front a of a grand fireplace, the oversize windows dressed in silky drapes and the baby grand piano and dim lamp light that makes it cozy and inviting. Most guests think it's romantic, but Grace has never given romance any thought, so she just smiles and nods when the guests gush over it all.

"My dad used to bring us here when we were kids. It didn't look like this," he says. She knows he means it's come a long way since the 1970s orange decor it was suspended in for decades, but she won't give him an inch.

"Is it not up to your standards?"

"That's not what I meant."

"Okay then." She holds out a brass key attached to a small leather loop.

"How quaint," he says, looking at it in surprise. Everyone expects a plastic card key, but that's part of the charm of the place. She doesn't respond. She clicks off a couple of lamps on the check-in counter and begins walking away—painfully aware of her awkward gait.

"Room 328. Breakfast is included, as you probably know. 7:00 a.m., otherwise I'll leave a plate and you can heat it up later. Checkout is at eleven."

"I'll be staying at least a few days, could be longer," he says, stopping her at the base of the stairs. She tenses but doesn't turn to him or argue this point.

"Good night," she says, and then calls for Hobbes and climbs the stairs to her room.

At 6:00 a.m., Grace brews a pot of coffee. She could leave him a bran muffin and banana, and he probably wouldn't complain about it or report to her superior that he wasn't offered the homemade breakfast promised with each stay, but cooking is one of her only joys in life. She taught herself everything she knows through cookbooks and Pinterest recipes, and so she decides to treat him like any other guest, still hoping he'll leave as soon as humanly possible and hoping he doesn't show up at seven o'clock so she can leave the plate and be left alone.

She poaches a few eggs and panfries thick slices of sourdough bread in a cast-iron pan. Then she stirs yolks and lemon into her hollandaise sauce and roasts the asparagus. She feeds Hobbes a slice of bacon and pours herself a cup of coffee, ready to wait two more minutes before she can take her coffee and breakfast back to her room when she hears footsteps echoing down the hall at exactly 6:59 a.m.

"Shit," she says, louder than intended. When Aden appears in the doorway, clean-shaven and smelling of woodsy cologne, her eyes linger on him a moment before she brings herself to speak.

"Morning."

"Morning," he says with a wide smile. "Smells amazing." She pushes a plate toward him. "Wow, thank you."

"Have a good day," she says, picking up her mug and moving toward the arched doorframe leading back to the lobby.

"Wait," he says, and she pauses and turns. "Do you have a few minutes?" She looks around, involuntarily turning her head slightly to each side, as if there is anyone else there he could be talking to, but still not convinced he's addressing her. It brings back a flash of middle school, and she feels more uneasy than she already had.

"Ahhh, yeah. Of course," she says dutifully and sits on the counter stool across from him at the kitchen island. Hobbes scratches Aden's leg in hopes of a bacon slice, and he looks down amused and pets him.

"Sorry."

"It's okay," he says, then to the dog, "You don't have a collar, buddy. What's your name?"

"He doesn't need a collar because he doesn't leave the property. And his name's Hobbes." She signals for Hobbes to go lay down. Sunlight streams through the crack in the drapes and he curls up in a long patch of sun on the floor of the old farm kitchen.

"So is there something you actually wanted to ask?" she says.

"Does the name Martin Coleman ring a bell for you at all?" he asks.

"No. Should it?"

"Well, you live here, so I thought you might have heard."

"Heard what?"

"That he's gone missing. There was a silver alert last night, and then…"

"A what, sorry?"

"Like an Amber alert, but for older people. Then it was on the local news, so I don't know…"

"I don't watch the news."

"Okay, well. Never mind."

"Oh. God. Coleman. So related to you then?"

"My father. Yeah."

"Oh, I'm sorry. That's why you're here," she says, feeling a momentary tenderness for him and a twinge of guilt for making things harder for him than they already are.

"Yes. It is. I'm helping my family look for him. I mean, I will be. I'm headed to my mom's place in a bit."

"So, you're not staying with…your family who lives here?" she asks.

"That's a no then?" He changes the subject. "Nobody has been talking about this—you haven't heard any gossip, anything?"

"Hobbes doesn't leave the inn because I don't leave the inn, and nobody has stayed here in weeks, so, no. Sorry." He doesn't ask her why she doesn't leave like she expected; he just gives a nod, picks up his fork, and takes a bite of runny egg.

"I wish I could be of more help," she says, but a wave of nausea makes her stomach lurch. She sees the word *missing* in her mind, spelled out on a poster every time she hears it—bold letters. She sees her own young face on the poster and bits of fractured memory come to her, unwanted, just flashes out of order—a dirt floor, yellow zip ties, dust particles floating in a sliver of sunlight coming through a crack in the soiled sheet covering the egress window, silence. Days of silence.

She has trouble walking at a normal pace, let alone quickly, so she turns her back to him, her hands clutching the sides of the kitchen sink for just a moment as she swallows down the bile rising in her throat. She takes a deep breath and looks up at the ceiling as she blows the air out, slowly through pursed lips. *You're okay*, she tells herself.

"Are you from here, then?" he asks. He hasn't noticed anything is wrong. He just eats a triangle of toast and scrolls through his phone.

"I hope you find him. Have a good day," she says. He looks up with raised eyebrows, surprised, she supposes, at her abrupt end to the conversation. Then she taps her leg, quietly, to arouse Hobbes's attention, and he follows her out of the kitchen and upstairs.

She limps slowly down the creaky hall floor to her room and sits on the edge of the bed with her head between her knees, trying her best not to throw up. Missing, abducted. People taken, people kept. She can't do this. She can't have him here. She's spent the last several years alone, avoiding people as much as she can, never leaving the inn, never inviting in news or the outside world and staying safely off the grid for the most part, surrounded by Pinterest images of pot roasts and nice tourist couples looking to see the lighthouses and go canoeing and talk about lobster and maple syrup. This has been her full-time job—to remain in the very small world she's created for herself. And *he's* ruining that. He's bringing it all back. She runs to the bathroom and throws up in the sink.

7

ADEN

Aden takes his time driving to his mother's house. He stops at Coffee Corner and sits at a two-top bistro table near the front window and watches people pass by—a woman from the salon next door steps outside with rollers in her hair and taps at her phone while she smokes a cigarette. A man with a small mushy-faced dog watches it pee on a bag of trash set out on the curb. He hates this town and he's not sure exactly why.

Maybe it's just the childhood memories that have been long forgotten until he steps foot back in town and is reminded of…what is it exactly? The loneliness, he supposes. The girl who broke his heart and how he made a fool of himself, crying, begging for her back senior year, the long winters spent in his room with his GI Joes and picture books as a kid, nowhere to go, few friends because he was shy, and too sensitive, his parents said. The square brick high school makes him shudder every time he drives by, and not for any life-altering reason—he wasn't bullied. He didn't eat his lunch alone in the bathroom like Randy Stevens, just to avoid the mean kids and being seen sitting all alone at the lunch table in the corner. He was just deeply unhappy for intangible reasons. Nothing ever seemed right here.

He orders a blueberry bagel with cream cheese from the teenager asking him if he'd like anything else. He can't believe how young she looks—too young to have a job. Way too young for the tiny shirt she's wearing. Was he ever that young? It seems impossible. It's almost ten o'clock, and his mother will start calling if he doesn't show up soon, but he needs a little more time to put aside his annoyance before he sees his mother.

He's on sabbatical for the semester, and he's supposed to be writing a book. He should be spending time with his daughter; he should be doing just about anything else besides enabling his mother's paranoia, but he can't say no to her. She's arguably the kindest woman who ever lived, and now, in the light of day, the more he thinks about it, the more he knows there is a rational explanation for his dad being away a couple days. If he leaves her with Brady and his batshit theories, this will escalate and she could end up with another breakdown and, goddamn it, he just has to go in and quash it. A day or two and then home, he tells himself.

He orders an Americano, cream, no sugar, to go and drives down Main until it turns into a no-name road that leads to his mother's house at the edge of town.

When he walks into the modest two-story colonial, the smell of casserole and cigarette smoke greets him before anyone else can. He wasn't informed his aunt Ginny and uncle Herb were going to be here, but their presence in the living room tells him how seriously they're taking the whole situation. Herb perches at the edge of an ancient brown leather recliner, balancing a plate of spaghetti on his knee (at 10:00 a.m.) and hollering at *The Price is Right* on the television.

"Oh, she thinks that Progresso is less than the cat treats. Those are ninety-nine cents at the Aldi. She's gonna lose. Loser!" Brady is draped across the sofa with beepy slot-machine sounds coming from his phone from his online poker game, and Ginny sits on the floor, feeding something to his parents' elderly Chihuahua.

"Where's Mom?" he asks.

"Oh, hiya, Ade," Ginny says when she notices him. Brady doesn't look up, and Herb gives a sort of wave, but it's probably meant to tell him to keep it down rather than a wave hello. His mother is nowhere in sight. He's sure he probably sounds like the rest of his family—a thick East Coast accent because he's still asked if he's from the Bronx on a regular basis, but when he sees them again, he can't imagine he sounds quite that extreme.

"Is that a Hershey's kiss?" Aden asks, watching Anderson Pooper eat out of Ginny's hand. "You can't feed a dog chocolate."

"Why not?"

"Because...it kills them?" Aden says, dropping his coat over the back of an armchair and turning on the ceiling fan to alleviate the suffocating smoke in the room.

"Nonsense. I always bring him kisses when I visit. It doesn't kill 'em. Look at him. He's fit as a fiddle. Aren't ya, Anderson? It's good for ya, I saw it on the *Dr. Phil*. It has antioxidants."

"What does?" Herb asks without turning away from the TV.

"Chocolate," Ginny says.

"Oh, that guy's fulla shit."

"Jesus," Aden mutters under his breath. He goes through to the kitchen where his mother stands at the counter, speaking to someone on the house phone, fidgeting with the mustard yellow cord and coiling it around her fingers anxiously. She gives him a weak smile when she notices him.

"Okay. Yes. Okay. Uh-huh. Thanks then," she says in a hushed voice and then hangs up. She goes to Aden and buries her head in his chest. He strokes her hair.

"It's gonna be okay," he soothes.

"Oh, honey," she whimpers.

"Hey, hey. It's okay." He sits down at the table and watches her nervously pour tea into her favorite rooster mug. "Who was that?"

"Levi Morris." She pulls a soiled handkerchief from her pocket and dots her eyes.

"Oh. Yeah, so he met Dad for a beer the other night, right? What did he say?" She doesn't respond, just looks down into her Earl Grey.

"Ma?"

"He said he didn't meet your father," she says, bursting into tears. "He lied to me. He said he'd be with Levi that night. Why would he do that?"

"Now, Ma. Come on. Maybe he just changed plans. That doesn't mean he lied."

"Levi said they never had plans to meet."

"Okay. Alright," Aden says, trying to calm her but running out of things to say. "Maybe he got his dates mixed up and forgot he told you that—had different plans instead—had his wires crossed. He does that sometimes. He's doing a lot of things at once all the time, ya know. He's forgetful," he says, but knows she's the one who's forgetful, and wishes she would remember which hunting or fishing destination he said he'd be going to for a few days. After going back and forth about the situation a handful of times since he left the coffee shop, he decided on the drive over that this is the only explanation.

"You've been here five minutes, and you're making Ma cry," Brady says, a cigarette hanging from his lips, the jeans hanging off his impossibly skinny hips, showing his boxers. He opens the fridge and pulls out a plastic container of chocolate Yoo-hoo. Aden doesn't respond to this.

"Let's just—let's make a plan here, okay," Aden says, trying to keep control of the situation. "The police are aware. They're looking for him, so what can we do in the meantime? We're all here."

"Herb and Gin are gonna drive around—try all the places Dad and Herb went, camping spots and stuff," Brady says, putting his foot up on a kitchen chair and gulping Yoo-hoo in a bizarre gesture of dominance or something.

"Why don't I go talk to Levi? See what else he has to say, maybe it'll be helpful," Aden says.

"Why are you talkin' to him?" Brady asks. A sob escapes Penny's mouth and she sits down at the table and pulls some more napkins from the festive jack-o'-lantern-shaped napkin holder on the table and blows her nose.

"Levi said he wasn't with him. Now nobody knows where he could be!"

"Shit, really? Oh, that's not good. That's—that's not good. Shit. He was with Levi, I thought," Brady says, obliviously unhelpful.

"Okay then," Aden says, standing and pushing his chair away from the table. "I'll go have a chat with him. Mom, just try to stay calm. We're gonna figure this out. I'm sure he's at one of the cabins and that's why his phone's out, okay. Just try to relax a little…"

"There's black bears out there," Brady says. "Ticks that'll kill ya. I heard about a lady who had one burrow in her tongue and lay eggs and then! Then…her tongue swelled so big she choked on it in her sleep. In her fuckin' sleep. When they found her, there were swarms of the babies crawling out of her mouth. Shit."

"Brady," Aden says sharply.

"Coyotes. Or—OR…he could have slipped at the cliff's edge. That's not good. He shouldn't be going out there by himself." Penny's shoulders shake as she silently cries.

"What the fuck is wrong with you?"

"What? We're brainstorming here."

"Are you kidding me?"

"Ma wants to know! She wants to think through all the possibilities. I'm trying to think of said possibilities so we know where to go—where to look. What the fuck is actually wrong with *you*?" Brady puts his arm around Penny—one-sided solidarity. Anything Aden says will escalate this and he can't do that to his mother right now.

"Well, we have a lot of places to start looking then. Ma, call me if you need me. I'm gonna go see what I can find out." He kisses her on the head. "Okay?" he asks, and she nods and squeezes his hand on his way out.

The truth is, Aden thinks as he picks up his coat and walks out to his car, that it's true his dad shouldn't go out by himself like that, but he always has. It's one of the luxuries of living out here—the main reason most people live out here is space, air, wilderness, the quiet. Safety isn't really a discussion.

The guys from the Eagles club are usually sitting around Wally's Waffles on late Sunday morning, drinking coffee and playing checkers and gin rummy. Aden drives down to Wally's, not having any idea what he really has to ask Levi if he sees him. Seems like an open and closed deal. They never had plans. What's there for him to even ask really? Still, he feels compelled to do something. He drives past the storefronts on

Willow Lane. The drizzle has cleared and the day is crisp and sunny. He spots a few older men sitting outside at the picnic table in front of Wally's, hunched over what looks like a game of backgammon, and wearing jackets too thin for the weather. He doesn't see Levi among them, so rather than going in and being roped into questions he doesn't have answers to, because they must have heard by now, he drives on and heads the few miles to Levi's house. As he rounds the corner onto Blue Ridge Street, he sees the expanse of the Morrises' weathered picket fence. A chestnut tree with a rope swing hanging from an outstretched branch rests in the distance near an east-leaning whitewashed old horse barn. Aden can see the outline of a figure sitting in an Adirondack chair, facing the small backyard pond. He pulls up the dirt drive and gets out of the car, shielding his eyes against the sun's glare to make out the person in the distance. He puts on a ball cap from the glove compartment and walks out toward the pond.

"Jesus and Mary!" Levi says, clutching his heart when Aden calls his name from only a few yards away.

"Sorry, I thought you heard me pull up."

"Oh, Aden. Sorry. No. It's okay, I just—I did, but I thought it was Millie coming home from the grocery shopping. She never comes out here. You gave me a startle. Please sit," he says, nodding to the second chair perfectly placed to take in the breathtaking view.

Aden notices a scotch or whiskey drink in his hand, and thinks this seems a bit off for a Sunday before noon.

"I wondered if you had a few minutes to talk," Aden says, sitting down. Levi sighs and hangs his head—not the reaction Aden was expecting. "Is everything okay?"

"I'm so sorry about your father... I..."

"Look, I'm sure he's fine," Aden says, "I just want to try and help Mom, get to the bottom of it. He's out fishing for

the weekend, I'm sure. It's not the first time he's done this."
He keeps saying this like a knee-jerk reaction—trying to be
comforting, and part of him believes it. But although his father had done this before, it was never for this long. The usual
scenario was that Penny would assume he was out for beer
and cards with the Eagles club or church guys until late, fall
asleep, wake to realize he wasn't there, panic, blow up his
phone, and there he would be. He'd tell her he was fishing
with Earl or Kenny or whatever. But this is two days now. He
reminds himself not all the good spots have reception, and so
he keeps repeating his soothing line, more for himself probably than others. "He'll turn up."

"Yeah. Of course," Levi says, then swirls his drink and
takes a sip.

"He says he was out with you, I hear. And you say you guys
didn't have plans, so Mom's freaking out, but maybe he just
said the wrong friend, ya know. All of you guys get together
all the time, so."

"Look, I need to be honest with you here, Ade."

"Uh. Okay. Yeah. What is it?"

"It's just, ya know the police talked to me—asking if Martin was with me..." He stops and runs his hand through his
hair. "I don't know if I did the right thing or not."

"Jesus, what is it?" Aden asks, and Levi shakes his head and
looks out at the glossy stretch of pond.

"I didn't know he said he was with me. I feel like I betrayed him, I guess, but I just told the truth 'cause, I mean,
it's the police."

"Of course. You did the right thing..."

"No. But that's not it. On Fridays—most Fridays he goes..."
He stops, flustered, and then starts again. "They asked me if I
knew where he was. And the thing is, he goes to... The Landing...a lot of Fridays," Levi says, his cheeks flushed.

"I'm sorry. What?"

"I mean, sometimes he meets us for a while, but then he goes down to The Landing," he says again, and Aden lets out an involuntary humorless laugh.

"The, uhh…strip club? Is that what you're saying? Levi, come on."

"Morty sees him down there sometimes on Fridays, I guess—you know Mort, he's always getting himself into something. He turned into a ladies' man when he got divorced. Anyway, so, he brought it up at a card game one night—Mort did, about seein' your dad, and your dad looked pretty white when Mort was sayin' it, and then he just made it into a joke—like I'm married, not dead. You know how the guys are—there's a sort of code. No one was gonna say anything—it's *his* own business. I pretty much forgot about it until I was asked where he might be."

"Wait. He actually admitted that he went there. This is not a joke?"

"Yeah. I mean, at first he said something like—I don't remember exactly—just something to the effect of he was surprised that the church guys would go there—like he didn't think anyone he knew would ever see him—that's how it felt, but then he tried to blow it off like it's just a normal guy thing, no big deal. I was surprised, don't get me wrong, but shit, I sneak a little porn. Who doesn't? It was just none of my business, but now he's gone. I had to tell them the truth. What if it helps them find him?"

"Of course. You didn't do anything wrong, I'm just… I don't even know."

"I didn't tell your mom. Don't worry. I wouldn't do that."

"Right, good," Aden says, distracted. He rubs his eyes, straightens his ball cap and stands. "Well, thanks for telling me about this. I…" Aden is at a loss for words.

"Yeah. I know. I'm sorry."

"No, it's okay, Levi. Thanks."

"I'm sure he'll be back tomorrow. He's probably just fishing and this is nothing," Levi adds, countering Aden and standing.

"I'm sure you're right," Aden says, holding his hand out. They shake hands and Aden pats Levi on the back and walks to his car.

Aden drives directly to the Rock Harbor Police Department because he needs to make sure this rumor about his father—and that's what it was right now—doesn't circulate and get back to his family. It's not that he doesn't believe Levi… But no, it was that. There was no way his father hung out at seedy strip. It was ridiculous. Could he have had a few beers on gin rummy night and let the guys think it was him—that Mort was being serious and just went along with it, sure. Mort is always three sheets to the wind when Aden sees him. He was probably just mistaken, but it made Martin feel kind of cool in the moment. Possible. But that's it. That must be it.

When he enters the station, he realizes that in all his years in Rock Harbor, he's never stepped foot in the police station before. He doesn't feel right being here now, but he wants to talk to an actual police officer and learn what they know and hopefully hear from them that it's likely nothing to worry about.

He approaches a middle-aged woman with 1980s bangs and penciled-in eyebrows and asks to talk to someone about his father. When he tells her his father's name, she looks up from her furious typing, raises her eyebrows at him, and says she'll be right back. She disappears into the back, and when she returns, there is a new expression on her face. What was once a mild look of annoyance at being interrupted is now replaced with pity, he thinks.

"If you'll have a seat, Detective Hendricks can talk to you. It's his case, but he's at lunch. Should be back in a jiff though."

"Detective? He's been missing two days. There's a detective assigned?" Aden asks.

"All I know is what I just told you. You'll have to talk to him," she says, returning to her desk.

Aden sits on a green vinyl chair and stares blankly at an American flag next to a dead ficus plant across the small lobby. He thinks about all the detective movies he's seen and wonders if all cases like this automatically get assigned to one, or if this is more serious. He has no idea how any of this works and it's making him anxious and he suddenly wants to leave, but the woman with the bangs calls his name and escorts him down a beige hallway and now he's stuck. He wishes he'd just called. What is he doing here? It seems so outrageous. Will they laugh when his father drives up the street with his fishing poles sticking out the back of his truck bed? Brady would, and his mother would cry with relief and make Martin sleep on the couch for a week, and Aden would go home and see his kid, and he just needs to get through one more day of this and have it done with.

Hendricks's office looks like an HR cubical, not at all what he expected a police detective's office to look like. Just an L-shaped desk covered in paper piles and Styrofoam cups and a bulletin board room divider surrounding it. He's tall and very lean, like a runner, Aden thinks, with salt-and-pepper sideburns and a full head of hair. He shakes Aden's hand and offers him a seat. Aden explains that he just got into town and his mother is worried but maybe overreacting and asks what they know.

"Not a lot," Hendricks says. "It's only been a couple days. Your mom mentioned you were coming in and I planned to stop in to see you this afternoon. Just to get a statement—get your thoughts on what you think might have happened. Have you talked to him recently?"

"Yeah, I mean we talk all the time. He called Monday or Tuesday, asking about Leah's birthday next month—what to get her. I mean just normal stuff."

"Leah's your daughter."

"Yes."

"And he sounded fine. Nothing you can think of that was off? Did he mention anything at all that you remember that could help us figure out where he might be?"

"No. No, he was—so you really think he's like—you think something bad happened? You don't think he's out fishing? His camping gear and fishing stuff are always in his truck. He goes off like that a lot."

"We're just looking into all possibilities right now, like I told your mother. Anything helps at this stage."

Stage, Aden thinks. The word feels incongruous to the laid-back tone of *just looking into all possibilities* from the moment before. This is a *stage* of an investigation.

"I talked to Levi Morris," Aden says. "He said he mentioned to you that my father...hung out at—" Aden lowers his head and his eyes shift around, making sure no one else is in earshot "—The Landing, or around there. You know, in that area. And I just want to tell you that I highly doubt that's true and I would hate for it to get back to my mother—she's going through enough already."

"Right," Hendricks says with a tight-lipped smile. "Well, it's very early and we don't know if that's at all related, so it's not something we'd be sharing. We certainly don't want to cause panic or assume anything."

"You don't know if it's related? So, you're saying you think it's true—you're assuming it's true."

"We have security footage from the shop across the street that shows him there recently, yes…"

"Wait. You already have that? You—is there something you're not telling me? Shouldn't you be considering him a forgetful old man who forgot to tell his wife he was going away a couple days like all the other old men around here? Security footage? Why?"

"We're doing our job, Mr. Coleman."

"You know he spends a lot of time witnessing."

"Witnessing what?" the detective asks, and Aden scoffs involuntarily and gives the detective a sideways look.

"Not like… I mean telling people about the Lord," he mumbles the last part, a bit embarrassed at the presumptuousness a man must have to go around trying to tell people their beliefs are wrong and his are right, unprompted, and trying to change them. "He hands out water bottles and sandwiches to homeless people with the youth group for God's sake. He was probably down there trying to do some good—I mean his version of it."

"Which is why," Hendricks says, calm and unmoved by Aden's outburst, "we are not jumping to any conclusions at the moment. We don't know what he was doing there."

"Right," Aden says, awkwardly triumphant.

"But he lied about where he was, and if you want to find him, which I assume you do, we have to follow up on our only real lead," Henricks says. Aden sighs and leans back in his chair. He bites at his cuticle, unsure what else to say.

"Are you familiar with a Mr. Harry Flynn?" the detective asks, and Aden feels a twinge of something like dread run through him. His mother called Harry *missing* yesterday, and Brady said he was just having sex with coeds on a Mexican beach or yacht or something like that, but why does this detective know about him?

"Yes. Sort of. Why?" is all Aden manages.

"You've heard he's also unaccounted for," Hendricks says, and he has a kind way about him, but he makes the man sound like a lost shoe.

"He's—he travels. He has a yacht. I heard he was…away," Aden says, confused.

"Well, we've not released any details yet, and he has no living family that we know of. Now, I am not saying that the cases are related. It's too early to know anything, but he's a man your father's age, missing under mysterious circumstances, they were friends—so we are just trying to dot all our *I*'s here and make sure to really take in all information."

"Mysterious. He's not sailing through Mexico or whatever the hell everyone says he's always doing?"

"Perhaps. But most people would take their cell phone and ID with them. Most people would need access to a bank account and his hasn't been accessed, so we don't believe he's on vacation, no."

"Holy shit," Aden says, the gravity of this news pulsing a dull ache across his shoulders.

"Now, we're not getting ahead of ourselves here, but you see we need to gather any leads we can at this point. Your father's phone hasn't had activity since Friday night, but as your mother and Brady have said, maybe that's reception or because it died. So, I wish I had more to relay to you, but I'll be in touch if we get anything definitive."

Aden had more questions swirling in his mind, but the news of his father on Seedy Strip and Harry being gone under *mysterious circumstances* was rendering him mute. As Hendricks thanked him for coming in, Aden nodded and stood. He shook his hand again, silently, feeling somewhat lightheaded as he walked out of the police station.

Aden spends the evening in his mother's living room eating

spaghetti and meatballs off the good china because somehow this was a special occasion. Brady is draped over the recliner slurping noodles like a Neanderthal, and his aunt and uncle sit side by side on the love seat with plates on their knees while they watch *Wheel of Fortune*. He can hear Penny crying softly in her room, but she's asked not to be disturbed, so everyone is staying close in solidarity or whatever else you can call Ginny and Herb's awkward presence. Aden assumes the second his mother told her sister what was happening she insisted on "helping," but it seems to have the opposite effect.

Someone buys a vowel and Vanna turns over two O's. Aden thinks about telling his family what he learned today because he hates being alone with the information, but he knows his mother would lose her mind and Brady would probably start threatening people on Seedy Strip for information with a shotgun or something and get himself arrested. He's pretty sure Hendricks also has a hunch about his mother's and brother's unique but equal fragility as well, and chooses carefully what and who he tells things to.

Aden types with one hand on his laptop balanced on the end table next to an overflowing ashtray and looks up Harry Flynn and Martin Coleman, but as expected it's just the generic missing alerts he already knows about. A little more elaboration in a couple local newspapers, but still very little. Anderson Pooper throws up on an afghan next to him, and Aden gags and puts his plate down, and goes to sit at the table in the dim kitchen. The air is heavy with the smell of marinara sauce and cigarette smoke, and he hears Herb loud-whisper (in respect for his mother) at the television that the idiot shouldn't have spun the wheel and now he deserves to be bankrupt. Aden looks around at the yellow floral wallpaper and ugly wicker baskets hanging above the sink, and he thinks of all the Easter egg hunts and Christmas morning cinnamon rolls in this kitchen and misses his father.

He takes a deep breath and before he closes the laptop and goes back to the Windmill Inn for a little bit of sanity, he thinks about Grace Holloway. He feels guilty, silly even for thinking of her right now—her long pale hair pulled back carelessly, her thin frame, her boyish clothes, and standoffish manner. There is no glossy-lipped, selfie-taking Instagrammer girl in Grace Holloway like all the women he seems to meet in Hartford. She'd actually probably punch you in the balls if you called her *sweetheart*, and he'll be damned if he didn't find that intriguing. She was decidedly not looking to meet anyone—in fact, she's gone out of her way to isolate herself. Why?

He looks over both shoulders first, as if he might be caught, and then quickly searches for her name—just curious about this mysterious woman who so eagerly wanted him the hell out of her space.

He expected a thousand options and that he'd have to scroll endlessly through thumbprint photos on social media to try to match the face to figure out which one was her, and eventually give up, unsuccessful. But she isn't on social media. Of course, she's not.

Instead, it takes only seconds to find an endless stream of articles about her. His hand flies to his mouth and he gasps when he finds out who she is.

8

KIRA

I don't catch him. The box truck makes a sharp right and I get stuck behind an Uber letting a touchy-feely couple out of his back seat onto the corner. Maybe I was imagining him running. I don't know because I feel like I've lost all perspective at this point.

I know there is nothing else I can do tonight, so I drive, exhausted, to our family's cabin ten minutes outside of town. My dad spends most weekends there since retiring, and now he's there all the time to stay in town and help search for Brooke. As grateful as I am for this, I just wish I could be alone right now. My head throbs, and my body aches. At the beginning, it was sobbing and screaming, but eventually that gives way to something else—a kind of emotional numbness, a dull heaviness—the edges of everything are soft and hazy. Everything feels slower and slightly surreal. Like knowing you're dreaming but not being able to wake up. I walk through each day somehow. I drink coffee and brush my teeth and it's outrageous—doing these stupid, meaningless things when my baby is out there. And there is just not a goddamn thing more I can do.

I pull into a gravel patch in front of the cabin. My father sits out front in a camping chair, smoking a cigar and drinking a Bud Light. Pulling up to the cabin and seeing camping chairs by the fire outside used to mean boxed wine and hot dogs and fighting over who got to play deejay with their Spotify while we talked about nothing in particular and got tipsy and poked sticks into the fire until late into the night. Now, my father has learned in only a month's time how to tiptoe around me and not ask for updates unless I bring it up. He just gives me facts if he has them and tries to make the right faces when I speak, because how would anyone know how to respond to all of this?

I shut the car door and sit next to him on a log bench next to the fire. He hands me a blanket to put around my shoulders and there is a bottle of pinot and a mug on the ground next to me. It's his way of taking care of me. I pour myself a glass and we sit in silence for a long time. He wears a wool cap over his silver hair and tugs at his mustache as he puffs on his cigar.

"What is it?" I ask, knowing he wants to say something. He hands me a piece of purple construction paper.

"Some lady came by and left this for you," he says and I look down at an address written in marker. I stare at it, confused.

"She had a ton of kids in the car, so..." he says, thinking I'm contemplating the silly paper rather than the address.

"This is Connie Reed's address. I've been there a dozen times, she won't talk to me."

"Said she will for a fee. I guess she finally realized she could capitalize on it."

"What a psychopath," I say, tossing the paper into the fire, because I know the address by heart and don't need it.

"Yep," he says, staring into the fire as the specks of charred paper pop like glitter in the flame.

"I'll go in the morning," I say softly, because of course I have to. Connie's the foster mother of one of the two girls who were missing and then found dead a few years back. Amelia Beck was her name. I've called, left notes, knocked on her door. I need to know if it could be connected and for that I just need all the information I can get—more than what the police gave, more than the articles online. Anything. She probably can't help me, but how can I not grasp at every straw even if the possibility is remote?

"And Dana?" I ask, knowing that he's gone to knock on Dana Rossi's door as many times as I have, in hopes to learn something about her daughter Heather, found dead a year before Amelia. She's never there, and I don't have a working number for her. She's kept to herself for years, so nobody seems to know anything about her other than she wants to be left alone.

"Nobody home," he says with a sigh, extinguishing the butt of his cigar on the metal leg of his chair. Long after the police presence and human chains combing the woods, and the divers and the dogs are all gone, Leo Everett will still spend his days driving to every far-fetched possible place a person could go—go to do what? Camp alone after an argument with her boyfriend, walk home from wherever she went and fall down a cliffside? Get taken and dumped somewhere? We don't talk about the what-ifs, but every day he goes to search, and then he'll sit here with me at night, both of us a little less ourselves with every passing day.

I pick up the wine bottle, tuck it in under my arm, and go inside. A fire flickers in the fireplace and fills the glowing living room with a musty cedar smell. I walk into the small room Brooke used to call dibs on whenever we stayed here as a family. I see a text from Matt as I plug my phone in to charge, and I ignore it. I lay down on top of my grandmother's appliqué quilt, placing the wine on the nightstand, and stare at the ceiling a moment, intending to open my laptop to continue my work, but I fall into a heavy dreamless sleep within minutes.

Connie Reed's cabin is thirty minutes northwest of ours on a strip of road the locals call Felony Lane. A row of small two-bedrooms that used to be a camping hub for tourists but was modified and made into permanent housing years ago. Each one the same, with five concrete stairs leading to the front door, tin roofs, and weathered siding. I pull up the dirt drive along the side of the house and see an overgrown backyard with a rusted swing set and several children playing—a few packing plastic buckets with wet mud, an underdressed toddler crying at the back door, a ten-year-old girl sitting cross-legged on top of a metal slide, arms crossed, pushing off the younger kids if they try to climb the ladder.

Then I see Connie in a green sweatshirt with the hood up, holding a baby on her hip and smoking a cigarette. She's hollering at the toddler to shut up and go play, scarcely looking up from the phone in her free hand.

"Who the fuck are you?" she asks, startled to see me walking toward the chain-link fence surrounding the backyard. "I'll call you back," she says into the phone, then stomps her cigarette out and puts the baby in a bucket next to the sandbox.

"What the hell do you want?" she asks, as I stare at a baby... in a bucket. She stands in front of the bucket with a hand on her hip.

"You the law or somethin'?"

"I'm sorry. The what?"

"The LAW. A cop? 'Cause I got my license up to date now," she says. I realize she must mean day care license the way she waves her hand around indicating all of the kids. "Four of 'em's mine, so they don't count."

"I'm not—I'm Kira Everett. You left a note saying you'd speak to me." Her eyes almost light up as she assesses me for signs of someone with the ability to pay her or not. She looks me up and down, then to my car, and I can see her processing—deciding how much is too much to ask a desperate woman for.

"You have a reward for information," she says matter-of-factly, not adding the rest that says *information leading to the safe return of Brooke Everett.* I don't add it either. I am desperate. She knows it, and I don't care. Whatever she wants is fine.

"I just got kids to feed, ya know. So it's only fair."

"Yeah," I say, not really knowing what approach to take.

"Five hundred dollars and I'll tell you whatever I can," she says, glossy eyes flitting from my face, then self-consciously to the ground, probably thinking I'll barter down, but I don't fucking care. She can have everything I own if she can help me.

"Fine," I say, and her eyes widen.

"Watch the kids, Lottie!" she yells to the ten-year-old. "And change Alex. He smells like shit." The girl on the slide climbs down and picks the baby out of the bucket like it's an everyday normal thing to do. Connie opens a squeaky screen door and leads me inside where a small galley kitchen sits to the left of the back door. The yellow linoleum is peeling around the edges and a garbage can is overflowing with cans and diapers and pizza boxes piled up next to it. Beer bottles and half-eaten peanut butter and jelly sandwiches on paper plates are scattered around the small counter space, and plastic sippy cups and *Sesame Street* bowls fill both sides of the kitchen sink. I sit at a card table with a Folgers can for an ashtray and hold my hands in my lap, trying to take a deep breath and keep my nausea at bay. The diaper and cigarette smoke mingling together in the heavy air make me want to wretch, but I have to just focus and stay centered and not react.

Connie pulls a Bud Light from the fridge and pops the top against the edge of the counter in one swift and practiced move.

"Want one? We got Coors too, if you're fancy." I shake my head. She shrugs, peeks out the screen door at the kids and then sits across from me and picks at her beer label.

"I'm sorry about your daughter," I say, trying to get the conversation on the right track.

"Foster daughter," she corrects. "The girl was barely here six months."

"Right, well, is there anything you can tell me about her—about the night she went missing?"

"I mean, I don't really know what I can say. The girl was a mess. A dozen foster homes, a shitty attitude. She stole the goddamn TV in Kyle's room and pawned it. Cost me two hundred bucks and she sold it for goddamn twenty. Snuck out damn near every night. I gave up trying to stop her. She was sixteen, old enough to take care of herself, so I let her go," she says with a wave of her hand. *Let her go*, I think, a sob trying to climb out of my throat, but I swallow it down. She was a child who looked like a woman at sixteen, but she was a child, and the state paid Connie Reed to watch over her, and she took the money and *let her go*. I dig my fingernails into my palms and swallow hard.

"Do you know where she hung out…where she went when she'd sneak out?" I ask, keeping calm.

"Oh, Lord, I don't know. All over. She had some boyfriend—some delivery guy named Vinny she talked about sometimes. A skinny, pimply thing. She didn't have no real friends. She was pregnant, so…"

"What?" My heart races. They never released this information. Maybe because it could be a motive—an ex-boyfriend and they didn't want to make it public. Jesus.

"Yeah," Connie says. "She was planning on getting emansycated," she says, and she must mean emancipated, but I don't correct her.

"She wanted to make her own money, so I think she was probably hookin'. The boyfriend, what's-his-face, Vinny's store is that Coastal Grocery down on The Strip, so I know she hung out down there at least—God knows what else she did. This girl looked high whether she was or she wasn't, crazy eyes—so damned if I know what the hell she was really doing," she says, and I think of the box truck at Coastal Grocery and how it sped off.

I feel my heart in my throat, and a burst of adrenaline that makes my hands shake. This is something. This is the only tangible connection I've discovered since the beginning. A dead girl who was also at the last place Brooke was seen—a guy in a fleeing truck who might know her—a boyfriend, pregnant. The edges of my vision blur and my head is light.

"Hey!" Connie screams, pulling me out of my near blackout and back into the room. My hand flutters to my heart, startled.

"Get Tommy-Jay out of that goddamn pool. It's fifty degrees outside. You'll kill him!" From the screen door, I see a boy of about eight pull a diapered one-year-old from a hot pink kiddie pool filled with an inch of dirty water and wet leaves.

"Vinny what?" I ask. "Do you know his last name?"

"No idea. It's the only person she ever mentioned, but I don't know much. I told the police about him though."

"Did they talk to him?"

"Yep. He denied knowing her. There were no texts, social media, nothin' between them, so that was that."

"Wait, but he was her boyfriend?" I ask, trying to make sense of it all.

"Well, somethin' like that—a thirty-somethin' guy hangin' around a teenager—she's pregnant, doin' drugs—whatever you call all that—hell if I know," she says, and I am in disbelief she wasn't arrested for child neglect in the process of the investigation.

"Thirty-something?" I say.

"Look, she was here a short time, and was off doing whatever most of that time. I only saw this Vinny guy in a photo the cops showed me. I really don't know what else to tell you. I barely knew her, really." She takes a swig of her beer, never mind that it's before noon and she has nine children to look after. I think about poor Amelia. Missing twenty-two days and found in the root cellar of an abandoned house with a cattle castration band still tight around her neck. Her last moments filled with terror while her larynx and trachea were crushed, the bright flash of white before the world went dark forever.

She was a girl nobody loved. I try to imagine this. No parents, no friends, no one. In her photo that circulated statewide, she's in a yellow sundress sitting on a picnic table. She's holding a can of Pepsi—her chipped pink nails bit down to the quick. She's not smiling, but her green eyes still sparkle in the sunshine. She was just a kid. A kid who got Connie Reed in some stroke of bad luck. Connie Reed who...*let her go*.

I have an overwhelming urge to hurt Connie. I imagine kicking the bottom of her beer bottle into her mouth and knocking her front teeth out. She didn't even report her missing; she just kept collecting the check from the state and forgot all about her. A teacher at the school finally asked about her after days of not showing up for class. That I do know from the press. I dig my nails deeper into the palms of my hands and remind myself that Amelia Beck is not my daughter, and hospitalizing Connie Reed will not accomplish anything.

"So, she was last seen July sixteenth, three years ago, at 10:14 p.m. on a security camera near the Hill Top Motel," I ask, reiterating the basic facts, hoping she might inadvertently add something. The Hill Top Motel is half a block from The Landing, which is next to Lucky's where Brooke was last seen around the same time of night. And it makes no sense. Brooke was not a poor lost girl who no one loved. She wasn't on drugs; she wasn't anything like Amelia. And she's not dead. I know that for a fact. *I know it.*

"That's what they tell me," is all she says.

"Is there anything else at all you think could help? What about her things? Did they look through her room—did you find anything missing or did they think anything was out of the ordinary—anything?"

"She didn't have a room. She slept on the couch. She had a hefty bag of clothes she kept in the coat closet. They looked through 'em, but I threw those out ages ago. Except this." She pinches the drawstring of her hoodie tighter.

"That's her sweatshirt?" I say, trying to mask my disgust.

"Only thing worth keeping. You can have this if you want," she says, walking over to a junk drawer next to the sink. She rifles through pencils and paper clips and take-out menus and pulls out a silver split heart locket.

"This was hers?" I ask, taking it gently into my palm.

"The police didn't think anything here was evidence, they didn't take nothin'. I brought it down to Big Bob's Pawn, but it wasn't worth nothin'." I open the locket and see a tiny photo of Amelia inside. She's just a kid, maybe seven or eight in the photo but the white-blond hair and green eyes make it unmistakably her.

"She has a photo of herself in her locket?" I ask, trying to understand if it could mean anything.

"Her sister what died in the car accident with her parents had this side of the locket with Amelia's photo I guess, and Amelia was wearing the other half of the locket with her sister's photo in it. Kelly, Katie—something like that."

"Do the police have Amelia's half of the necklace in evidence?" I ask, making a mental note to look up a car accident and Amelia Beck for more information later. I put the locket carefully into a zip pocket in my purse.

"They never found it. I thought she pawned it for drug money, but since it ain't worth nothin' I guess not, so I don't know. She never took it off, so it's fuckin' creepy, that's for sure. Some sicko out there probably has it," she says, pulling out a Camel Blue from a pack inside her hoodie pocket and lighting it between two bony fingers. "You know how those sickos are.

"Welp," she says, "I gotta get back to them kids. I don't know anything else. I really don't. It's a sad thing, but that girl—I mean something like that was bound to happen. She was trouble from the get-go." And as much I want to punch her right in the throat, she actually was helpful. At least it's something—a place to go next. And I *will* make an anonymous call to child protective services, but for now I pull out the cash I took out of the ATM on my way over and place it on the table, in five one-hundred-dollar bills. I took out a lot more than that, willing to give her anything, but she doesn't know that.

She snatches it up, shoving it inside the plastic of her cigarette pack and into her hoodie pocket. She walks outside, quickly busying herself by hollering demands at the children, as if she doesn't get me out quickly, I might change my mind and not pay up.

On my drive back, I think about what Amelia was doing on The Strip—The Landing, Lucky's, Hill Top, Coastal Grocery. The whole street almost gray and invisible during the day, and at night a blur of streetlights and booming bass music coming from the back doors of clubs, girls with hair extensions and fur coats, men drinking Old Milwaukee from bottles in paper bags, patrons stumbling out of doors, urine on the sidewalk. I know how a poor soul like Amelia could find herself here, but not Brooke.

The police don't see any threads connecting two murdered girls to Brooke, so they certainly aren't giving me information about these cases I have no right to know about, so I'll have to find out for myself. This boyfriend should be easy to find. He says he never knew Amelia. Will his face give him away when I show him this half of her locket? Does he know Brooke? My pulse beats in my forehead and bile rises in my throat. I drive too fast through the windy cliffside roads and directly down to The Strip to find Vinny from Coastal Grocery. And this time, there's no way he's getting away from me.

9

GRACE

"Jesus, Vinny!" Grace says, leaping to her feet from her place at the kitchen counter, hand to heart. "You scared the shit out of me," she half laughs because it's Vinny and she was expecting him after all, but she's also genuinely annoyed that he always lets himself in the back door no matter how many times she asks him to knock first.

"Sorry. My bad," he says, unloading bags into the kitchen. All his other delivery venues are open-to-the public sorts of places—bars, clubs, offices, and you just walk in, he tells her, so he forgets. The owner gave the Donatto family a key years ago because they'd been delivering to the inn for decades. Grace hates the idea of anyone having a key, but of course the staff does, the owners do, the cleaners do, and Vinny Donatto does. He's the only one who comes by in the off-season though after the staff are long gone, so it's especially jarring when he's not on time and scares the living shit out of her.

She is also required to leave the front unlocked so her guest can access his room, which makes her spend the day in a perpetual state of anxiety, more than usual. Vinny she trusts though, relatively speaking, after all this time. He's always been very kind to her, and she's quite happy to see a case of cabernet on the counter, if she's honest. Vinny places the rest of the week's groceries inside.

"You're delivering late tonight, huh?" she asks.

"I was gonna push it till tomorrow, but you're my favorite stop, so I wanted to make sure you had what you needed," he says, handing her an invoice to sign and rubbing his hands together to warm them up.

"Well, thanks for doing that," she says, not knowing how to take whatever compliment he seems like he's trying to give.

"Let me help you put these away." He begins pulling items out of a box and opening cupboards.

"Oh, no. You don't have to do that. Really." But he's already placing cans of tomatoes and bags of rice on the pantry shelf like he's done so many times before.

"My pleasure."

"Okay then," Grace says, and pulls a bottle of wine from the case. She pours a glass and sits at the counter while she watches Vinny work.

"I wish my family had gotten into the inn business instead of groceries. It's so quiet out here, you get all the time to yourself—don't have to deal with too many nutters. I'd kill for that."

"You get a lot of weirdos, huh?" Grace asks, because Vinny always comes with entertaining stories he loves to tell.

"Last week," he starts, "some dude stumbled in from one of the bars and asked where the pickle chips were and I told him we don't sell pickle chips and he said every shop sells fucking pickle chips, and I said well we don't, and he pulled a knife on me. Had to call the cops and the whole nine yards." He is talking more to himself than to her, but she sips her wine and listens, finding herself amused.

"There's no way," she laughs.

"I shit you not. People love fuckin' pickle chips, I guess. Then, some lady comes in yesterday morning—still wearing slippers. I guess people just go out in public in their fucking pajamas these days, excuse my French…and anyways, she's asking me if she can buy six eggs, I say lady, they come by the dozen, come on. She says she only needs six. I say, ya gotta buy the whole package, it's only a buck forty-nine, I don't know what to tell ya. So she counts out a dollar and forty-nine cents in coins to pay for 'em, and then when she gets outside, she throws six eggs at the front door and takes the six she needs with her."

Grace spits her wine back into her glass as she chokes on a laugh. He finally stops moving and looks at her. He laughs too and she's suddenly grateful for his company. She knows Vinny's a lonely guy and likes to talk, and she genuinely likes to listen, but never really knows what to say back.

"People are messed up," he says.

"Well, you could write a book at least. Sounds like you have great material."

"I really want to," he says. Not at all what she expected. "I've been doing some poems and stuff, and like some lyrics, you know. Like that would be—I don't even know. You're so lucky. You have all this time, quiet."

Time, she thinks. The one thing that's wrong with such a solitary life is all of the time—time to think, time for memories to surface. Images so vivid she could paint them in the dark: the green radiator, a padlocked utility closet, five plastic storage bins along the brick wall, the smell of mold and urine, the skeletons of long-dead mice that look like tiny scaffolding in the corners of the dirt floor. She closes her eyes for a moment and replaces the unwanted images. She fills her mind with new ones—happy ones, the way she'd practiced: strawberry gelato, French manicured fingertips, origami turtles, a blue mood ring, sunflowers in a vase, a seashell necklace.

"It is a little…lonely for you though…maybe," he says.

She forces a weak smile. Vinny sits on the counter, his legs dangling, and looks at her intently, which makes her momentarily uncomfortable.

"Ya ever get scared out here all by yourself?" he asks, and she doesn't answer. How could she begin to verbalize the paralyzing fear from one day to the next? She wouldn't, she doesn't want to talk about it, and now she wishes he would leave. He continues before waiting for an answer though.

"'Cause I could always keep ya company whenever you need, and I always have a gun. You just—you have my number, so you just call if you ever get scared or anything. I mean it," he says, and she thinks he's about to say more, but then they both look up at the sound of a voice coming from the front lobby.

"Hello? Anyone here?" the voice calls, and then Grace sees Aden appear in the doorframe of the kitchen. Vinny jumps off the counter like he's planning to attack whoever it is.

"This is Aden," she says quickly, almost before Vinny gets to his feet.

"Oh, sorry," Aden says. "I didn't mean to interrupt. I just wanted to make sure you knew I was back so you can lock up." Vinny looks at Grace with a mix of confusion and disappointment.

"I didn't realize you had a…friend coming over. Sorry."

"No. Aden is a guest. He's staying in one of the rooms."

"Oh, yeah, you look familiar." Then, "I thought the inn was closed," he says, looking to Aden and back to her.

"It's not closed," Aden says with a tight-lipped smile.

"Not officially," Grace adds. "Anyway, thanks, Vinny, so much…for helping unload too. I appreciate it. I should lock up," Grace says, moving to the back door to escort him out.

Vinny gives Aden a once-over and then whispers to Grace, "You sure you're okay?"

"Yes. I'm perfectly fine. Promise. But thank you," she says, and he gives a hesitant nod.

"Oh, I almost forgot," he says and pulls out a tiny paper box from one of the grocery bags. He hands it to her, and she gives him an uncertain smile and then opens it.

"It's your favorite, right?" he says and she looks in at the slice of coconut cake with a single pink rosette on top, neat as a pin, looking like it could be on an episode of the *Great British Baking Show.*

"How did you know that?" she asks. He just shrugs and picks up his invoice clipboard and opens the door.

"Thank you," she says, and he tips his ball cap at her and leaves.

"Sorry if I interrupted," Aden says again, lingering.

"No, he's the delivery guy. Comes every week. You didn't interrupt." She can smell his woodsy cologne again from across the kitchen and she feels her edges soften at the sight of him— the sandy hair that he pushes away from his eyes all the time, the wide smile and cleft chin. The size of him—he's tall and broad-shouldered. She chides herself silently for thinking any of this, not just because it's a brand-new feeling she has no earthly idea what to do with, but because of why he's here, what he's going through. She's ashamed for even looking at him this way.

"Vinny brought wine, if you'd like some," she says. *God damnit. What is she doing?*

"Um. Okay, yeah, sounds nice. Thanks," he says and sits at the small eat-in table as she pours him a glass.

The tick-tick sound of little claws on the hardwood echo through the lobby and in through the French doors leading to the kitchen as Hobbes hops up from his dog bed and comes in. He sniffs Aden's shins.

"You smell my pup, huh?" he says, scratching Hobbes's chin.

"You have a dog?" she asks.

"My parents do."

"How did it go today?" she asks, not knowing if she should, feeling like she wouldn't want someone to ask her that question, but feeling simultaneously rude for not asking because that's what a normal person would do.

"A good question. It's hard to say. He's still missing, so I mean… I don't know," he says, sipping his wine and looking at the floor. Grace sits across from him and doesn't speak. They sit in a moment of silence.

"So Vinny seems like a nice guy," he changes the subject abruptly.

"Yeah. He is."

"He's the delivery guy?"

"More of an owner, I guess. He inherited his parents' grocery store…that he doesn't particularly want. You know Coastal Grocery. There's a little deli counter inside, but mostly they deliver to most of the small businesses in town. That's about all I know about him."

"Well, he's definitely sweet on you," he says, and Grace finds herself once again laughing. Twice in one night. This rarity is not lost on her.

"Why would you say that?"

"A guy can tell. It's the way he looks at you. All of it, I don't know. Trust me though."

"I don't think so," she says, picking the corner off a biscuit on the table and dropping it on the floor for Hobbes. "He's just nice to everyone," she says, meaning it. The thought of anything romantic had never crossed her mind. It's ridiculous. She feels the familiar pull to excuse herself and go to her room. She doesn't know this person who is initiating conversation, but somehow she doesn't go. She traces the rim of her wineglass with her finger and asks him if he's hungry.

"We had spaghetti," he says. "A neighbor brought it over, actually. In a casserole dish covered in tinfoil. Everyone is tiptoeing around and sending *thoughts and prayers* like there's been a death. There hasn't. I'd still bet the house that he's out fishing for the weekend." Hobbes goes over to him and makes two circles, then rests his chin on the top of Aden's boot.

"I'm sure you're right," she says quietly. He reaches for her hand, resting on the table next to her wineglass and squeezes it.

"Thanks," he says, but all she can feel is an electric pulse— something that starts like a pinprick and then rushes through her. Their eyes meet and then she pulls her hand away.

"I'm so sorry you're going through this," she says.

"I'm not worried about what I'm going through. I'm worried that I'm wrong and that he really is… I don't know—hurt, suffering. What if one of my brother's idiotic theories is right? What if he's in danger, you know? I mean what if someone really has done something to him," he says, and she swallows so hard it's audible. Then she gives a nervous sigh and shifts, ready to get up and leave the conversation, the room, in which she has no business being—all of it. She hasn't spoken more than a dozen words in weeks, and all of a sudden she feels like she's been thrust into someone else's life tonight.

"I'm so sorry," he says, gently grabbing her wrist before

she can stand. "I didn't mean—I'm sure nothing's happened to him—I… God, that was—I shouldn't be saying that after all you've been through." Her eyes widen and he lets go of her wrist.

"What?" she says, and he immediately closes his eyes and drops his head to his chest.

"Oh, God," he says.

"What the hell do you know about what I've been through?" she asks because she knows that he, of course, knows everything. It's all over his face. He's searched her name. He looked her up and now he's read every humiliating, graphic, horrific detail about her life. But she doesn't understand why he would even care to remember her name let alone look her up. For what?

He's seen the headlines she has etched into her memory. "Twenty-year-old found alive after being missing for thirty-six days."

"Young woman kept in basement in remote cabin escaped: her captor never found."

He's seen photos of her being rescued from a bear trap her leg was caught in after running hysterically through the woods when she was finally free after reportedly incapacitating her captor, who still somehow fled the scene before she was found. How is it legal for the press to make all the private details of her tragedy public? It was eight years ago, and the permanency of the internet means that a simple search of her name will allow anyone in the world into the most intimate and devastating time in her life.

Now he knows she was moved around from foster homes her whole childhood until she aged out of the system and then moved from Bangor because one of the foster girls she used to be homed with had a shitty duplex at the edge of Rock Harbor they could share. She got a job cleaning motel rooms, until one night when she found herself locked out because her roommate forgot to leave the key under the mat for her, and she wandered around until she found an all-night laundromat down on Seedy Strip, and fell asleep.

She woke up in that basement with no knowledge of how she got there—they speculated chloroform, or that she blacked out the trauma. Each news source had its own spin on the horror of the conditions and sexual assaults. Which version did Aden read? Her cheeks redden and pinpricks of heat climb her spine. She feels tears forming behind her eyes, and she quickly stands so he doesn't see her vulnerable in this moment. He's seen enough.

"I'm so sorry," he says. "Shit."

"It's okay," she says, because how can he be faulted for simply looking up a name? He didn't know what he'd get. It's all the vultures who preyed on her tragedy that are at fault—it's the reason there is no TV in the lobby or in her room—why she's never looked at a paper or turned on the news since she saw her own face reflected back at her every time she turned around those eight years ago. She's worked hard to be left the hell alone, and he's not going to bring it all back up for her.

"Grace," he says as she picks up her box of cake and pats her leg for Hobbes to come.

"It's okay," she repeats quietly before walking out of the room, doing her best to control her gait and keep as much dignity as she is able to.

In her room, she sits on the edge of the bed and thinks about that key her roommate forgot to leave under the mat. She's thought about this key every day of her life ever since it happened. They were so broke they hadn't wanted to spend the bus fare to Home Depot and then the three dollars to make a copy of the key, so they decided to just share it for a while. What if she had just spent the three dollars and made a key?

She opens the cake box and sees that Vinny has written her a poem on the back of a deli receipt. She drops the cake and the poem in the small wire trash can and lays down on top of her covers, refusing to let the tears come.

10

KIRA

Coastal Grocery is a small shop with a giant warehouse off the back that they do most of their delivery business out of. Inside there is a glass case filled with Bavarian salami, liverwurst, prosciutto, fat handmade sausage links, bistro ham and pickled onions. They specialize in sandwiches and there is a chalkboard on the wall with the daily special written out in blue chalk. Today it's a Reuben. I think of the tubby wiener dog named Reuben that Brooke fell in love with at the dog park and my chest tightens. I order a coffee and a pastrami to go, and ask the guy behind the counter if he knows a Vinny.

"Yeah," the twenty-something with ripped jeans and a sweatshirt says as he assembles my sandwich. "Like Vinny Donatto?"

"Yes," I say because how many Vinnys can there be here? *Donatto*, I make a mental note.

"He works here, right?"

"He's the owner's son. Well, the owner now, I guess. He's out delivering all day though. Is it about an order? I can call him."

"No, no. That's okay, I'll come back later," I say. I need to catch him off guard. He can't run again.

"You sure? He gets back pretty late most of the time."

"Yeah, thanks," I say, taking my sandwich and heading to my car.

It's after 11:00 p.m. and I've been sitting across from the Coastal Grocery parking lot for three hours. I look up Vinny Donatto, but there isn't anything alarming. Little social media, a few paper write-ups about the deli, a photo of him just as Connie described, pale wispy hair, impossibly thin with a pockmarked face. He's smiling in front of the deli storefront as a younger kid, next to his parents that the caption says are deceased. He's very unremarkable-looking and doesn't scream psychopath to me, but you never really know, do you?

I hear my phone buzz. It's Matt calling, and I hover my thumb over the Ignore button, but there are only so many times I can put him off before it will turn into a something-we-need-to-communicate-about conversation that I have no time for, so I answer.

"Are you okay?" he asks before I can say hello.

"Fine, I just—I'm in the middle of something."

"I called your dad when you didn't answer all day. He said you're still out. Did you find anything? Do you want me to come up there?" he asks, and I don't tell him about Connie or Celie or Vinny. I don't know why. It's his stepdaughter and he deserves to know, but I don't need to hear that it doesn't mean anything—that Amelia is not connected, that the box truck didn't really try to flee at the sight of me. I just can't hear it right now. There is some connective tissue here. I know there is and I'm trying to wrap my brain around it. I don't need another voice contaminating my thought process.

"It's better if you stay there. We need someone home just in case," I say.

"Well, we could get Jen and Bobby next door, or your dad could come and stay at the house. You need someone with you, Kira."

"My dad is here. He's helping look in new places during the day. Plus, you need to work. They won't give you any more time off. It doesn't make sense. I mean there's nothing else you can do being here…"

"Look," he says, and the silence that follows lets me know that the next thing he says will piss me off.

"The most good you can do is online and through the media. I mean you've physically done all you can there. Keep the word out, keep posting on the forums, but like, what are you doing by driving around all day? It's not—" Before I can wind up all of the pent-up rage I've been carrying all day, and hurl it at him, I hear something—a word coming from the low hum of the car radio on in the background, the word *missing*.

"I gotta go," I say and hang up, turning up the radio.

"Local man Martin Coleman was reported missing by his family on Friday has still not returned home. There is concern that seventy-three-year-old Coleman could have been in an accident because they've discovered his heart medication along with other necessary medications at home, and without them, Coleman could have become disoriented and perhaps driven his truck off the road or even suffered a heart attack. If you have any information about this case, please call…"

The announcer rattles off 1-800 numbers and a website.

I turn down the volume and feel my stomach lurch. Harry Flynn is around the same age as this Martin Coleman. They are both missing. I know it sounds like they think he left his medication behind, but who would do that? Unless they didn't know they weren't coming back? I mean, it's not a major city; it's Rock Harbor. How could these all be unrelated and co-incidental…? But on the other hand, how could two elderly men be connected to a series of missing teens?

They probably can't be, but it still feels wrong. It feels like this matters and I can't let it go without looking into who these men are. I can't explain why. There is just a heightened sense when your child is out there somewhere—when there is not enough room in the world for your pain—nothing is coincidence. Nothing is left unexplored… Or am I just being desperate? Am I wasting time?

Suddenly, I hear the rumble of a garage door opening. The loading dock across the street is dark until a square of yellow light appears from inside the warehouse and a Coastal box truck rounds the corner and pulls up to it. I wait until he turns the ignition off and I see a figure open the door and step down out of the driver seat, then I leap out of my car and run quickly across the narrow street until I'm right behind him and he can't take off.

"Hey!" I yell, and he screams as he whips around and puts both his hands in the air.

"What the hell!?" he says, then upon seeing me, he lowers his hands and rests his hands on his knees a moment to catch his breath. "Ya scared the living bejesus outta me. I thought you was the lady with eggs again."

"What?" I ask sharply.

"Christ. What are you sneaking up on me like that for? I almost took a shit in my pants."

"Are you Vinny?" I ask, just confirming what I already know—wondering if he'll try to lie.

"We're closed, lady. I can't handle no more crazies today," he says, and walks inside the loading dock and clicks the button on the wall so the giant steel door begins to slowly close.

"Do you know Amelia Beck!?"

"You got the wrong guy, lady."

"Do you recognize this?" I hold up the locket desperately. "Vinny!"

"I don't know what you're talkin' about," he says as his face disappears, and then all I can see are his feet, and then nothing at all as the gap closes. He's a liar.

I beat the steering wheel until the heels of my hands ache. I wait another hour in my car, but he doesn't come back out. I'll follow him next time—confront him in a place where he's not alone. Where he can't hide. I'm not giving up.

Before I go back to the cabin for the night, I drive past Ryan's apartment like I do most nights and look for any sign of movement. Has he been back? His things are still there, so I don't know if he's abandoned them and ran or if he is just a master at avoiding me. He's cleared, so it wouldn't make sense for him to run and make himself look culpable in any way. But if he did something, maybe he's just getting as big of a head start as he can until they figure out he did have something to do with it.

I have a notebook in my purse where I keep the dates and times I have stopped by Ryan and Brooke's apartment over the last month. Ninety-seven times, each with a date and time next to it. One of his buddies I cornered told me he was coming back from Maryland after a couple weeks with his parents because he wasn't a suspect and this is where all his friends are. I went to the docks where he worked and he hadn't gone back there, and I never saw his car in the parking lot of his apartment, but I knew he was around and making it his mission to avoid me.

A crack in the blinds lets me see a narrow view of the messy living room where there is always an Xbox on the coffee table with the cords tangled, but in a certain configuration that I have memorized, and four beer bottles, one crammed full of cigarette butts. The ninth time I peeked in the window, the Coffee Corner cup on top of a full trash can, visible just past the living room dividing wall in the kitchen, was gone—the garbage had been taken out. Six visits later, the yellow laundry basket full of video games, and a pair of socks with the faces of little sloths on them next to a brown recliner (Brooke's socks) were no longer there. Someone is accessing the apartment. If it's not Ryan, then who is it and why is Ryan hiding from me? The most reasonable explanation is that he is avoiding becoming a suspect again and wants to stay as far away as possible, but what kind of boyfriend wouldn't do all he can to help?

Tonight when I pull into the apartment parking lot for the ninety-eighth time, something is different—off. There's a small parking lot in the middle of a U-shaped two-story complex with a walkway wrapped around the second floor and private entry doors for each unit. I stare up at number 201. There's a light on!

Somewhere in the apartment, a dim light is illuminating the window just slightly. That's never been there before in my ninety-seven attempts to catch Ryan and make him talk to me. My hands tremble, and I clumsily get out of the car, not taking my eyes off the door to 201. I can hear my heart thump and the blood rushing between my ears. I walk quietly up the stairs and peer in to see there is light coming from the back of the apartment. I grasp the door handle…and it turns. It's unlocked. The adrenaline pumps through me so violently

I can't control my shaking, and I see stars behind my eyes for a moment. Then I push open the door.

I hear a sound from the back of the apartment—water running maybe. I tiptoe through the living room. The smell hits me; something's rotting. And there is a sharp chemical smell like a cleaning solvent or gasoline. Then, there's a voice, a low reverberation. I can't make out what it is. The bedroom door is cracked and when I push it open, I can't comprehend what I'm looking at.

11

Today there is a tangerine and a slice of white bread on the top stair. I've been sleeping for hours and hours on a sheath of plastic I found on the shelf with the paint cans. I can wrap it around myself so I don't feel the noses of the rodents touch my body in the night. I have the strength today to push myself up the stairs and take the food.

At the top stair, I try to press my eye to the cracks around the sides of the metal cellar door above my head. I try to see daylight. I bang on it with my fists and scream until my voice is raw and no more sound comes.

I should have never gone to The Strip that night. I knew it was getting dangerous. I should have stopped going. I'm going to die in here.

12

ADEN

By Wednesday, Martin had been missing for too long for Aden to convince himself that he could be okay. Aden had spent most of that time at his mother's, avoiding Grace and feeling guilty over the information he's kept from his family. But his mother didn't need to know that his father went down to The Strip because for all he knows, he was there to save lost souls and hand out those little Bibles the way the church deacons did. It used to embarrass the hell out of him as a teenager when his dad gave checkout clerks or waitresses or whoever little Bibles, always with an insert for his church and a number they could call about getting "saved." Now he prays that's all it was. That was really the most plausible explanation, but still…he needed to know the truth. He needed to go down there and get some answers.

Aden makes the midmorning drive from the inn to his mother's house, thinking about where to even start his search later that night along The Strip. He's never even been there before, not really. He remembers once in high school he and his friends drove down there to a liquor store to see if they could buy some tallboys or vodka without getting carded. It didn't work and instead they stole some peach wine coolers from Jason Beckstrom's dad's garage. That's all he recalls of the area. He just knows that now it's one of Maine's plentiful meth hubs. It's why it gets the bad rap. The strip clubs and bars were supposed to have been good Saturday night fun at one point, but now people get shot over dime bags and girls don't give blow jobs in back seats anymore for a hundred bucks—they get sold and never come back. Out of all the strip clubs, if that really was his father's secret, why this one? The one that could get you killed if you looked at someone the wrong way.

The sky is overcast and gusts of wind kick up the leaves from the maple tree in the front yard, making his parents' house look even more bleak than it has the last few mornings he's approached it. The neighbor's wind chime tings and the flagpole out front makes a dinging sound as the small cleat hook strikes against the metal pole. It's a lonely sound—the soft ringing in the otherwise silent street. He remembers as a kid making an igloo out of snow and then smashing it and laying on top of the snow hill it created. All life and vegetation were dead in the middle of January—no birds or leaves rustling on trees, no buzz of insects—just ear-ringing silence and the ping of the flagpole. Now it makes his stomach turn. It feels like an omen, somehow.

Inside the house, there is little hope left. There is no excusing away Martin's absence as a weekend trip his mom forgot he mentioned. It's been six days. It's the middle of the week. There has been no phone or credit card activity. His truck hasn't been spotted by anyone since last Friday. Reality has officially set in.

When he goes inside, there is no game show playing on the television. No Herb smoking and yelling at *Family Feud* or *Wheel*, no Ginny making casserole, none of Brady's incessant rambling and handheld poker game beeps and trills. They are all huddled around the TV in the living room, watching channel five showing an image of Harry Flynn standing on a boat deck with a sailor's cap on. Next to the image is a news anchor's solemn face.

"What's going on?" Aden asks, coming into the room, but he's immediately shooshed and waved over to sit down.

Mr. Flynn's body was found in a wooded area approximately thirty minutes outside of Rock Harbor, Maine. Although his death is being ruled a homicide, the police are not offering up any details at this time. Mr. Flynn, seventy-five, had been reported missing nearly three weeks before he was found. We'll keep you updated on any new details of this story as it develops.

Aden sits next to his weeping mother and takes her hand in his. When she called hysterically a couple days ago to tell him that she noticed Martin's prescriptions were all still in the cabinet and it hadn't dawned on her to look before, it became pretty clear that it was unlikely he'd be coming back Monday morning, fishing poles in hand. They knew it wasn't going to end well at that point, but an accident is one thing—losing your bearings and going into a ditch and hitting your head was a terrible, heartbreaking thing to have happened, but Harry Flynn was murdered. A man gone missing days before his father was just found murdered, and now everyone in the room is thinking the exact same thing, but Aden hopes no one will say it.

"Oh, honey," Ginny says, sitting on the other side of Penny and putting her arms around her.

"Ma, listen though," Brady says, standing up and pacing the floor. "Harry was… I mean you know the guy, right? He's a party dude. He has a pet weasel for Christ's sake. He's weirdly tan. A guy with a fake tan can't be trusted, Ma. He gets himself into some crazy shit, so it's not totally surprising he got himself, you know…into trouble. But that's not Dad. Come on. Dad's fine. I know he is. Come on."

"Brady's right," Herb said, "It's totally different. Don't worry, Pen."

"Back when I was drinking," Brady says, and Aden always finds it amazing that after nine rounds of rehab for meth addiction, he likes to only refer to himself as a recovering alcoholic, pretending the rest never happened. "You know, I was at the bars and stuff. Harry fuckin' Flynn drank an entire bottle of ranch dressing once on a bet to get some girl to go back to his place. He was in his seventies and still doin' Jell-O shots. He has a freakin' waterbed. C'mon. Let's just agree that some chick's husband finally got ahold of the guy. Let's just keep lookin' like we were," he says, and even though he never knows when to stop talking, what he's saying is oddly comforting.

Aden wants to ask how Harry was killed—if the news said anything else before he caught the end of it, but he doesn't. Not now. His mother has agreed that he'll be the one in communication with the detective. It wasn't said out loud that he's the only levelheaded one of the bunch besides her, and that she just can't take anymore right now, but it was silently agreed upon with a hand squeeze between them. He's just glad he can filter some of the information before it gets to her.

Penny goes to her room and quietly closes the door.

Herb and Ginny were supposed to go back home today.

They live less than an hour away, but wanted to support Penny. Nobody ever thought this would truly go on this long—that he wouldn't be back. Herb goes to the porch to smoke his Swisher Sweet and Aden watches Ginny walk to his parents' bedroom door and ball up a fist to knock, then think better of it and go upstairs.

Aden goes into the kitchen where Brady has the refrigerator door open and stares inside. Two cases of his dad's Guinness rest on the bottom shelf, and he knows this kind of stress is a trigger for Brady. But he doesn't take one. He's not drinking. Aden pats him on the shoulder.

"I'm proud of you," he says, and then sits at the kitchen table. Brady takes a grape soda from the fridge door and sits across from Aden, but doesn't respond.

"Fucking Harry Flynn," he says, shaking his head.

"Did they say any more about what happened?" Aden asks.

"Naw. I know what I said in there, but fuck me. Nobody's husband would go after Harry. He looks like a raisin, and I got a glimpse of his prick once at a house party. Yikes—like a Fruit Roll-Up. No guy's goin' to prison 'cause his wife banged that guy in exchange for a Gucci bag or some shit. What if it's like a serial killer—like for real?"

"Okay," Aden says, but Brady continues.

"A serial killer who goes for old men though... I mean they're slower and can't fight back as much maybe, but weird. Ya think?"

"I think we should talk about Mom going to stay with Herb and Ginny for a little while."

"Why?"

"Because a second elderly man missing after what they just discovered..."

"A second?" Brady says, confused.

"Dad?"

"Oh, right. Yeah, I thought you meant. Okay, yeah. You're right."

"The press is gonna be all over this place. She's barely coping as it is," Aden says.

"Good point. Yeah," Brady says.

"They don't live far. We'll make sure she knows someone will always be at the house and we will update her all the time. She's going through enough. We can't put her through anything else."

"And her heart's bad," he adds, dropping his head and fidgeting with a cuticle.

"Listen," Aden says, "Why don't you try to bring it up to Ginny first, they can help talk her into it. I'm gonna go see if I can talk to Hendricks—see if they can tell us anything else," Aden says, knowing how much Brady loves to have a task and how seriously he takes said task, like a child. He wasn't always that way. Things used to come so easy to him back in school—basketball, grades, stealing a little action from Kelsea Waters on the weekends, getting invited to parties. He admired Brady then. But now, after years of drug abuse and subsequent brain damage, he feels like he babysits him. He's volatile and unpredictable, and Aden resents that it feels like he's carrying this burden on his own.

On the drive to the police station, Aden thinks about his daughter. How can he keep all of this from her? Will the local news stories reach her? Will it turn into more than a local story? What more can you lay on the poor kid?

When Aden's girlfriend became pregnant, they were only seventeen. Shannon wanted to keep the baby, but Aden wasn't ready. He made it clear he thought neither of them were ready. He pleaded with her to give them the gift of their youth and their future and not keep it—even if that meant adoption—whatever she needed to do, but Shannon refused, and so Aden was a father as a teenager, and the two married after college. Not for love, but for Leah.

He tried over the years to convince her that he was committed, happy, but she never let him forget that he hadn't wanted to be a father—she'd spewed it at him like venom in arguments. *You didn't even want her!* she screamed at him one night, taking off her shoes unsteadily and throwing them at him. She had come home from a girls' happy hour and was drunk. He was in the backyard on a deck chair asleep when she came in. He was sunburned from a day at the beach with Leah. The cicadas buzzed in the trees, the night was windless and humid, and he was happy...until she came home and ruined it.

He doesn't recall how the fight started. Did he start it because she was so late? Was she angry at him for leaving takeout containers and empty Miller Lite bottles for her to clean up? Whatever it was, it escalated into something ugly, like it often did.

Somehow it took a turn and became about Leah and the school trip he'd signed off on—that she said they both should have agreed on. It took on a life of its own from there. And when she said it—when she screamed, *You didn't even want her*, Leah was sitting on the top stair, curled up—forehead to knees, listening. Shannon thought she'd gone to a sleepover, and the argument surged so rapidly he didn't even have a chance to tell her that she was home.

Everything was different after that night. Shannon resented him more for what happened—blaming him for being irresponsible, not herself for saying the words. And Leah took the words to heart and distanced herself from him.

It was only eleven months later when Shannon died in the accident. Leah has been impossibly defiant ever since. And when he decided boarding school was the only solution that could help her get away from all the reminders of tragedy, she has refused to forgive him.

Aden picks up his phone from the center console and calls her. She'll be in class, but he'll leave a nice message—tell her he's thinking about her and suggest a shopping trip to the outlet mall she loves on her next school break over Thanksgiving. She surprises him when she picks up.

"You should be in class," Aden says instead of hello. *You know what your problem is,* Shannon used to say, *you have no sense of timing. You don't think. You just say whatever.* He finds this ironic in a way, since her words are what ultimately tore them all apart. But she's not wrong. He knows the relationship between him and Leah is fragile and he should have asked if she was okay, or made a slight effort at small talk before jumping down her throat.

"I'm sick," she says.

"What do you mean sick?"

"God, dad. Seriously. Just sick—like not feeling well."

"Well, where are you? The hospital?"

"Oh, my God. I'm in my dorm. You're such a drama queen."

"Did you go to the nurse, are you okay?"

"Yes, it's just a sore throat. Is there anything you actually wanted to say?"

"Well, is there anything you need?" he asks.

"Sure, please drive three hours to bring me some Theraflu and soup, seems reasonable." He can almost hear her rolling her eyes at him.

"If you need, I—"

"I'm going back to bed if that's okay with you," she says, cutting him off.

"Sure, okay," he says and hangs up, then calls the grocery delivery service near her campus and orders Theraflu and tea and soup to be delivered. He questions his decision to send her away to school every day. Did he do the right thing? What if this is the start of the behavior she began displaying last year when she was still home, and she faked sick or skipped class altogether for weeks, and he had to find out from the neighbor kid that everyone in school saw the nude photo she sent to Randy Boswell, a senior at her school.

Aden had snapped. He didn't think. Shannon was right. After everything Leah had been through, and this fucking Boswell kid with his boy-band hair and smug smile thought he could not only humiliate her but ruin her life—threaten that if she didn't do what he wanted, the photo would go up—forever to be searched and found somehow because that shit never truly goes away, does it? But Aden humiliated her further by finding the kid after school and punching him in the jaw. There were no broken bones, but he was still charged with assault and battery on a minor, and if she didn't already hate him, he secured permanent damage that day. He'd just wanted to protect her even though he reacted like a Neanderthal. She was happy to leave that school to be fair, just not happy to be sent away. He wonders if she actually did do "what Randy Boswell wanted," and if the kid posted the photo anyway. He thinks about that a lot. She has a lot of reasons to be angry at the world, but that one would kill him.

I hate you. I didn't want you either! Her words reverberate in his thoughts and the knot in his stomach tightens. He couldn't control her though. He tells himself it was the only thing to do, but now he worries she's not safe there either—not safe anywhere in a world where people can ruin your life with a few keyboard clicks and old men can disappear without a trace.

When Aden walks into the station, he doesn't really expect Hendricks to be there. If he's honest, he hopes the guy is out looking for his father, doing his job, but the police station is buzzing with a quiet energy, low voices and a lot of movement between cubicles.

"Oh, good," Hendricks says when Aden's escorted back to him. "I was going to call you. There are a few things I want to talk to you about. Please, sit."

"What? Has something happened? Did you find him?" he asks, the knot growing, hoping deep down there isn't news because the look on the man's face tells him whatever it is, it is not a good thing.

"No, I'm sorry. No news on your father."

"Then what?"

"Well, there's some other news. You mentioned you heard about Mr. Flynn. Maybe you've also heard about the two young women reported missing and found dead—it was a few years ago, but Rock Harbor isn't a huge city, so…"

"I mean, I don't know. No—I live in Hartford, so probably not."

"It's not uncommon for young women to go missing. There are plenty of unsolved cases, runaways and, well, much worse situations, of course. Amelia Beck and Heather Rossi were unfortunate cases. These two particular young women were last seen in the same part of town, same time of night, both known to be sex workers—both found in a rural wooded area eight miles apart. We have a clear link between the two cases…"

"I'm sorry, but what does this have to do with my father?"

"Well, it doesn't really. But some information has leaked to the press unfortunately, and we had planned a press conference already, but before it blows up, I just wanted to inform you."

"What? Am I suppose to understand what the fuck you're talking about? What leaked? What?"

"The two women died by strangulation, and we linked them because the… Well, the murder weapon was what most people would recognize as a zip tie—but it's actually a castration band for cattle. It's very unusual, and we haven't had much luck on the two cases, but now Harry Flynn has been found in the same manner with the same color and brand of band."

"Holy shit."

"We have a responsibility to at least offer some information for public safety. We want to mitigate the panic response about there being some opportunistic serial killer on the loose."

"But that's what you think it is?" Aden says, a wave of anxiety washing over him at hearing the word *panic*.

"That's what the press might spin it into. We honestly don't know. Look, there is no reason to think that this means your father is…in danger of the same fate. It's unusual for two young women and an older man to be linked like this. So again, I can't say we really know what's going on, but I just wanted to give you this information so you heard it from me first and can ask any questions."

"Christ almighty. How am I gonna tell my mother this?" is all he can say.

"I want you to really think about the odds though, Aden. It's far, far more likely that his truck broke down somewhere remote. And your mother said he has a truck bed full of supplies at all times—water, everything. We intend on finding him alive and well," Hendricks says. Aden doesn't know what to say. He has a dozen questions and then none at the same time because he knows there are no answers to his questions.

When Aden leaves the station, he doesn't know where to go. And for some unknowable reason, he wants nothing more than to talk to Grace—Grace who wouldn't even see the news or paper or have any idea that his life was falling apart. Again.

Before he can decide where to go—how to process what he's just heard, he gets a call from Brady. He pushes Ignore because Brady called twice already, asking him to bring back spicy Cheetos, and he needs to think right now and not be interrupted—he drives along Coastal Drive, wondering how this is happening. Who would want Harry Flynn dead? Two teenage girls and a seventy-something eccentric man. He can't wrap his head around what this could mean. Brady calls again, so he answers this time.

"They found something," he says in a quiet and pensive voice that sounds nothing like his brother.

Aden speeds through the narrow winding road up Fisherman's Bluff toward the landmark Brady gave him. He doesn't know what to expect, but the same image plays in his mind; his father wrapped in emergency blankets in the back of the ambulance, drinking a Styrofoam cup of water from the medics, embarrassed at all the fuss he's caused. His truck fishtailed out and he's been stranded but he's okay.

When he pulls up to the dusty dirt clearing at the top of the bluff, his heart is in his throat. He sees half a dozen cop cars, the sheriff, and an ambulance. Brady is there already, standing with his arms crossed. Aden leaves his car door open and runs over to the edge of the eight-hundred-foot cliff that's taped off, keeping anyone from getting too close.

"What is it, is it him?" Aden asks desperately.

"I don't know. They don't know yet, they won't say anything," Brady says, his voice cracking. He lights a cigarette and runs one hand through his hair anxiously.

They stand silently for several minutes. The shouts of police and medics swirl around them in a surreal and dizzying haze. Then Aden realizes that there are divers in the canyon below, but the tape won't let them see down to what's happening. Then, Brady mumbles, "Fuck this," and pushes past the tape. Nobody else is there besides the police who are not paying attention to them. Brady runs up to the cliff's edge and Aden runs after him. They both freeze a few feet before the drop-off and look over the edge, and they see it.

Their father's Chevy Silverado being lifted by a mechanical crane out from the bottom of Wolf Lake. Martin Coleman nowhere in sight.

13

KIRA

I stand inside the bedroom doorframe and stare a moment, taking in what I'm seeing.

"Ryan," I say, his name getting caught in my throat. He's sitting on the bed, shoving clothes into a backpack. Blankets cover all the windows, paint thinner and drain opener and pseudoephedrine clutter the surfaces in the room. A propane tank sits on a crowded dresser. The stench is overwhelming. There are lesions on his skin, up his arms and on the sides of his mouth.

"Jesus. Get the fuck outta here," he says weakly, and I can see a missing tooth and bloodshot eyes. He's nearly unrecognizable. But I have him. I finally have him. Before I can talk myself out of it, I slam the door shut and pull a kitchen chair over, shoving it under the doorknob to trap him inside the bedroom.

He's cooking meth in here. Brooke's fairy lights are strung above the bed frame, and her blue ballet flats still look like they were just kicked off next to the dresser. The bedspread we bought together for her new grown-up apartment is still on the bed, full of burn marks. Her presence is still there along with her things and he's turned it into a meth lab.

"What the fuck are you doing!?" he screams, pounding at the door.

"Calling the cops unless you talk to me," I say, and I desperately don't want to call the cops because I need him to finally tell me the truth. And since they cleared him, he doesn't have to speak to me or anyone else. But he's fucked now. He's trapped.

I want to believe that this is Ryan going off the deep end out of grief, but it's hard to believe that he couldn't look the way he does in such a short time—gaunt and decaying.

"Fuuuuuck," he screams, beating the door.

"I don't give a shit if you wanna kill yourself with this shit. I really don't, so I don't plan on turning you in as long as you cooperate with me," I say. There is a long silence.

"Then let me out first and I'll tell you whatever you want."

"No," I say. I can't risk him running. It does me no good if the cops find his drug den after he's long gone and I get nothing out of it.

"Jesus. Fine. What!?"

"For starters…do you know where she is? Ryan. Please. Do you know anything?" I say, sliding down the door to the floor.

"I swear to God. I don't. You think I want all these shit cops asking me questions—you up my ass? If I knew, I'd tell you."

"Did she know you're doing drugs—cooking drugs, whatever the fuck you're doing?" I ask, and he laughs.

"You're like, just as oblivious as she said you were," he says. I remember how defensive I was when the police asked me about Brooke's lifestyle, when Celie said she was using. I don't want to know what he has to say. I want to keep telling myself that my baby would never allow this, but I have to know the truth.

"She was last seen around 10:00 p.m. on The Strip. You told the police you didn't know where she went."

"I didn't. I know she went there for pickups sometimes."

"Pickups?" I ask, and he sighs.

"Score some meth." And there it is. The undeniable truth. Two girls dead. Both are girls from The Strip and drug users and now I have to swallow this truth. The urge to wail and beat my fists into the door until it breaks down and I can claw Ryan's face off with my own fingers for getting my daughter into this is overwhelming. I try to control my shaking hands and breathe.

"So you did know where she was?" I ask.

"I didn't. She said she was gonna run an errand and then she never came back. I was partying with my friends, I didn't notice. I assume she went down there and scored something good and partied with whoever—whoever she got it from. I didn't lie. I don't know for sure 'cause she didn't say."

"How would she—how did she get drugs, the drugs? Did you get her into this?" I ask, suddenly realizing this is probably who he was all along and put on a good front that I never suspected. His complete silence is my answer.

Is this why she started calling me less and talking about putting off college in the fall? She was on a music scholarship. My sweet cello-playing honors student. This cannot be happening. I feel my cheeks go numb. I can't have a panic attack. I need to stay strong. I need to take in every piece of information. I don't want to ask the next question. I feel tears forming behind my eyes.

"How do you get the money for it?" I ask, and I hear a quiet bitter scoff from behind the door. He doesn't answer. I don't need him to.

"That's all I know. I had witnesses with me all night, I offered DNA and a polygraph—whatever they needed—but you already know that, 'cause you can't leave me alone, so what else do you want? I can't tell you what I don't know and that's all I know," he says, and at this moment, I believe him.

This is what he was hiding from me—not information about Brooke's whereabouts. He wasted weeks of my time. If I knew. If I knew this is what she'd gotten into, I would have been looking in a totally different direction. I hate him more than I've ever hated anyone. I think about calling the cops on him anyway. Then, I think that I might want to keep this tucked away in case I need to blackmail him in the future for more information.

I look in every room and closet and shelf in the apartment before I leave, collecting anything I can grab that belonged to Brooke—her favorite travel mug, her sheet music, a stuffed unicorn, and her sloth socks, and I walk out of the apartment, leaving him locked in the bedroom. He can find a way out.

Tears blur my vision as I drive to Hemlock Lane. *The Strip.* I hate everything about this horrible place. I found a glimmer of hope in it until now because I thought there must be some crazy reason she'd be down here and if we could find it, we could find her. I held on to that because it's all I had. A simple explanation for why she was last seen there needed to make sense. Now that it does, it's worse than I ever imagined.

A storm is gathering as I pull into the parking lot of White Horse Tavern and stare at the blinking neon sign across the street that says Live Nudes. Brooke loved the autumn storms in Maine. They've become more frequent and severe in recent years and she always had a soapbox speech about how it was because of global warming. She cares so much about that stuff—will argue toe to toe with anyone who disagrees.

The ache in my gut feels like a pang of hunger, acute and distracting. I don't know where to start. I feel like nobody wants to be involved, and so even if they *have* seen her, they'd lie. They don't want to have a cop around, asking questions. This feels futile, but what else can I do? This is where she was. It's where the other girls hung out. There has to be a clue here.

I decide to drive behind the row of bars and tattoo shops and clubs—down the alleyways and see if girls like Brooke make their transactions there because nobody in the bars seem to know her.

The alley is wet and narrow. I see a mattress on the ground next to a dumpster. The man sitting on it glares at me. He has a shopping cart next to him filled with empty soda bottles and plastic bags. He places a hand on it as if to guard it from me. Two young girls wearing miniskirts and too much makeup are sitting on the stoop of a shop, sharing something from a bottle. They open a steel back door and hurry inside upon seeing me. A middle-aged gap-toothed man in a trench coat smacks the hood of my car as it crawls over the potholes and navigates the narrow clearing.

"Heya, baby!" He grabs his cock and laughs, but moves out of the way with his hands up in some mock surrender as if I was the one accosting him. I watch the splinters of lightning illuminate his face and the rows of metal trash cans behind him. I think of Brooke here, and the shame swells in my chest. I didn't protect her.

Before I reach the end of the alley, I see a figure, all bony legs, resting elbows to knees and smoking a cigarette on the back stairs of a shop. I recognize him. It's Vinny Donatto.

I stop the car and turn off the ignition and he looks up at me. As if instinctively, he stands, tosses his smoke and starts to go inside.

"Vinny," I say, exiting the car and closing the door behind me. My car blocks the alley, but I don't care. I can't imagine any other idiot would be driving back here for any reason. "You're Vinny," I repeat.

"Yeah," he sighs as if caught red-handed doing something bad.

"I need to talk to you."

"Yeah, yeah, aright," he says in his thick East Coast accent, taking a second cigarette out of his pocket and sitting back down on the stairs. "Come on."

"Do you know who I am?" I ask, following him, hesitantly.

"Yeah, I know. You're on the news and stuff. I know who ya are." He holds a cigarette out, offering me one. I shake my head and sit down on a concrete block across from him.

"Then why did you run from me?" I ask, expecting a lie to begin to form on his lips.

"'Cause Connie fucking Reed, that's why. She got the cops all over my ass after Amelia went missin'. It was a nightmare. I don't need any more trouble," he says.

"I don't want to cause you trouble," I say, and I hope he doesn't detect the desperation in my voice. "I just need answers. I—I know that you were cleared and there were no texts or social media between you and Amelia—no calls. No connection just like you said. I believe you," I say, having no idea what I believe, but needing him to trust me too.

"There's no calls or texts because she's a teenager and I was thirty fucking years old and not a complete pervert. Because there is no relationship even though looney tunes Connie

Reed wants to flap her jaw and tell everyone there was. She was a kid for God's sake. She shoulda never been down here at all, but that bitch didn't care a thing about Amelia, or she'd still be alive. That's the truth and I don't feel bad sayin' it," he says, and maybe it's because he pegs Connie for who she is so accurately that I begin to actually trust what he's saying.

"Then how did you know her?"

"She came back here doin' what every other girl is doin' back here, and then, on her way to the bus stop she'd stop by my shop, bum a smoke or ask if there was any day-old bagels she could have, and I'd give her some Camels and a couple a' onion and chives and we'd sit and talk while she smoked. We chatted about stupid shit—skateboarding, bands. I tried to tell her to get the hell outta here while she still can is what I did—unlike fucking Connie who didn't give two shits about her," he says, pitching his cigarette butt with all his might across the alley.

"I met the woman," I say, hoping to gain trust. "I see what you mean about her."

"Real piece a' work, that chick. Real fruitcake."

"Yeah," I quietly agree.

"I see a zillion girls just like Amelia. I hate to say it, man. But this shit pit I'm forced to work in, ya see it all. You know sixty years ago, when my grandpa opened this business, it was a nice place to be, man. There was a prairie across the street. Can you believe that? A fuckin' prairie with flowers and shit. No Juicy Lucy, no Doggie Styles Cabaret. Just some nice mom-and-pop shops selling newspapers and yo-yos and shit."

"I'm sorry what you had to go through with Amelia," I say and mean it. There's something about him that feels genuine. The rain falls in torrents now and we both stand simultaneously and move back farther under the awning to escape the splashes from the fat drops hitting the cobblestones below us.

I don't want this natural shift to serve as his cue to end the conversation. I need more.

"I know what you want," he says, taking me completely off guard. "And ya gotta understand, I didn't run from you 'cause I knew anything important. It's 'cause a' what that bitch put me through. I can't do it again. I don't know anything, but I did know her."

"What?" I say. Momentarily paralyzed, the pounding of the rain loud and hissing and his words filling my head and making it feel light and dizzy. "You what?"

"Not *know* her exactly, but I talked to her a few times. Most of the girls that come around hear from other girls they know that I always give out leftover deli food and smokes—I did that to try to help them, and so lots of 'em stop by. A couple I did convince to go back home and get the fuck out. I thought Brooke would be one of those," he says, and her name in his mouth is shocking. He continues, "Funny, huh? Not the mission in life I thought I'd have. I was gonna write great books. Now I give bagels to hookers and tell 'em to go home. Life's a sneaky snake like that." The word *hooker* feels like a sharp stab to the heart.

"You…knew her," I say, swallowing, my breath shallow, aching for more information.

"She came by two or three times. Same thing as all the others…" he says, and for the first time I want to punch him—scream that she is not like all the others, but I do not. I keep listening.

"She drank a forty of High Life and talked about music school," he says, and I try to keep my facial features arranged in the right configuration and my pulse steady. I can't react. I need to hear it all.

"She wanted to go to school, but something about a boyfriend who didn't want her to, so she was trying to get out of the relationship. I mean, honestly, the story isn't new, so I don't remember the details," he says and a lightness washes over me. She wanted out. She lost her way and she screwed up but she knew it, and she was trying to get out. Of course she was.

"Did she…" I swallow and control my shaking voice. "Did she say anything else at all?"

"No, that night she said she was gonna go do *somethin' wild*. And I says *didn't you do that already?* Assuming what I assumed is the only reason she was down here, and she laughed and said *no, I'm gonna go to the cabin and get some money off my creepy stepdad. I have a plan.* And that was it. I told her to be careful and she giggled at me and walked away."

I open my mouth to speak, but nothing comes out. My jaw remains gaped and I just stare at him.

"What?" he says.

"It's just her stepdad—my husband…wasn't at the cabin that week. He wasn't even in the state, so that doesn't—I just—she called him creepy? I don't—"

"I told you all I know. That's what she said, said she was stopping by Lucky's and then going to get money off him. I swear to God I don't know anything else. I never saw her again," he says and then hangs his head. "I wish I had. I'm sorry."

"Thank you," I say, and then turn and run through the rain, covering my head with my purse, to my waiting car. *Gonna go do something wild* repeats in my mind. What does that mean? I drive around the corner of the alley and back to Lucky's parking lot where I turn off the ignition and stare up at the security camera that caught the last glimpse of my beautiful baby girl. I think about his words—*creepy stepdad*. She was going to see him at our family cabin, but he wasn't there, so who was she going to see?

Exhaustion and confusion and rage take over as the rain pounds down on the roof of my car in deafening cracks, and I scream and beat the steering wheel with my fists.

14

GRACE

Grace stands at the stove in the inn's boxy farm kitchen and chops garlic at the butcher block island. She crushes basil with a pestle and mortar and listens to Billie Holiday's voice warm the room. She tries to tell herself she's safe, but when the wind catches the screen door and whips it open, slamming it into the siding outside and making a crack that almost stops her heart, she is back on edge and panicked.

She opens the back door and pulls the screen door behind it closed, latching the hook-and-eye lock. She looks out into the vast woods and shudders. When the lightning flashes, she sees the shed and cellar in the stretch of backyard being pummeled with heavy rain. The trees are illuminated and look like skeletons in a Halloween movie since shedding most of their leaves. She thinks of that figure she saw, running through the trees last week and double-locks the door. It was a hunter or a jogger, she knows. She's safer than she's ever been, she reminds herself, taking a long breath in and blowing it out with her cheeks.

She wonders if Aden will come back. After her reaction, maybe he's too uncomfortable. There's an indescribable emptiness in his absence. She's carefully carved out a life for herself that allows her as little interaction with other people as humanly possible, but as the years pass by and her loneliness is swallowing her whole, she longs to be normal at the same time.

She resents all of the things she'll never have—a college roommate, getting drunk at a bar, a first love exploding into her heart, a fight, a breakup, a road trip, a friend—she resents the life that man robbed her of when he found her asleep on a laundromat bench and thought she was an object for the taking.

She can't explain why she needs Aden gone but wants him to stay all at the same time, so she tries to push away the thought of him. She tosses the garlic into a sizzling saucepan and the sharp smell permeates the room, mixing with the earthy smell of rain that gushed through the back door minutes earlier, and she sits at the table with a glass of wine and lets it all wash over her. *I am safe*, she repeats to herself as Hobbes blinks at her from his bed in the corner. Everything is fine.

Just then, she hears tires pull up onto wet gravel; she pulls the hot pan off the burner and hurries to the front door, which she also double-locked, unsure of Aden's return, and peeks out the side window. When she can see it's him, she quickly unlocks the deadbolts and runs back to the kitchen so she doesn't look like she's been waiting for him. She turns down Billie and puts the pan back on the burner, adds the pasta and tosses it.

"Hello," she hears him call as he comes into the kitchen

doorframe, drenched. He puts down a stack of papers he's carrying and pulls his messenger bag off his shoulder and sets it all down on a kitchen chair.

"Oh, my gosh," she says at the sight of him, doing her best acting to appear as if he startled her. "Here." She pulls a few towels out of a low cupboard and hands them to him.

"Thanks," he says, taking them and sitting down. He runs one over his face and through his hair, then takes off his coat and places it across the back of the kitchen chair. He looks exhausted and pale.

"You okay?" she asks, and he rubs his eyes with his palms and nods. "Hungry?"

"It's okay. Thanks. I'll get out of your hair." But before he can get up, she places a wineglass in front of him and begins filling it.

"You look like you could use this," she says, and he smiles and takes it.

"Thanks."

"Are you sure you're not hungry? Because you look starving," she says, and as she does, she is slightly horrified at her own words and the unrecognizable sound of her voice. Is she... flirting? Gross. What the hell is she saying?

"Little late to be cooking, isn't it?" he asks.

"Yeah, I'm a night owl, I guess," she lies, not wanting him to know she was worried about him—waiting for him.

"Well, I am actually starving," he says, and she scoops her famous *aglio e olio* with shrimp onto two plates and sets them on the table. They eat in silence until Hobbes comes over and puts a paw on Aden's leg, hoping for a scrap. They both smile at this and he hands the pup a piece of shrimp.

"Any progress?" she asks, knowing she needs to, but hoping to avoid getting any details. She can see in his face something has happened. He looks older, somehow, in the space of a day.

Sadder—a totally different person than the man who arrived a handful of days earlier. She can't imagine he'd tell her what the thing that happened is, now that he knows her past—has seen the way she responded to it all.

"Still don't know anything concrete," is all he says. "Let's talk about anything else right now if that's okay with you."

They eat quietly again, the distant hum of Billie Holiday's voice nearly drowned out by the rain, heavy on the roof.

"Look, I'm sorry for yesterday. It's not against the law to look someone up. I shouldn't have—"

"No, I'm sorry," he interrupts. "It was a stupid thing to say." He fiddles with the stem of his wineglass. "This is delicious, by the way."

"Thanks."

"How'd you learn to cook so well?" he asks.

"I have a lot of time on my hands." Her mouth twitches into something resembling a smile.

"My brother's a chain-smoker," he says, seemingly out of nowhere. She pauses the bite of pasta she was about to take halfway to her mouth and looks up at him with raised eyebrows.

"Oh. I'mmm...sorry?" she says, and he gives a weak laugh.

"To answer your question about why I don't stay with my family. He's a recovering addict and lives with my mother, so the house smells half like an ashtray and half like tuna casserole, and one hundred percent like childhood memories. I wasn't popular if you couldn't tell—not a lot of great recollections in my childhood bedroom. And it's constantly full of people—like all his AA friends playing poker in the garage, Mom's bridge pals, relatives that seem to never leave. It's the embodiment of an anxiety attack. Hard pass. So, since you asked, that's why."

She smiles and stifles a laugh.

"Well that's a lot of reasons," she says, but the only one that's sticking is that he wasn't popular. Actually she couldn't tell, and would have guessed the exact opposite, but it makes them more...the same, and she likes that.

"And I have a feeling it's about to turn into a media circus," he says and then quickly adds, "Sorry, we don't need to—never mind."

"No, it's okay. It's—I can't imagine what you're going through. And your poor mother. God. It's awful."

"Yeah. She's like that last person who should have to deal with this, ya know? She's literally everything good in the world—like Sunday school and brownies and hugs and Christmas Eve all wrapped up together," he says. "You'd really like her," he adds, and their eyes lock. She smiles affectionately at him for just a moment until she has to look away because she doesn't know what to do in a moment like this. He leans back in his chair and fidgets with his fork, winding noodles around it and then unwinding them.

"It's killing her," he says. Grace nods.

"I'm so sorry," is all she can think to say even though it's not enough.

"Listen," he says. "I'm talking her into staying with my aunt and uncle for a little while, so I can get out of your hair and leave you be if you—"

"No," she says, more quickly than intended. Then she feels like an idiot, and so she nervously stands and walks to pick up the wine bottle from the counter.

"I mean the smoke and tuna smells. Sounds..."

"Like a form of hell," he says, completing her thought.

"Yes, you should stay," she says. "If you want." Then she picks up the bottle, but when she glances down at the stack of papers he's placed there, her heart almost stops completely. There is a girl's face looking back at her with the words *miss-*

ing above her head. A girl who looks a lot like her, and it's so unexpected and triggering that she drops the bottle. It shatters, splashing deep red liquid all over the light wood floors. It immediately looks like a crime scene, and Aden leaps to his feet to grab the towels he dried his hair with and help sop it up. But she doesn't move to clean it up—she just stands there, frozen.

"What's wrong?" he says, urgently throwing towels on top of the wine threatening to run all the way over to the white throw rugs. Hobbes whimpers, makes two circles before laying down on his bed and watching them.

"I'm sorry, I'm—"

"Hey, it's okay, I can get this. Why don't you just sit…" he says, touching her elbow to help her sit down, but she instinctively jerks it away.

"Sorry."

"No," she says. "Sorry." She can't form any other words, so she sits down as instructed and watches him clean up the shards of glass and bloody-looking wine. While he's cleaning, she can't slow her heart rate down. She's trying to breathe in—one, two, three, four—and out with an eight count like she was taught. She's actively trying not to have a panic attack.

"Who is that girl?" she asks, and he stops what he's doing and looks at her. She points to the missing persons poster on top of a stack of papers he brought in.

"God, Grace. I'm so sorry. I know you go to a lot of trouble to not see the news and the paper, and I should have brought it to my room first, I—"

"No. It's—I just want to know why you have that."

Aden picks up the dripping towels, places them in the sink, and rinses his hands.

"Are you sure you want to talk about this?"

"I want to know why you have that," she says again, impatient now. He walks over, picks up some of the papers, and sits down next to her, spreading them across the table.

"This is Amelia Beck and this," he says producing yet another face of a missing girl on a poster, "is Heather Rossi. They were missing and then showed up...well, dead. You probably heard about—oh, right. Sorry. Well, the cases were similar, a few years apart but they were last seen in the same part of town, found in rural woods, have a similar look..."

"But what does that have to do with you?"

"My father..." he begins.

"What could these girls possibly have to do with your father?" she asks, trembling, unsure if she can continue the conversation—but now she needs to know.

"They think there might be a connection—well, they're not saying that, but some guy my dad's age, Harry, a friend of his actually—was found dead, just like these two girls. All of them, I guess... There were similarities, so I have no fucking idea how two teenagers and an old guy are related, but it looks like they are, so now my dad, who is the same age as Harry is missing, and it looks...bad," he says, and Grace feels a tingle like fingers running up her spine. She steadies her breath. A string of people disappearing and her being this close to it is her worst nightmare, but she can't shake how much the girls look like her. Maybe not now because she's years older, and Aden can't see that because she's changed so much, but Grace's stomach twists as she waits for his reply.

"What kind of similarities?" she asks, staring at the faces of Amelia, a pale-complexioned thin redhead who she thinks looks just like Anne of Green Gables, and Heather, with her green eyes and smattering of freckles across her nose. Her heart throbs, her pulse quickens even more.

"Grace, hey," he says, moving his chair over to her and

placing a hand on top of hers. "I can't imagine what you must be feeling. I…"

"I need to know. Please. I'm fine, just tell me what happened," she says, and Aden takes a deep breath, picks up his wineglass and takes a sip, then looks down at the missing girls' faces.

"They were all…killed the same way."

"How?"

"Grace…"

"How?"

"Strangulation."

"But how does that link them? Lots of people are choked, I…" She almost says it. *I was choked and there are still scars on my neck under all the wooly sweaters and scarves I wear,* but she does not. She stops and changes gear. "That doesn't link an elderly man and two teens."

"Well, right. But the same…weapon was used," he says haltingly, obviously uncomfortable telling her this.

"What does that mean?"

"They're these yellow zip ties except they're not actually zip ties like for storage, they're castration bands? For cattle, I guess. And that's a very specific thing to find on all three of them," he says, and she cups her hands over her mouth, willing herself not to throw up.

She can't tell him yet what she just realized. She stands and then hunches over, resting her hands on her knees, trying to breathe. He moves to her and puts his arm around her. She wants to run like she has every other time, pushing him away, but she doesn't. She lets him pull her into his body and allows herself to bury her head in his shoulder.

"Oh, Grace," he whispers, and something is happening. She's making a connection that she has spent years praying she'd never have to face. She knows those yellow bands. They hung on that basement wall—a couple dozen on a hook next to an old dartboard and a poster of Johnny Cash.

But she didn't know there were other girls. She never imagined that. She thought she was in the wrong place at the wrong time and some psychopath got a hold of her, but that she won. She escaped.

But they're dead. And she should be dead too, except that she was lucky and she got away. She's just realized that she holds the key to all of this, but she needs to be sure she's right before she tells him anything. Her hiccupped cries soften and he holds her tightly against him until she pulls back. He looks at her, and there is a strange electricity between them—a longing that has no right showing up in this moment. He touches his forehead to hers and she lets him. She wants so much to reach up and touch the side of his face and let her lips brush against his—such a foreign feeling, a terrifying possibility, but still she wants it. Of course, after what she's just discovered, she knows she can't.

"Are you okay?" he asks as she pulls away.

"Yeah. Yes. I just—it's just a lot. I'm gonna go get some sleep." She forces a final weak smile, and he squeezes her hand one more time before letting go.

"Of course. Again, I'm…"

"Don't be sorry," she says, and taps her leg so Hobbes gets up and follows her. She walks slowly so her limp is less pronounced, and exits the kitchen. When she reaches the stairs to her room, she sits, holding her chest, clenching her fists and suppressing a wail. There are other girls. Could she have saved them? All she knows for sure is she has to do something now—something that will stop this from ever happening again.

15

ADEN

Early the next morning, Aden drives again to his mother's house. As expected there are a couple of TV station vans, and eager reporters ready with microphones and cameramen standing by to see if they can get a statement from one of them. He's glad his mother agreed to go to Herb and Ginny's for a few days, but he's also worried about how Brady will handle it. He's fragile, Aden thinks, more so since recovery, and he's quick to anger, always has been. He does not need the Channel Five anchor popped in the nose, aiming the spotlight even closer on his family.

After he parks, he mimics what he's seen on dozens of crime shows and looks straight ahead, shielding the side of his face with his hand, nonresponsive to any of the vultures in his yard until he's safe inside the house. On *48 Hours* or *Dateline*, he always wondered why the people didn't just say something to the press to get them off their back, but now the violation of privacy is infuriating. What kind of people harass a family in the middle of a crisis? It's animalistic. How do they go home like everyone else and live with themselves after spending the day tormenting a grieving family?

When he closes the door behind him, he expects Brady to be smoking and eating a pile of Toaster Strudels like he has been every other morning, but the house is dark, the drapes closed. He hasn't been inside the house without his parents here since he was a teenager—it's eerily quiet and joyless. He calls for Brady, but there's no answer. They were going to go over all of the facts of the case and make a plan of who will look where for the day, like every day since his father vanished.

"Brady?" He walks down the stairs to Brady's basement room and taps on the door with his knuckles. No answer. He pushes the door open with his index finger and pokes his head in. This is his brother's life. Almost forty years old and the room looks like a college apartment. He has a DVD tower for God's sake. A television set up on an overturned box that it came in instead of an entertainment center, a round, braided area rug to cover the cement basement floor under the bed, and an overflowing ashtray, for some reason, sitting inside a pizza box on his neatly made bed. He keeps his clothes in plastic storage bins and has an *X-Files* poster next to his bed, no frame—just tacked to the wall, teenaged-boy-room style. It's really quite a depressing sight.

No career, no apartment, no girlfriend, just a collection of He-Man memorabilia and an Xbox. When he's asked Brady why he's not working as a car mechanic anymore, he says something about disability. Aden doesn't think one can get disability for frying their brain with 8-balls, but what does he know? He's pretty sure their parents give him an allowance and that he's full of shit, but he's decided that it's none of his business. He knows Brady works very part time at a retirement home, and with all his free time, Mom has someone to go to church with her and dad has someone to do jigsaw puzzles with, so if everyone says they're happy, then he'll leave it be.

When he walks back upstairs, he opens the front drapes a crack and sees Brady's car that must have just pulled up, and there's Brady, just chatting away with the reporters.

"Oh, fuck me," Aden mutters. Brady could say absolutely any wild thing—he could incriminate himself without knowing it or simply make shit up because he lives in a world of his own, and this is exactly why Aden cannot tell him about Martin being seen on The Strip. He can't even imagine.

Aden rushes out to the ABC News van with a giant satellite on the roof and a very young woman standing in front of it wearing a pantsuit that's a size too big and makes her look like she's playing dress up.

"Brady, come on," he says, taking his elbow.

"Mr. Coleman, we just have a couple of questions for the concerned public..."

"What's wrong?" Brady asks him. "They're nice. They're askin' about Dad," he says and turns back to the pantsuit woman and finishes his statement.

"Just 'cause they pulled his truck out doesn't mean he's dead. He's a good swimmer, and they're looking into his phone records so they know where he was just before. So, we're gonna find him. We're not worried," he says, and Aden closes his eyes and shakes his head. He looks to the camera.

"We're definitely worried," then to Brady. "Let's go," he says, pulling his brother away from the reporters. Brady follows behind, childlike.

"What's wrong with you? I'm trying to help the concerned

public." Aden closes the front door when they get inside and closes the gap in the drapes.

"You told them we weren't worried."

"Yeah, 'cause you gotta stay positive. You gotta show that you know he'll be found. What if Ma saw it?"

"You can't—do you think it looks good for his family to *not be worried*?" Aden asks, walking into the kitchen and pulling out coffee grounds and a mug. Brady follows him.

"They know what I mean, sheesh. It looks bad if you don't talk to them."

"Says who?" Aden asks.

"It looks like we have something to hide if we don't." Aden ignores this and shifts gears.

"Speaking of looking bad, where have you been all night?" he asks, praying Brady isn't using again. But judging by the dark circles under his eyes and his sallow skin, he's not sure.

"All night?"

"Your bed doesn't look slept in, so…"

"First, what are you doing in my room, Nancy Drew? Second, I made my bed before I went to AA this morning, what's it to ya?" Aden thinks about the ashtray and pizza box on the bed and can't imagine a scenario where he places that there after making it, but he's not going to press the matter.

"Okay, glad you went to AA," is all he says, hoping it's true, afraid all this could easily trigger a relapse.

"Ya want a Toaster Strudel?" Brady says, rifling around in the freezer.

"No, thanks," Aden says, taking his coffee to the table and sitting. He feels as though talking to Brady about this is as good as talking to a brick wall, but there's nobody else here and he needs the questions in his mind to be out in the world and sorted through.

"I don't know what to make of Harry and the two girls—

the connection. I can't get my head around it." Brady lights a cigarette and sits across from him, the smell making Aden's stomach churn.

"I know, I mean what do two teenage girls have in common with Harry that got 'em all killed? So the girls are like stripper-types, on dope, and then Harry…well. You know what he's like."

"Yes. Okay," Aden says before he goes on a tangent about him.

"That guy should be at the retirement home playing chutes and ladders all day and eating Nutter Butters, but he's at Mexican swim-up bars banging smokin' hot Spanish chicks."

"I get it, thank you," Aden says.

"And then someone strangles him. Of all things. God, I mean…what if—if like, okay, so now Dad's truck was found and his phone was in it, and he's nowhere around, like what explanation could there possibly be? I've gone over it a million times in my head," Brady says. "Aliens? Mafia? Are there mafia in Rock Harbor, ya think? What if someone has him? Is he a spy? Ya think he's selling meth like—ooh, like *Breaking Bad* and the Mexican cartel has him. Oh, shit, 'cause Harry was always in Mexico—oh, my God. I could be on to something!" he says, getting excited. "What if he was smuggling drugs and got Dad into it?"

Aden considers this a moment and it's not actually the dumbest thing he's ever said, because something absolutely insane is going on here, but he can't fuel this fire with Brady right now.

"Why don't we try to focus on what we can do today, because we're not going to Mexico on a hunch at the moment," Aden says.

"But I should tell Detective Hendricks this. Don't ya think so?"

"Sure," Aden replies because what could it hurt and it will

give Brady a task for the morning. "And then here's the map for today. The red is places we've already looked but should circle back to and the blue is downstream of where his truck was found. These are the lookouts or camping spots along the canyon. I'll go to them today and you stay in town and talk to Hendricks."

"Yeah, yeah, okay," he agrees.

"Tell Hendricks, NOT the press, your drug cartel theory though. Promise?"

"Okay, but I'm on to something." Aden squeezes Brady's shoulder, then pours his coffee into a travel mug and sets out to spend another day searching for his father.

By the time darkness falls in the late evening, and Aden has driven to every clearing and RV park and lookout downstream, along the bluffs where the truck was found, he knows that it's time to drive down to Hemlock Lane—The Strip— and try to see if he can get any answers there.

Reluctantly, he parks his car on the south end—the main area with shops and bars and clubs is only a few blocks long, so he'll just start on one end and go into as many places as he can—show Martin's photo and see if anyone recognizes him. He starts at a sex shop called Good Vibrations and the heavily mustached, plump forty-something working behind the counter tells him he needs to make a purchase before he'll talk. Aden bumps into a rack of various sizes anal beads and double-sided dildos and his face reddens. He doesn't really know what to even ask this guy, so he just leaves, figuring he is going to get absolutely nowhere with this. After wandering down the sidewalk for some time, he musters up the courage to begin showing his father's photo to passersby, a guy sitting on a stack of tires outside a closed down mechanics garage, and a clerk at a liquor store. He can't believe that this is his life at this moment—showing photos of his dad. *His dad*. To strangers. In sex shops. It's surreal and disturbing and Aden desperately does not want to be here.

He walks a little farther and shows the image to a few more people, and nobody seems to know him. Then he stops outside of a strip club called Babeland. He hesitates a moment, deciding whether he should go in or if this is completely futile, when a woman with pink hair and the longest eyelashes he's ever seen walks up to the side door of the strip club with a duffel bag almost the size of her body and pauses to light a cigarette.

"Excuse me," he says, thinking if she's never seen Martin, and she obviously works here, maybe he won't even bother going in.

She looks up, startled, but then arranges a pleasant look on her face and says, "Sorry, hon, I can't help you until we're inside."

"No, sorry, it's just—I'm looking for someone."

"Well, in that case I don't know her and she doesn't work here," she says, blowing smoke in his face.

"No. Please, that's not…" He waves the smoke away and pulls out the eight by ten photo of Martin, because he doesn't know if the missing persons poster will scare people away from talking to him.

"This man," he says and she squints and looks at it more closely.

"Oh, well, yeah, I see him a lot when I'm walking in for my shift on Fridays. Never saw him *inside* the club, but down there at the Cliffmere intersection. He's so cute, isn't he? He gave me a Bible once." She giggles.

"He did?" Aden laughs suddenly with an overwhelming sense of relief.

"Yeah. Super nice guy—I mean if you don't mind religion being forced down your throat or whatever."

THE VANISHING HOUR

"Yeah," he laughs awkwardly again in agreement. "So he was handing out Bibles?"

"Yeah, well, I mean. He was. Technically."

"What does—technically—what do you mean?"

"I mean he was standing there—over there." She points to the corner. "You know, inviting people to church and handing out tiny little New Testaments, but I always wondered if he was down there for the guys, ya know?"

"No. I don't know—what?"

"Well, it's like kinda notorious, I guess you could say. Abbott and Fifth Street—the corner where the married guys come to find…you know, a guy for the night. It's easy for a girl to make a buck down here. But the male junkies, gay or not, mostly not, gotta suck a dick or two themselves if they want to score some cash or a little meth or whatever. I wondered if that's what he was always doing—in the same spot and all—never coming inside where most guys would end up if they wanted…a girl."

The look of horror on Aden's face must have registered with the pink-haired woman because she rearranged her features again and gave a wave of her hand.

"But I'm sure he was saving souls and shit. No, for real. That's what it looked like. I never saw him do nothin' weird. It's just he'd be like *literally* the only guy down here not looking for…a little something."

"Right," Aden says in a whisper, at a loss for words.

"Is he okay? Why are you looking for him?"

"No. He's…missing."

"Oh, my God," the woman says, stamping out her cigarette and taking the photo out of Aden's hand and staring at it.

"Is it your dad? He looks like you." Aden nods, still processing what she's told him.

"Oh, honey, I'm sorry. I wish I could say I'm shocked but

139

this place isn't the safest place to hang out. You think he went and got himself into some trouble, huh?"

"I don't—I don't even know what that means. I don't know."

"Not everyone takes well to being told they're sinners and invited to church."

"No, I'm sure they don't," he agrees.

"I don't know what's worse for him—if he was looking for guys or telling people they were going to hell, but either one can get ya in trouble down here. I'm sorry. I really hope you find him," she says, and then hands the photo back and pulls her giant duffel bag over her shoulder. She gives a pouty lip and a little wave as she disappears behind the side door of the strip club.

Aden sits down on the shallow concrete stair in front of the door and stares at his father's face. How, in the space of one day, can this have taken such a turn? This morning, he was still a guy who probably got confused without his medication and now it's been suggested that he had a secret life as part of a Mexican drug cartel or a closeted gay man and Aden just can't believe any of it. He knows his father and none of that seems possible. But he can't shake the nagging feeling, despite how much he rejects the idea, that he did get himself into trouble down here. That he pissed off the wrong person, and that it definitely does not look good for Martin Coleman.

16

KIRA

Before the sun comes up, I sit outside the cabin on a camping chair, smelling the smoky remains of last night's campfire that my dad must have put out late, because the embers
are still simmering. The horizon is painted with pink streaks
through the red spruce trees, and it's a morning Brooke would
love. The bite in the air, coffee before dawn. I want to wake
up my father and ask if he was here that weekend, but I know
he's said a dozen times he was at Moosehead Lake with the
guys. So why would she tell someone she was coming here?
Matt was in New York, and I have to wonder if this Vinny
kid just has it wrong. But what reason would he have to make
anything up? Why would he know the detail of the cabin, or
that she had a stepdad?

It's too early for most places to be open, but I decide to

drive around and find anywhere that is open—ask at gas stations and truck stops—ask if anyone saw her or recognizes her car, anything. I've exhausted my options, I know, but I can't not keep moving. I can't just sit around and hope and pray.

By the time the sun comes up, I decide one more time to drive past Dana Rossi's house. Amelia's foster mom led me to Vinny, which led me to new information. No matter how much I didn't want to hear it, it's valuable, and maybe Heather's mother could offer me some thread of direction she doesn't even know she has. She hasn't answered the door in weeks, and it's probably a waste of time, but I need to keep stopping by every few days just in case I can catch her. Ask her why she seems to be hiding from me like Vinny—like Celie—just because they don't want to be involved. It's infuriating.

As I drive the dirt road to Dana's house, I pass acres of cornfields, the stalks now browned and brittle. The trees look like bony fingers reaching up to the sky, having shed most of their leaves, which allows me a decent view of the red farmhouse in the distance. My heart jolts when I think I see a car parked next to the dilapidated barn. Plumes of dust lick up behind my tires as I speed up, my eyes fixed on what I think, yes, is definitely a car, until I'm close enough to see the old Toyota Corolla. A sign of life. I park next to it quickly and rush out of the car, terrified that I could lose her—that she could run out and drive off before I can even speak, but there is no movement.

I walk up to the front door and tap it lightly, calling out, "Hello? Dana?" I don't hear anything, until suddenly the front door swings open and a slight middle-aged woman with a close-cropped haircut and something of a scowl on her face is standing in front of me. Not Dana Rossi.

"Yes?" she says impatiently.

"Hi, uh… I was looking for Dana? Isn't this her house?"

"She isn't expecting visitors," she says, drying off her hands with a tea towel and tossing it on her shoulder. She puts one hand on her hip and looks me up and down.

"She's here? It's just, I've been trying to…"

"Who is it?" a small voice from somewhere in the back of the house calls.

"I don't know!" the woman calls back, then to me. "Who is ya?"

"I'm Kira Everett. I've been trying to get in touch with Ms. Rossi for a few weeks," I say and then I realize what this is. The woman's shirt has an embroidered logo on the pocket that says Full Hearts Hospice, the stale air and medicinal smell are pungent, and I suddenly understand that Dana must be very ill.

"You're a nurse," I say, and she just sighs.

"I'll ask her if she's up for visitors, but we just got back from the hospital yesterday, so I can't promise. What's it about anyway?"

"Heather," I say, wondering if I can really burden her in this way—bringing up her dead child right now. But I have to. The woman raises her eyebrows at me, then turns and disappears down the long hall next to a neglected wooden staircase. After a moment, she comes halfway back down the hall and waves me in.

Inside the living room, mustard-yellow drapes cover the oversize front windows. Specs of dust dance in the sliver of light coming through the crack between the fabric and dimly lit small room. Dana is lying in a hospital bed set up in front of the television where low canned laughter erupts from a rerun of *Ghost Whisperer*. She looks very frail. She wears a daffodil-yellow nightgown and a knit cap pulled down over her pale forehead. She smiles brightly at me.

"You have to be Kira," she says weakly, and I nod, surprised she knows who I am.

"Would you like to sit down?" she asks, and I sit in the armchair next to her bed. I wonder if losing her child is literally killing her. I see a flash of my future in the giant sippy cup with an accordion straw, an IV taped to my arm, the slight odor of urine in the stale air. Did her body just start shutting down the day she got the news?

"My neighbor brings me my mail now and again. I got the notes you left in the box. I'm sorry I couldn't respond."

"No, of course. I didn't—no one told me you were sick," I say.

"Tell me, what can I do for you? I can't imagine I have anything important that will help find your daughter, but I can try," she says, and her openness and kindness are so unexpected I feel tears prick my eyes, but I blink them back.

"Thank you," I say almost imperceptibly. "I don't know what I'm looking for, I just know that the cases are similar—the place, the age. I just, I guess, would you just tell me about her? I don't want to upset you, I just…"

"It's okay. I love to talk about her." She forces a smile and shifts in her bed to sit up a little bit. "She wanted to be a chef." Her eyes glisten when they catch the beam of light through the curtains. "She planned on volunteering in Thailand, teaching English for a year so she could trade for culinary training in this program she got into. She was so excited. She said traveling the world would be her college, and that was okay with me. She knew what she wanted," she said. I hand her a tissue from the box on the side table next to her bed.

"But she never went?" I ask.

"I thought she was clean. She struggled. I know many young people out here do. It's a big problem now—an epidemic, the police told me. I got her into rehab twice, and she was set and determined to stay clean—get outta this town for a fresh start, and I thought she would. I thought she'd do it. My sweet girl."

"I'm so sorry, Dana," I say, squeezing her hand.

"That stuff takes over—it's a disease. It was stronger than her. She was just a girl. It wasn't her fault," she says, and the tears begin to stream down her cheeks, the skin so papery-thin and pale I can see the blue of her veins.

"The thing I'm most angry about now is that whoever did this to her took everything from her, ya know? And it's a small thing, but I'm just so damn angry that on top of it all, they took the bracelet I gave the Christmas before. It was gold with little elephant charms hanging from it. It was supposed to remind her of Thailand and following her dreams. She never took it off. It was her favorite thing in the world and they even took that from her—from me. Why? It might be a small thing, but I wish I had that of her. And now, they said on the news that that old man was killed—they think it's related. The whole town's freaking out, right? Is it just some serial killer and no one's safe?" she says, wiping her tears as fast as they come.

"I don't know," I say softly.

"I don't mind not living in a world like this one," she says, placing her tissue on the side table and pulling her hat down farther around her face. I don't know what to say, but she breaks the silence by speaking again.

"Do you think that guy—Harry Flynn—on the news, you think that's related? You think he was down on The Strip too? It's all so strange."

"I know. I don't really know what to think. Did you know Heather went to Hemlock Lane that night?" I ask, hoping to not push her over the edge, but needing to know. She just looks at the ceiling and shakes her head slowly. I'm sure she's had to share every painful detail with police over and over, but they don't tell me this sort of thing.

"No. She said she was going for pizza with her friend, Lexi, and then to her house after, but she didn't—Lexi says they never had plans and her parents say she was home all night watching TV. She lied, and the only reason she would have gone there was to buy, and I gave her money because I thought she was better—I didn't know, but maybe it's good I gave her money so she didn't have to do what a lot of other girls do down there for a fix." She starts to cry again, and I worry, suddenly, that I'm upsetting her too much in her condition. My concern is validated when the nurse comes in from the kitchen, her brow furrowed.

"No disrespect, ma'am, but I think that's probably enough for today. Ms. Rossi can't take this much excitement," she says, and Dana doesn't protest, only blows her nose and wipes her tears. I stand up and squeeze her hand one more time.

"Of course. I'm really sorry if I upset you. I appreciate you talking to me," I say.

"I hope you come by again," she says. "It was nice having a visitor. It was just me and Heather, and you know how it is... Friends start to disappear when your life is a constant tragedy. Well, maybe you don't know that yet. Anyway, Kira, it was nice talking a while. I'll be praying for you."

"Thanks. I will visit again," I say, and the nurse walks to the front door and opens it for me as if I need an escort out of the house, but I simply thank her and walk to my car.

As I drive around the outskirts of town, the way I do every day to search every clearing, every ditch, every forest I can find, I think about Dana's words—the elephant bracelet. Is Harry missing an item? The secrecy of the girls going down there without anyone knowing, the drugs. How does it all fit? What does it all mean? Was it simply bad luck because they put themselves in danger and got unlucky, or is there more?

And the biggest question I can't shake are Vinny's words.

Creepy stepdad. She never said she felt that way. Matt's been in her life since she was a kid. They got along wonderfully. Could he be wrong? Maybe it was another one of the many girls who stop by his shop for freebies who said this and he's mixing them up? Why would she go to the cabin if nobody was there?

Matt was in New York visiting his sister. He left Boston with a packed bag two days before Brooke disappeared. He went to Albany. He called from fucking Albany, so how does this make sense? I need to know for sure. I trust him, but there is some nagging in my gut that is telling me to confirm it.

His sister and I have never been exceptionally close, but certainly friendly, friends even. She flew in for the first ten days after Brooke disappeared to be with us. She stayed and held things down at the house, making stews and cookies and staying close to the phone. She was as supportive as she could be until she had to go home. She never mentioned Matt's visit, but why would she at a time like this? Matt came home immediately from Albany when he heard, and she came a few days later. It makes sense it wouldn't have come up, because nobody talked about anything besides Brooke and what to do. Would I even have remembered? Now I need to ask her, but I can't come right out and make it sounds like I'm checking up on him, so I make up a story in the ten seconds it takes to push dial on her number.

"Kira, hi, sweetheart. Is there news?" she asks eagerly. I know she is in touch with Matt every day about the situation, but is letting me have my space.

"No, sorry, I just—I can't find Brooke's old...iPad. She never uses it, but Matt sometimes does when he flies to watch movies on the plane, and I thought...maybe he left it there when he visited in August? He doesn't remember," I say, white-knuckling the phone, my stomach in knots. Am I really trying to catch him in a lie? Am I just paranoid and losing it?

"You mean May?"

"What?" I say, my hands beginning to tremble, my breath catching.

"Last time he came out was that Memorial Day picnic in May, not August, but I can have a look around," she says, and I sit in stunned silence. "You there?" she asks.

"Uh…yeah. Yes. I must have gotten my dates wrong—with everything going on."

"Well, I don't blame you. I'll look around and call you back," she says.

"Thanks, Jenny," I say because I worry that if I say anything else anger will take over and I'll say way too much, so I hang up the phone, and I feel numbness wash over me, then rage.

When I get back to the cabin, my dad isn't home, so I pull out my laptop and quickly log on to our AT&T account to look through our phone records from late August. I find the date she went missing and scroll through all of the calls from both of our phone numbers. Matt makes more calls than me for work, so there are pages and pages. They tell me it takes time to acquire phone records from a missing person's phone, so I don't know her activity yet, but I never thought to look at his. Why would I? Why the fuck would I?

He was never a suspect. He said he was in Albany, I confirmed he was, and his friend Russ, who he often stays with there to avoid Jenny's little kids 24/7 also confirmed his alibi. That was it.

I'm saddened for a minute at the memory of Brooke asking to get on her own phone plan when she turned eighteen. She wanted to not be monitored, and now I wished I'd said no. I could have seen who she called, where she was, and we might be a lot further along.

After a few pages, I see it. I feel as if my body can't take anymore shock, anymore surges of adrenaline, but my whole being trembles when I look at the two calls from Brooke's phone to Matt's phone the afternoon she disappeared.

With shaky hands, I call AT&T customer service. I need to know if there is a way to see where the phones were— the tower they pinged off of to show the area they were in. I know they won't tell me Brooke's legally, but Matt and I are on a family plan and I'm authorized to see anything I want.

I can barely keep my voice steady as I ask the customer service woman where I can access that information, and in a few easy clicks I can find it. I always thought accessing these kinds of records was a weeks' long ordeal, but it turns out if it's your own phone, it's quite easy. And all the truth I need is right in front of me.

Matt was in Rock Harbor the day Brooke disappeared.

17

GRACE

In the early morning, Grace walks the perimeter of the property with Hobbes by her side. She doesn't know what she's looking for—maybe footprints in the mud or the side gate unlatched, but she just wants to feel safe—make sure nobody has been lurking around.

When she's satisfied that there is nothing out of place, she gets a mug of coffee and a blanket from a storage chest inside the back door, wraps it around herself and sits on the back porch swing. The trees go on forever, and the closest neighbor to the inn is at least a mile away. She wonders where she'd run if she had to. She can't run though, can she? Walking is difficult enough, and she'd never make it through the rugged terrain all the way to the next property if someone were after her. If someone were lurking around, and if they were really after her—*overpowered* her.

Right now, she's in control. She's safe, she reminds herself. She stares out at the treetops that look like they are burning as the blazing orange sun begins to peek through behind them. She looks at the cellar door in the ground and remembers being kept in a basement like that. She's never brought herself to go inside it, and she's never stepped foot in the inn's basement either. But now…she thinks this debilitating fear has caused harm. She thinks about those other two girls, and how maybe he wouldn't have gotten them if she'd paid attention—the monster who took her because it has to be the same person.

She never thought about other people being taken, trapped like she was. She was just a kid back then. She was focused on surviving. And then when she did survive, she was still focused on surviving—surviving the day to day of a life that was no longer hers. It was taken away from her, and she could only retreat into herself to make it through a day. No one could fault her for that, but now…she blames herself. She never mentioned to the police the yellow zip ties she'd seen on the wall. It was just something in the room—a room that was full of things, of junk and trinkets, and shelves of tarnished, useless knickknacks, canning jars, and rotting paint cans. She wouldn't have even recalled the zip ties if it weren't forced in front of her face—the detail that they were larger than normal, and then the detail about them actually being cattle castration bands. She remembers the label on an unopened bag on a rusty low shelf next to the utility sink. There was an image of a cow head on the bag. It's all making sense now.

She spent most of last night on the front desk computer after Aden went to bed, looking up what she could about these cases. It's something she would have never imagined herself doing even twenty-four hours ago, but what she'd learned changed things. What kind of person would she be if she didn't try to get to the truth—to help these families? She thinks she knows something that would crack these cases wide open. But she can't tell anybody until one: she's certain she's right, and two: she leads someone else to discover her epiphany and go to authorities, because she is not the most credible source. She knows how she comes off—a traumatized foster kid, a recluse, a weirdo who never smiles. That all equals unstable. She can't make a wild accusation and have nobody believe her. She never saw the face of the man who held her captive. But there are things she knows—there are things she could tell that would help, but that would also shatter lives, so to be sure is her first priority.

She second-guesses herself when she thinks of the man Harry Flynn. It doesn't track. It throws off her whole theory. Maybe if he weren't connected, she would be more certain she's right. She knows what these other girls went through. She knows the brutal and unthinkable things that were done to her—the way she was violated. If he likes teen girls, why would he do the same to a seventy-something man? Do the castration bands prove it's the same killer though? There are a lot of farms and cattle around the area, and she wasn't strangled to death. She wasn't murdered. Was she just lucky or is this a different man? She just can't wrap her head around it all. It's dizzying and nauseating.

It could be an excuse. An out for her. She could tell herself that she's right. That it makes no sense about Harry, so she's probably making giant assumptions, and then she could run as far away from this whole thing as possible. Let Aden stay at his parents' like he offered. Shut down the computer, close the doors until the spring reopening, and be left in peace. But there is one thing that isn't letting her do that.

There is another girl, Brooke Everett, who might be connected. A girl who is still out there. Same age, same area of
town. What are the odds in a town this size? It's also not lost
on Grace that the two dead girls and Brooke all look similar, and they all look just a bit like her too—same build, same
age when they were taken, same fair skin and slight frames.
If there is any remote chance that Brooke might still be alive,
she has a duty to act on this hunch and do something.

"Grace," a male voice calls from somewhere behind her and
she leaps to her feet with her heart in her throat.

"Jesus Christ!" she screams involuntarily. She knew Aden
left early this morning. Nobody else should be here.

"Vinny. You scared the shit out of me. What are you doing
here?" she asks, holding her hand over heart and shaking the
spilled coffee off her forearm. Vinny has come around the side
of the building, box in hand. He sets it down on the edge of
the deck.

"Sorry, I just came to drop this off," he says, and she can
see in the open box that it's full of crab apples. He always
brings her the extra in the fall so they don't go bad because
she'll bake with them, but he usually does this at a regularly
scheduled delivery time.

"Sorry," he says again. "Can you use these?" he asks.

"Of course. Thanks. Let me pay for them," she says, going
to pick up the box.

"Naw, just have 'em," he says, but he doesn't move to leave.
He lingers like he has something to say. She puts the box on
top of a picnic table on the deck and sees he's fidgeting with
his ball cap and looking at the ground; it all feels a bit odd.

"Can I…get you a cup of coffee?" she asks.

"Oh, I mean, yeah if you're making some, sure," he says,
a nervous smile playing across his lips. She nods and goes
through the back screen door to the kitchen and pours an-

other cup for herself and one for him from the already-made pot. She watches him from the window over the sink as he perches on the edge of the picnic table bench and looks around as if expecting someone.

She returns to the deck and places two mugs on the table and sits across from him.

"You okay?" she asks, looking in the direction he's looking in.

"Oh, yeah. I just wasn't sure if you still had company—that guy."

"He's not exactly company. He's a guest. And he's not here right now." She wishes she could take that last part back as soon as she says it. He's making her uneasy for some reason.

"You're out and about early," she adds.

"I like to drive around before other people are up. People ruin everything. It's nice and quiet before sunrise."

"Yeah," is all she can think to say. Vinny sips his coffee and looks out into the woods.

"You know I'll always look out for ya, right?" he says.

"Uhhh. Sure." She smiles, uncertainly.

"It's that guy staying here…"

"Aden."

"Yeah, I just wanted to make sure you're safe. It's different when it's on season, but it's just the rando guy here with you—out here all alone, ya know?"

"Oh," she says, feeling a little relieved that that's why he's acting paranoid. "Well, I appreciate that, but no, he's fine."

Vinny does always look out for me. He always makes sure I'm stocked with supplies before a winter storm, he checks the chimney flue and the pipes, he adds wine to my orders and never charges, and I know he knows my story but he's never mentioned it. He just tries to protect me. Today though, he's going slightly overboard worrying about Aden.

"Okay," he says. "Good. I mean. Yeah… It's just that… I don't like the guy," he says, and Grace gives him a look—a smirk—a *you don't even know him.*

"Oh," she says instead, her silence leaving him room to continue.

"It's just someone you don't need to be messed up with right now. He's got a lot going on is all." And that's the closest he's ever come to admitting that he knows who she is.

"I know about his dad," she says.

"Well, oh. You do? Well. I just—I can ask him to find another place to stay if you're not comfortable. I mean… If you need—if you don't wanna deal with all that…"

"Vinny, it's really okay," she says.

"My parents used to go to church with his parents," he says, putting his mug down and looking her in the eye for the first time since he's arrived. "They're good people. I only met them a couple times after church. Super nice people and all, don't get me wrong, but him. Aden. I don't know."

"I really do appreciate you looking out for me—" she begins to say, but he interrupts.

"I know how it sounds. Like, I'm just… I don't know. But did you know about his wife?" he asks, and Grace is suddenly filled with an overwhelming feeling of dread at the mention of the word *wife.*

"I didn't realize he was married," she says, her eyes downcast and her heart speeding up.

"He's not. He was, but she died," he says, and Grace opens her mouth to speak, but nothing comes out.

"I'm not tryin' to say anything. Alls I'm sayin' is it was like a freak accident and they never figured out what happened. She went over a cliff when she was hiking," he says, and Grace takes a sharp inhale of breath and tries to conceal her shock.

"See, you didn't know that," he continues, gesturing to the

look on her face. "His kid got into some trouble too and was shipped off to boarding school. He's bad news bears, I tell ya. That's all I'm trying to say. You don't know the guy. Bad luck follows this guy around maybe, okay. Fair enough. Or maybe it's something else," he says, pushing his mug away and folding his arms as if he's proven a point.

"I'm sorry. How do you know this?"

"I looked him up, asked around a little. I don't get a good vibe from the guy is all," he says, and she thinks about how Aden looked her up and found out so much so easily, and how it would never have dawned on her to do the same. She's been away from technology for so long it just never even crossed her mind.

She's not sure what to think. She certainly knows what it's like to be judged by things that happened to her—as if she should have done something different—not been in that part of town, fought harder, dressed differently, known better. She finds herself, instead of fearful about what Vinny is saying, annoyed with him for spreading the rumor.

"Well, I mean he's a guest and it's my job to let him stay as long as he pays for a room, but thanks. I mean I don't really know what to say."

"I don't like it. Ya want me to stay here a few nights? Make sure nothin' fishy's goin' on?"

"Vinny, thank you, really. I know you're just looking out for me…"

"I am. I'm always gonna look out for ya, Grace. I told ya that."

"Thank you, but I'm fine. I promise," she says, and sees the disappointment behind his eyes but doesn't really understand why he's so emotionally involved.

"Okay then," he says, standing. "But I'm gonna stop by and check on you till this clown leaves though, alright? Deal?"

She mirrors him and stands.

"Deal." She nods, and he steps in as if he is about to hug her. He knows she doesn't like to be touched, and she sees him quickly think better of it and then awkwardly pat her on the shoulder instead. He reluctantly turns to leave, pulling a pack of cigarettes from his back pocket and jostling one loose as he walks to the side gate.

Aden has a troubled daughter and a dead wife. He's right. She doesn't know him at all.

18

KIRA

On the interstate from Rock Harbor to Boston, I white-knuckle the steering wheel, radio off, thoughts reeling. I don't tell Matt that I'm coming. I just tucked the phone records in my purse and got on the road within minutes of discovering his lies. No thinking, just action.

My body seems to have acclimated to a constant state of stress over the last weeks—the panicked breath and elevated heart rate, the trembling hands and perpetual edge-of-tears feeling is morphing into a kind of numbness. As I pass the familiar cliffs and truck stops and rows of white pines on my way back home, I try to play out any possible scenario where Matt's being in Rock Harbor the day she disappeared has any explanation. And I can't find one, no matter how I curve my thoughts and create scenarios that could be plausible… The lie is too big. What could he possibly say to explain himself?

I think of calling Wes—Detective Hendricks—right now and having them haul him in for further questioning. It dawns on me that he lied to the goddamn police too. But I would rather catch him off guard first—see what excuse he comes up with, and then see how it unravels when he tries to continue lying to the police who have much better resources for fact-checking than I do.

The miles are mostly a blur until I pull into my driveway. A wave of resentment swells as I think about the compromise I made moving into this suburb of Boston, my wanting to stay in the city, him arguing the benefits of how far a dollar can go out here. It's so irrelevant I'm embarrassed the thought even passed through my mind right now, but it begins a domino effect. Would Brooke even have met Ryan if she stayed at her high school in Boston? Or would she have been busy with all of her friends and track and college prep like the rest of them to care about coming to the cabin with us and running into that bastard in the first place? I'm grasping at straws, I know, but just—what if? What if she hadn't been unhappy here? Maybe it would all be different.

I see his car in the garage as I get out. I pass the side window, and my knees feel like they might buckle beneath me for a moment. The house seems foreign, like it belongs to someone else, and that it's so far from home. There is no home without Brooke, and my husband is a liar, and maybe worse than that. The loneliness in this moment feeling like a stone in my chest, heavy and suffocating.

When I fling open the front door and walk in, Matt is on the sofa, a ham sandwich and Pepsi on the coffee table in front of him, and he's playing *Skyrim* on the Xbox. He's playing a fucking video game—he's sword fighting a goddamn warlock while my world is collapsing, and Brooke is out there somewhere.

"I thought you were working," I say, and he startles and jumps to his feet, wiping sandwich crumbs off his jeans.

"Hi! Oh, my God, what are you doing here? Did something happen? Is everything okay?"

"No," I say, and he moves to me, taking my elbow and guiding me to sit down in the rocker recliner.

"No what? What's going on?" But I just stare at him a moment, this stranger to me now. Then I look at the scattered Bud Light bottles and sandwich and back to him.

"I gave the guys the day off because of the rain," he says matter-of-factly, as if I care about any of that—as if it's not outrageous that he's not spending the day helping me look for her if he had the time.

"Can you sit down, please," I say, and I see the color drain from his face as he reluctantly sits across from me, back on the couch.

"What is it? Something happened. Tell me what—" But I cut him off with one swift move, pulling the phone record from my bag to the coffee table in front of him, then I just wait. I watch to see the myriad of emotions shift from confusion, then shock, then something like embarrassment, then defensive anger.

"What's this?"

"Just don't. There's no time for bullshit," I say softly, then jab my finger into my chest and raise my voice, choking on my words. "I don't have the time for bullshit!"

I pick up a green pen from the cluttered coffee table and circle the dates and calls from Brooke's phone to his and the location. He knows exactly what I'm asking. He leans back in stunned silence and his face and the tops of his ears redden.

"It's not whatever you're thinking it is, I'll tell you that," he says and picks up a half-full beer and takes a sip like this is a casual conversation—like it's about something as comparatively trivial as cheating or our sham of a relationship. But it's not. This is about *my daughter.*

"Then before I shred your face off with my bare hands, please tell me what the fuck it *is*," I say, trying to keep control, needing to hear the words he will say before it escalates too far and I've lost him behind a wall of self-preservation.

"Jesus, Kira, it's really nothing. I promise. It was just a change in plans. We were arguing… You and I were arguing. Things were… I just wanted to get away for a little while. I was gonna go to Jenny's, but she said it was a bad time and I really didn't want to deal with flights and her kids, I just needed a little time away and I needed it to be for a reason you wouldn't be pissed about—start an even bigger fight—so I went to the cabin. Big deal. Your dad said he wasn't gonna be there that weekend, so that's it."

"That's it?"

"Yes. I stayed one night and then went to Buck's Head fishing a couple nights. Ask Colby, ask Mike… I know how it looks—"

"Do you? You lied to me this entire time! You lied to the police! Do you actually know how it looks to lie to the police or how serious that is? Do you know how it looks to be in the same area she disappeared from and caught lying about it!? Do you really?" I stand, gesturing with the phone record printout before flinging it in his face.

"Okay," he says in a calm tone, trying to be soothing but having the opposite effect. He comes to me, placing both his hands on my shoulders, attempting to make eye contact. "Hey, I'm so sorry." I jerk away and move across the room.

"It was a bad-timing thing is all. I knew that if you heard I lied to you about Jenny's, you would think the worst—everyone would think the worst, but the only reason, Kir, I swear to God, the *only* reason I didn't come clean is 'cause I didn't see her that night. Like, I had no information that would change anything, so I didn't say anything. Kir, Kir, come on—you've seen all those shows. They all think it's the spouse or step-father or whatever male is the main one in their life—they would have focused on me instead of figuring out what actually happened. They'd have fixated on it. It would've hurt the case, not helped."

"She's not a case!" I wail and then bury my head in my hands. I sit on the edge of the couch, catching my breath.

He's silent for a few moments, and I can see his eyes shift—like he's thinking about what to say next, but if it were the truth, he wouldn't have to think so hard.

"I'm sorry I didn't tell you. I was in an impossible position."

"Why would she call you?" I ask, because she doesn't call him. He's not her father. They get along, but they're not close and they don't "chat." So if she called him at all, it would be a rare occasion and certainly for a reason.

"She was asking to borrow money. Said she saw my truck at Mike's that afternoon, and knew I was in town and could she borrow a hundred bucks. That was all." He sips his beer and turns away from me, looking out the window into the back garden where the drizzle taps on the surface of the small pond and creates a pattern of ripples. The pond where Brooke and her friends glided across the surface last summer on their Flamingo-shaped pool floaties, sipping iced lattes and sunning themselves.

"And you said no. Because you said you never saw her that day, so you must have said no. Why?" I ask, rage surging through my body, my fists clenched at my sides.

"Because you told her if she was taking this time off school to be independent, she needed the job and to do it herself. You didn't approve of her being up in Rock Harbor, I know—so I knew you wouldn't like it if I was giving her money behind your back," he says, standing, agitated. He goes to the fridge and pulls out another beer. He pops the top and tosses the cap into the sink harder than he needs to.

"Why did she want the money?" I ask, but I already know the answer. Does he?

"How the fuck do I know? She's nineteen. Makeup, clothes, I have no idea. She just wanted to see if she could play me behind your back, probably. I don't expect credit for trying to do what you'd want me to do, but—"

"Oh, you don't? You don't want a fucking *award* for that?" I yell, and I don't know why. I am so exhausted and I don't even know what else to say to him.

"Kira—"

"So you never saw her?" I interrupt.

"I promise you, I do not know anything else that would lead to finding her," he says, and I stare at him.

"That's not what I asked."

"Jesus Christ, you're impossible. If I could help—if I knew one thing that would help, I would tell you. I would have told the police. I was there briefly and didn't mention it because of how it would look. Like I said. That's all I know. I'm sorry. I am. I really am sorry I didn't tell you, but like, how could I?"

"So my dad knew you'd be there?" I ask, just realizing how many people have been lying. Covering their asses.

"Well, I mean, yeah. I told him I'd use the cabin if he was out, so…" he says. He comes to sit on the ottoman in front of my chair. He puts his hands on my knees and hangs his head. I want to punch him in his pathetic face, but instead I push him away and stand.

"What else have you lied about?" I ask. He sighs and flings his arms in the air—an exasperated gesture of giving up. I walk past him and run up the stairs, taking two at a time. I go into our bedroom and begin stuffing the rest of my clothes into a bag, a tablet and charger, some shoes from the closet, a photo of Brooke at graduation. I open the cupboard under the sink and swipe my arm inside, pull out all its contents and drop them into a beach bag I find hanging on the hook.

I hoist the bags over my shoulder and go down the stairs. Matt sits on the couch, his beer on the coffee table forming a white water stain in the dark wood surface. He doesn't look at me as I pass him, and I don't say goodbye, but we both know I have no intention of coming back.

19

ADEN

Aden hasn't a clue where to begin searching for his father's secret male lovers or evidence of a drug connection. It's all so ludicrous, but something very sinister is going on, indeed. And he has to admit that to himself, even though the thought of his father out there somewhere—hurt, suffering…dead—is almost too much to bear. He has to really absorb the fact that seeing his father again may not happen. He wants to call his mom. In a pathetic, childlike moment, he feels like he desperately needs hear her familiar, sing-song voice telling him it will all be okay, until he snaps out of it and remembers she's the one who needs him. There is nobody to comfort him. That's his job now. The weight of that realization steals his breath. He pops three more antacid pills from the car console and chews on them, the fizzy grape flavor dissolving on his tongue. It goes down thick and chalky as he swallows.

Brady mixes too much powdered vanilla creamer into his cup of gas station coffee and squirms around in the passenger's seat, never able to sit still, as they drive around the outskirts of town and search every ravine, bluff side, and fishing spot they come across because they have no idea what else to do. Aden just knows that he can't stop moving—he can't just wait at home and hope. He has to do something. After what he learned from his visit on The Strip, he thinks this approach is even more futile. Another part of him thinks that they might find his father's body discarded in a ditch somewhere, the revenge of whoever wanted him dead evident from the state of his remains. He feels like he could be sick.

"You okay?" Brady asks, fidgeting with the glove compartment handle and digging around in its contents. He pulls out a pack of cigarettes and lights one. He cracks a window and Aden thinks he might actually throw up.

"Yeah, I'm fine," he says.

"I think I might know what happened to him, but you won't believe me," Brady starts, and Aden is already uninterested in what conspiracy theory follows.

"I'm not saying it's aliens…" he starts.

"Then don't. God, Brady, please."

"Just hear me out. I watched this documentary about all these missing people who disappear in national parks and like rural outdoor places, right. Like a lot of them. They always have shit in common—they're older or have like a disability—a vulnerability."

"Brady."

"And they search an area like a hundred times, and then one day, some hiker finds their backpack or shoes or even their body in this wide-open place that was checked over and over."

"Okay," Aden says impatiently.

"It's very convincing. That's all I'm saying. It fits." And just then Aden's phone rings. It's a number he doesn't recognize with a 617 area code.

"Who's that?" Brady asks, looking down at it in the cup holder, then picking it up and answering.

"Aden Coleman's phone."

"Brady. For God's sake, just give it to me."

Brady cups the speaker in his palm and loud-whispers over it, "I'm makin' sure it's not a reporter."

"Kira who?" he says. "Kira Everett, what can I do for you…? No, this isn't Aden. Can I tell him what this is regarding?" he says, and Aden swipes at Brady for his phone back. "Hold on," Brady says and then hands it over. "God, here. Take a pill."

"This is Aden," Aden says reluctantly, hoping it's actually not a reporter, or maybe worse—someone from Leah's school. Or worse than that, a cop with information he doesn't want to know.

"Hi," the voice says. "I'm… I heard about your father, and…"

"What's this about? We've already made a statement. We just want to be left alone right now."

"No, sorry. I'm not… Let me start over."

"How did you get this number?" he snaps, remembering that his number is on posters all over town to call with any information. He hears her sigh and collect herself. She speaks calmly.

"Look. I'm calling because…my daughter is missing. Brooke Everett. You've probably heard about it," she says, desperation in her voice. He remembers seeing her face on the news, but it blends in with all the other missing girls, countless smiling faces—snapshots. A moment of life, just before it was stolen from them.

"Uh, I think so, maybe. Sorry, I don't…"

"I think we should meet," she says, not explaining further.

"Meet?" he stutters, still not understanding what she wants from him, too distracted by his own pain.

"Maybe it's nothing, but I've been studying the other cases like my daughter's—the other victims, the similarities. Then I heard about Harry Flynn, and maybe it's meaningless, but I've been finding lately that the leads I think are the most far-fetched and pointless have given me the most…interesting information. It's worth comparing notes at least," she says. He hears her voice break. He hears a woman in utter despair, just as he is, longing to find someone they love.

"Yeah. Yeah, okay," he says.

"Put it on speaker," Brady says, nudging his arm, but Aden has no intention of telling him about this, just like he has no intention of telling him anything about their father being spotted on camera outside a nudie bar. He's too unstable. Aden needs to put the pieces together himself and have actual facts in his hands before his mother or Brady can be exposed to maybes and partial theories and unhinge.

"Just text me when and where," he says and quickly hangs up.

"Who was that?" Brady asks, flicking the butt of his cigarette out the crack in the window and shifting in his seat.

"Leah's school. Don't worry about it," he says and Brady nods and puts his feet up on the dash. He knows better than to comment on Aden's daughter or ask nosy questions. They drive in silence for a while until Brady gets fidgety again and starts poking around at the buttons on the radio. First, a scratchy country station comes in and out. George Strait sings "Amarillo by Morning," and then it fizzles out and a Cat Stevens song pipes through the car speakers.

It reminds Aden of their childhood road trips to Crescent

Beach in the summer—the two of them, just boys, kicking each other in the back seat. A cabin with a long dock and rusty nails popping through the wood, scraping their feet; dead sunfish washed up on shore; a life vest with Snoopy on it driving a red boat with a bunch of little Woodstocks waterskiing behind it; and the gift shop where they bought night crawlers in a cup of dirt and Dr. Peppers and got to pick out a candy *and* a chip. His heart swells with the memory of the four of them happy together, his mom's hand resting on the back of his dad's neck while he drove and she would hum along to "Moonshadow" and "Peace Train."

When the station goes scratchy again, Brady scoffs and switches it. A woman's voice breaks through, talking in that strange artificial way he thinks all news reporters have—forced, with unnatural inflections—but it's the mention of the words *Hemlock Lane* that strike his attention.

"They're talkin' about Dad," Brady says, catching Martin's name somewhere in the static. It's hard to catch everything that's being said, but she is talking about a series of missing person cases over several years. How Heather and Amelia were last seen in the same area on Hemlock Lane, and how they've connected those two murders to Harry—even though he wasn't last seen there, he did frequent the area.

"Makes no goddamn sense!" Brady yells at the radio. The reporter continues.

"New information has local residents on high alert. In a shocking discovery, missing seventy-three-year-old man Martin Coleman was also seen in this same area between 10:00 p.m. and midnight on several occasions. The teen everyone is still searching for, nineteen-year-old Brooke Everett, was caught on camera at 10:19 p.m. at Lucky's on Hemlock Lane the night she went missing. This has some locals avoiding the area after 10:00 p.m., calling this the *vanishing hour*. Several businesses are closing early, and some are even calling for a curfew to be put into place. More on this story as it unfolds."

Brady turns the radio off. His face goes pale, but he doesn't speak. Aden pulls the car over. He can hear himself swallow hard in the sudden stillness. He's furious with Hendricks for not warning him that this information was going to come out. Maybe he could have been with his mother—tried to soften the blow.

"We'll go see Mom," Aden says after a moment, and he turns the car around and starts down the winding cliff road leading west, out of town. It strikes Aden as off that Brady is not ranting, asking dozens of unanswerable questions at lightning speed, and punching the dash and yelling about how the press are a bunch of "douche canoes." The silence is unsettling. Brady doesn't smoke or babble. He just looks quietly out the passenger window as they drive the forty-five minutes to Herb and Ginny's rambler, nestled under a canopy of chestnut trees near Augusta.

He wonders about Leah. Wonders again if this will reach her—if he should tell her the details before she hears it from strangers. She might not even know any of it's happening, and it could stay local. He thinks about his mother, crying in bed last time he saw her and if she's already heard about her husband lying to her and hanging around the outside of a strip club. What must she be feeling right now?

Herb is tinkering with something in the back shed as they park in the dirt drive and walk up to the house. He's drinking a can of Old Milwaukee and holds one hand up to greet them as they pass by, then continues twisting some wires around inside an old useless radio.

Inside the small house, the air is stale and the smell of sausage and onions wafts from the small kitchen as Aden and Brady reluctantly walk in, hoping their mother is okay.

She stands in a pink housecoat and matching slippers at the stove, pushing around meat in a frying pan. She startles when she sees them appear in the arched doorway.

"Oh," is all she says, neither surprised or happy to see them as if they've been there the whole time.

"Sit down and eat. There's potatoes in the pot. Brady, get the potatoes," she says, and Brady looks back at Aden with the same dumbfounded expression Aden is wearing.

"Ma," Aden says softly.

"What? Brady, they're in the pot," she says again, pointing at him with a spatula, and Brady goes to the crockpot and dishes some mashed potatoes out on plates with a frightened look.

"Hey, why don't you sit down," Aden says, his hand on her shoulder, attempting to guide her to the kitchen chair.

"Can't ya see I'm cooking? Sit down. You boys need to eat," she says, turning her back to him and pushing chunks of meat around in the popping hot oil. Aden and Brady look at each other once again, and then sit as they're told.

Penny piles greasy sausage onto old china plates and serves them. Then she pours milk into tall glasses with yellow daisies around the rim, and picks up the basket of rolls from the middle of the table and passes them to Brady on her left, nudging him with it to take it, acting as if it's Sunday dinner and not the middle of a Thursday afternoon in her pajamas.

"Where's Ginny?" Brady asks, obviously trying to find something to say to create any sense of normalcy.

"Working. She's got four highlights and two hair extensions today," she says, buttering a roll and shoving it into her mouth.

"Look, Ma. I just want you to know that…it's not what it looks like, okay. I talked to Detective Hendricks and…that video of Dad. He was down there trying to witness. You know, for the church. I talked to someone who works there, and they said so. They said he was handing out Bibles."

"You knew about it?" Brady raises his voice. "You didn't say you talked to the police guy. You went down there. What the hell? Why didn't we both go?"

"Boys. Keep your voices down," Penny says calmly, not looking up at any of them.

"I don't think this is the time—" Aden begins to say.

"If you know some shit we don't, then you need to—"

"Boys!" She slams her hand on the table. Aden leans back and rubs his hand over his face.

"I talked to Hendricks, Ma, and yeah, so they have this footage, but it's not what you think," he says, and Penny looks at Aden as if he's said something to greatly offend her.

"I don't want to hear anything more about it. Those cameras are grainy-blurry and you can't see what's what. He was never there. End of story. He was a good man." Her use of the past tense makes Aden stop chewing mid-bite and look at her.

"End of story," she says. "He's just fishing, so there's nothing to worry about." Brady nods and drinks his milk.

Aden looks from his mother to Brady and back again, and he feels like he's in a horror movie and that he's looking at two people he's never met before.

20

KIRA

When I hang up the call with Aden Coleman, I place the phone down next to me at the end of the dock and look out over the glossy surface of the water at the other cabins that dot the lakefront. It's a long shot—a seventy-three-year-old man and my daughter having a link, but talking to Dana Rossi felt like a long shot and led me here—to Vinny, to Ryan, and to the truth about Matt. At least part of the truth.

The more I think about Matt, the more I convince myself that there is no way he could be involved. He couldn't be a monster. There are so many reasons that's not possible. He'd have to be living another secret life. That's something from a movie, not real life, and I would know. There would be signs, secrets, a feeling, right? Of course, there would.

Also because what the hell would he want with elderly

men? And the links between Harry and the girls are there. There is no denying that. Matt would have had to be here in Rock Harbor when Amelia and Heather were killed. I can barely remember what I ate yesterday. How am I supposed to recall every weekend we came to the cabin over a five-year span of time. And besides that, these girls were gone for days before they were murdered. I don't know when they died—the exact time frame after they were taken—that information isn't something I'm privy to, so how can I possibly pinpoint if Matt was here in town? I can't, and it nags at me no matter how many ways I tell myself there is no way he'd hurt any-one—that there has never been one sign that he'd be capable of such horrific acts. He lied, and he kept lying, and the enor-mity of that lie makes me feel like I don't know him at all.

I think of the time we took a canoe out on Webber Pond, the jasmine-scented spring air, making love on a picnic blan-ket under a sunshade of poplar trees, the dinners on this dock with tiki torches flickering at dusk, the smell of campfire and damp earth filling the evening air. We laughed easily and ex-changed awkward stories of teenage years and lost loves.

Our life together has been easy until the last few months. Texts throughout the workday, saying nothing in particular.

The garbage disposal is clogged again.

Omg look at this cat video—it's doing the tango.

Can you pick up dinner? I didn't feel like cooking.

I love you, don't forget to get an oil change.

We're boring. We watch TV on the couch most nights like everyone else. He never had stretches of calling saying he'll be late or any odd behavior. I never had a sense he was hiding something. But if he really had a whole second life, I didn't know about it.

My dad didn't pick up when I called three times on my way back from Boston yesterday. Probably for the best since I was hot with rage and would have exploded on him—blaming him for lying to me—and I would not have been grounded enough to listen for any hint of a lie in his voice. Now that I am here in person, I can see how he responds—see what his body language has to tell me. Did he know? Is everyone I love conspiring against me?

I saw his phone on the clutter of papers on the small desk by the front door of the cabin when I got in last night and realized that's why he didn't answer. I know he just went over to Moosehead to catch northern pike because he does it all the time, and I know there is no reception, but still I wondered—and I hate myself for wondering—why would anyone leave their phone unless they didn't want where they were going to be trackable? But then I know he forgets it all the time. He's a different generation and isn't glued to it like the rest of us. And then the self-loathing comes when I let my mind go down that dark path. Wondering if he forgets it because he is up to no good and can't have a time stamp attached to himself—to whatever he is out there doing.

It's a sick thought. I'm so ashamed of even having it even for a fleeting moment. He's my father, and he's an incredible man, but all of this has me doubting everything I know.

His car pulls into the dirt patch next to the cabin at a predictable 7:30 a.m., and he gets out of the car as he always does, balancing a paper cup of coffee and a small box of doughnut holes. He closes the car door with his hip and walks down to the dock.

"You're back," he says. "Hungry?" He walks down to the

end of the dock and sits next to me, our legs dangling off the end. He opens the doughnut holes and takes one, then pushes the box to me.

"Did you know Matt was here the night Brooke went missing?" I ask quickly, like ripping off a Band-Aid. I keep my eyes fixed on his, searching his face for any look of recognition or maybe waiting for his features to change and reveal a flash of panic or a lie forming.

"Huh? Here where?" he says with authentic bewilderment across his face.

"He said you knew."

"Knew what? Ya gotta back up, Kira. What are you talking about?" he says in the calm way he always speaks. She's never known him to raise his voice—she can't actually think of a time where he has. He speaks slowly, in a low grumbly drawl—a boy from Kentucky transplanted to Maine as a teenager who only stayed for the solitude and good fishing, but still a laid-back cowboy to his core.

"Matt was in this cabin the night Brooke disappeared. He was here and he said he asked you if he could have the place—if you'd be gone or not, and that you knew," I say, trying to keep my voice even but feeling it quiver.

"He was in New York. They confirmed his alibi," he says, brows furrowed, shaking his head. "What are you talking about?"

"He lied. He had his buddy there vouch for him, but he was here. I found the phone bill that proves it and he admitted it."

"Holy moly," he says, "That son of a bitch! Why? Why would he—"

"He says he asked you if he could stay and you said yes—that you knew," I say again, and a humorless, sharp laugh escapes his lips.

"I always told you that boy ain't right. He asked me a few

weeks earlier which weekends the cabin would be available—if I knew my fishing schedule in case *you guys* wanted to come up. You guys, as in the family. So I told him the couple of dates I knew for sure I had plans. That's the only time I've talked to him and that's all that was said. He never asked if he could come up by himself, and he sure as shit never told me he did," he says, taking off his hat and angrily running his hands through his hair before replacing it. He sips his coffee and shakes his head, mumbling something about Matt being a son of a bitch again.

I feel an overwhelming relief wash over me because of course he didn't know. He would have told me. Why would he protect Matt? He doesn't even like the man. Then another feeling eclipses the relief, and I have to ask him...

"Did you have your phone with you that weekend?"

"My phone?" he asks, taking the lid off his coffee cup and blowing to cool it.

"Yes. Did you take it with you?"

"I have no idea. Only person who calls me is you or the guys, and I was with them, so probably not. Why would you ask that?" he says, his voice even, but a look of mild irritation flickering across his face. I think about how easy it was for Matt to lie about an alibi. If we weren't on the same phone plan, I'd have never seen the records. I wouldn't have access and I wouldn't know about any of this.

"I don't know," I say, changing the subject, quickly dismissing the absurd idea that he knows anything more than he's saying.

"The old guy, Harry, and the two girls were all known to frequent The Strip and are all connected—for some unknown, godforsaken reason. We know they were killed with the same..." I stop, unable to say the words *zip tie* or *castra-*

tion band because it makes me ill to think about it—to think about Brooke in danger.

"The same weapon. And now this Martin guy is gone. Did you know they found his car? It doesn't look good. He was last seen near where Brooke was. It's all there—it's all right fucking there and we're missing it. There has to be some predator that stalks that area, and we can't see him in plain sight. I bet he's all over those security cameras and everyone knows the guy and we're all just missing it. Three young women and two older men in a space of five or six years. What could that possibly mean? It makes less sense the more I learn, and I just—I can't—" I stop and force myself to take a deep breath.

"Hey," he says, putting his arm around my shoulder. "I know. It's gonna be okay. We're gonna find her." I flick the tears from my eyes and stand.

"I gotta go," I say. I walk down the dock and look back at my father before I go into the cabin to get my things. He looks small, his back hunched as he sits with dangling legs, looking down at the still water and sipping his coffee. Is he telling me the truth?

When I go inside, I look again at his phone. I pick it up hesitantly, then glance out the window to make sure he's still at the end of the dock. I see if it's unlocked and I'm a little surprised when it's not. I've never really looked at his phone before, but he doesn't seem like a guy who'd bother with a pin or password. He doesn't really understand or care about technology and goes along with the minimum amount of work it takes to get by in the modern world. But there it is, a four-digit pin needed to open it. My hands shake as I quickly try a couple of guesses. My birth year, my birth month and day, then the same attempts for Brooke's birthday and then his. The last four of his social. Nothing.

I glance out again to see him coming up the length of the

dock, doughnut-hole box tucked under an arm with the hazy gray sky a backdrop behind him. I look at him differently even though I tell myself I'm being paranoid and ridiculous. I put his phone back where I found it and slip out the front door, getting in my car before he sees me go.

I have hours before I meet Aden, and I don't know if I can stomach driving around the same places we have looked a thousand times. I don't know where else to try, who else to call. I just start on the narrow road around the lake and drive, and then something strikes me. Something I didn't think to ask before because I only just learned about what Vinny claims Brooke said to him.

I fumble in my pocket for my phone and scroll down until I find Ryan Lambros's number, and this is exactly why I didn't turn him in. If he were in jail, he'd have no reason to talk to me or answer any questions and I didn't know if I'd have any, but now I do. I call and it rings half a dozen times and goes to voice mail. I try again, no answer. Then I text: You can answer my call, or you can answer a call from the police. I wait a few minutes and try him again. I hear him pick up but he doesn't say anything.

"I just have a question I want you to answer," I say, not knowing what to expect.

"What?" he says and with only one word I can already hear the slurring. He's high. I pull over so I can focus. I stare out at a lighthouse that stands where the road curves ahead, the waves crashing violently against the jagged rock below, and I take a deep breath.

"Did Brooke ever say anything about Matt?"

"Who?" he asks.

"My husband. Her stepdad—anything…bad, I mean. Anything that stands out—like negatively," I say, and he laughs.

"Is that funny? Is there something funny about any of this to you?" I snap.

"No, it's just so typical that you would be clueless about it. About everything."

"About what?"

"'Course she said stuff about him. He was… What did she call it? Handsy. Always touching her too long—like lingering, staring at her tits. Said he grabbed her ass once, but she laughed it off and so did he—pretended it was an accident. She thought he was a total creep-show," he says, and she tries not to audibly gasp. She tries not to show her shock.

"Did he ever cross the line? Did she say anything else—anything that might have happened?"

"That's all she said. Most guys are disgusting though. Ya get a pretty girlfriend and you start to realize how much men are really awful. Fucking pigs, most of 'em." And then she hears some muffled voices in the background, and he must cover the phone with his hand when he responds. "I gotta go," he says and then hangs up.

I sit in my car on the side or the road, breathless. He touched her. That absolute fucking bastard touched my baby girl. What else has he done?

21
GRACE

Grace lights a fire in the brick lobby fireplace and pokes at it with a metal stoker until it roars to life. She pours three glasses of red wine and places the bottle on the low oversized coffee table in front of the leather sofa. She arranges a plate of hors d'oeuvres and sits on the edge of the armchair near the fire, nervously.

When Aden called to tell Grace not to bother leaving the lobby door unlocked for him tonight she asked if everything was okay, and when he said he was going to meet Kira Everett, she asked him to do it here at the inn. He hesitated and was silent for some time, but Grace said she wanted to help—that maybe she could offer some insight, and he agreed. Now, she is sick and anxious about the meeting and wonders if she can really do this, but she has information and even if Vinny is right and Aden isn't the nice guy he portrays himself to be, it's about finding these two missing people. She has to put aside her feelings. What kind of person would she be if she didn't at this point?

She hears Aden's door at the top of the stairs open, and a hushed voice finishing a phone conversation, then his footsteps are on the stairs. Before he even reaches the bottom, the front door opens, and a voice says, "Knock, knock." A thin very tired-looking woman with blond hair in a messy knot on the top of her head and a parka too big for her frame walks in. She carries a laptop under one arm and a box of papers in the other.

"Kira, hi," Aden says, clipping down the last two stairs and going to greet her. She gives a weak smile and shakes his hand. She's ready to get through any small talk and down to business, Grace can tell.

"This is Grace. She runs the place. She's also interested in trying to help," Aden says, and Kira shakes her hand and gasps ever so subtly. Grace knows she resembles Brooke. At least a little. Enough to think this kidnapper—no, *killer*—has a type. She wonders if Aden told this woman about what happened to her—if Kira knows she's one of the girls too.

"Please, sit. There's—" Grace gestures to the table. "If you're hungry or anything."

"I'm fine," Kira says, opening her laptop. "I just want to exchange any details we have. The cases seem so completely unrelated in some ways, but of course we know the links that might help or mean something," she says, and when she opens her laptop, her screen saver is a photo of herself with a much younger Brooke and two men. They are all standing on a dock, posing for the camera. Grace notices Kira looking at her as she stares at the photo. It feels like Kira is studying her reaction.

"That's Brooke with my dad and husband," she says. "Taken a long time ago." Grace nods and Kira keeps eye contact. "Maybe you know them, they're up here a lot. Leo is my father with the cowboy hat, and that's Matt," she says, pointing to each as she speaks.

"No, I don't think I do," she says.

Then the screen saver disappears and is replaced with photos of Amelia, Heather, and Harry side by side on her laptop—all their stats listed next to their faces. Then she pulls out current missing persons posters. An eight by ten with a color photo of Brooke smiling and making a peace sign with her fingers. She lays another down next to it. Martin Coleman, it says across the top. It's a three-quarter photo of a man wearing a suit, standing in a church.

"This is your father?" Grace asks, picking it up and taking a closer look. She's never seen a photo. They've only ever talked about him.

"Yeah," he says, taking the poster gently from her hands and looking at it himself.

"Who's this?" Grace asks, pointing to the man in the background sitting in a pew, looking at the ground.

"My brother, Brady," he says, handing it back to Kira who takes that as an invitation to begin.

"So what we know for sure is—"

And then there is a loud crash that comes from the kitchen and makes them all jump. Grace screams and begins trembling violently.

"Is anyone else here?" Aden asks.

"No. No—"

Aden grabs the fireplace stoker and holds it above his head, ready to strike. Hobbes is barking from his mat in front of the fireplace, and nobody else should be here. Grace is suddenly terrified that the shadowy figure she saw is there somehow, inside the inn, and is there for her.

Aden moves in front of her protectively and they all listen a moment, frozen. Then the kitchen door opens and Vinny walks in eating a crab apple. He freezes, wide-eyed, when he sees them in a strange tableau staring back at him.

"Oh, hey," he says, chewing, casual and smiling. "Ya got a dinner party or somethin'?" he asks. Grace exhales hard through inflated cheeks and holds her hand to her heart. She sits down on the leather love seat and shakes her head.

"What are you doing here?" she asks.

"I said I'd be checking on you," he says, giving a sideways glance to Aden. "Oh, hi," he says, looking at Kira. Grace catches Aden's eye and they exchange a look.

"You know each other?" Aden asks.

"We've spoken. I asked him questions because Brooke's last seen location was near his store. Hi, Vinny," she says.

"Heya." Then Grace sees Vinny take a closer look at everything laid out on the coffee table.

"Oh," he says, and folds his apple core up in a napkin as if showing respect to the seriousness of the situation. "Sorry."

"Thanks for checking," Grace says, punctuating the conversation so he'll leave.

"Did they tell ya about those zip ties yet? Said they wasn't gonna make it public, but maybe they at least told youse guys," Vinny says, and they all look over to him, wide-eyed at the same time.

"What?" Kira asks.

"I was deliverin' deli sandwiches to Malarkey's pub the other night. Corned beef, I think. Anyways, I was waitin' to get paid. Malarkey's a cheapskate, thinks he can keep pilin' up a tab, so I says, ya gotta pay it out if ya want the good pastrami next week, so he goes into the basement where his office and stuff is, and I'm waitin' forever, and I hear a couple a cops talking real low in a booth. They didn't know I was standin' around the corner by the back door behind them. Ooh, is that cucumber sandwiches?" he asks, pointing to the coffee table. Kira pushes the tray across the surface, her mouth agape, not taking her eyes off him, and he sits and eats one.

"What did they say?" Aden asks impatiently.

"They traced the zip ties back to a batch of like 250 made back in 2009. They're for sure from the same bag, but couldn't trace who they were sold to."

Grace is barely listening. She looks from Vinny to Aden, from the faces of Amelia and Heather and then Martin and Brady. The image of Brooke with the two men—Kira's husband and father—mingle with all these other faces. Her head swims. Something is happening. Something is coming together.

"Did they say anything else? We already know the link with the zip ties," Aden says.

"We didn't know they were confirmed though," Kira says, a gentler approach to get Vinny to keep talking, it seems.

"Anyone drinkin' this?" Vinny asks, pointing to the wine. He picks it up and takes a sip.

"Did they say anything else?" Kira asks, repeating Aden's question and picking up a glass herself.

"You guys might already know what they were sayin'. It was hard to keep it all straight 'cause they were back and forth, but alls I know is that the two girls were…you know…assaulted," he says, his eyes downcast a moment.

"Sexually," Kira confirms, and Vinny nods.

"But the old guy wasn't. And the two girls, they was killed within like thirty-six hours of being found dead. But they were missing for days, so they were held a long time first. The old guy, Harry, he was missing a couple weeks and they know that he was killed right away. Whatever the stuff they use that shows that—like the forensics? Showed he died two weeks before, and he was only missing two weeks, so no assault and he wasn't held like, whadya call it—captive. Plus, the girls had drugs in their systems and he didn't. That's the stuff they was sayin'. Makes no damn sense if ya ask me. They were clueless, the cops. Like no leads at all."

Grace remembers the traps. Running wildly through the woods, her eyes burning from the sunlight she hadn't seen in days, barefoot and clawing her way through brush and vines to get away. These girls were held captive like she was, assaulted like she was. She remembers the snap of metal, the crack of bone. She tries to calm her breath.

"No offense, but why should we believe you? I mean, you just come in and give us details nobody else knows. Ever think that makes you look bad? Like why do you really know this? Were you involved?" Aden says, getting heated. Vinny puts his wineglass down and looks at Aden.

"Why would I give you details if I was involved?" he says very matter-of-factly. Aden stands, frustrated.

"It doesn't change anything. It doesn't help these cases right now." But Grace knows that it does change something, and Aden and Kira must be thinking the same thing—that if this is actually a pattern, Brooke could be out there, still held captive in some basement, alive... And Martin would probably be dead. Of course, they are thinking that.

"Okay, let's just..." Kira says, standing and flashing her palms, a gesture that says settle down. "Is there anything else, Vinny? Anything else you heard?"

"Naw. That's it. But, man, I hope you find her. One of those girls was missing for almost eight weeks. You got a shot at finding her still," he says, and the corners of Kira's mouth twitch up like she might smile at this, or possibly cry.

"Well, thanks, Vinny," Aden says, walking to the front door and opening it even though Vinny came from the back. He takes his queue and stands.

"Oh, okay then," he says, popping one more mini sandwich into his mouth. "Call me if you need anything, Grace," he says and moves to the front door. Aden pats him on the back in what looks like a condescending way and then he's gone.

Grace hears Aden and Kira speak but only bits of it come through. "Can we really trust that guy, I mean come on," Aden says, and then Kira says something about being skeptical about him at first but then he helped her…something— she can't make out the details, and then the words dissolve and the room shifts.

All the faces jumble in her mind. The girls; Brooke who has her own light hair and freckles; the older dead man, she can't recall his name. And then Martin and Brady, and Matt and Leo. Vinny's words. It all comes crashing down, the weight of it stealing her breath and squeezing her lungs. She knew part of the story and she was hoping to confirm what she knew, but she didn't expect this—the blinding clarity.

She holds her chest. She can't catch her breath. She knows what a panic attack feels like, but this seems like something worse—like her heart might burst. She hears worried voices around her, but she can't respond to what they're saying.

"Grace? Grace!? What's wrong?" It must be Aden speaking, but all she sees is an explosion of stars behind her eyes. She hears the woman—Kira—say to call a medic, and feels a hand on her back, but she slips away from it and falls to her knees, still gasping to catch her breath. She knows who it is—who the killer is. She knows everything. The world goes dark.

22

KIRA

I sit in the waiting room of the hospital, drinking translucent coffee out of a Styrofoam cup until I get the news that Grace will be okay. She had a panic attack and fainted, and hit her head pretty hard against the edge of the end table when she went down. Thank God, she's not too badly injured.

When Aden explained her panicked reaction to the situation—who she really was—I found myself resentful that she was hurt because I wanted to talk to her. And then, of course, I felt guilty for feeling resentful. The poor girl. But I needed to know everything—everything she remembered, all the details she could tell me. She was a prisoner for weeks. She might have information that could spark something—could bring up some minute detail of the basement she was kept in that might be a clue to Brooke, anything. But I can't talk to her now, they tell me, and how could I really ask her to re-live all that? How can I expect her to tell me about any of it?

It's still a flicker of hope though. Knowing the other girls were alive for so long. And Grace escaped. Brooke is still alive. I know she is. I feel a lightness just for a moment that I for-got existed—a solitary moment free from the crushing pain of loss and uncertainty—but it only lasts a moment, and then my phone rings.

I fish it out of the bottom of my bag as I exit the revolving door and step out of the hospital and into the biting night air. The sidewalk is quiet save the buzzing sound of beetle wings under the fluorescent lights above the hospital doors. I start toward my car as I answer the call.

"Kira," the voice says, and I know immediately who it is. I drop my hand that was holding up the remote to my car and hear the high-pitched beep-beep of the door unlocking echo in the distance.

"Wes, what's happened? What is it? Why are you calling me, do you know something, did something happen?" I ask, my words repeating, the pitch in my voice uncontrollable.

"Kira, I wonder if you're available to come down to the station to talk. I'm here now," he says.

"Just tell me. Just fucking tell me," I whimper. "What!?"

"I can tell you that we found some belongings we believe belong to Brooke, but I really need you to come down and identify them," he says.

"Wh-why do you think they're hers? What belongings—her phone, her wallet? Why are you connecting them to her?" I say, and I'm already to my car, opening the door and starting the ignition. "I'm coming down, but what are the belong-ings? Please."

"It's some clothing, but I'd like to discuss it in person, please. You're on your way?"

"Yes," I say, my voice breaking. I hang up and throw my phone into the cup holder. I think about Brooke's clothes as I speed through the wet streets, going too fast over railroad tracks and blazing through stop signs and past shop windows. I could paint her in the dark I know her so well—her dimples, the pale freckles across her nose, her cheap bangles she wears up her wrists and the collection of sundresses it's always too cold to wear, the Old Navy jeans because designer is stupid and a waste of money, the shell necklace we bought together on the Jersey Shore one holiday.

What clothing, and how are they connecting it to her? Will I recognize the items? What was she wearing under the fuzzy hooded coat she was last seen in on the security footage? I hadn't seen her in a few weeks, and she lived a whole different life out here.

At any other time I'd call Matt or my dad to meet me there, but now...

I hurry from my car to the police station doors and my head feels light, like I could float up and away from myself. I wonder if this is it. Is this the moment they will tell me something that will steal all my hope—that will change everything?

There is an earthy pungency and heavy sweetness of the dying sugar maples meeting a smoky grease smell escaping from Biff's diner next door. I have a sudden strong desire to just sit right down in the road and breathe it all in—stay in this moment, not know anything more—just hold my hands over my ears and close my eyes and keep her exactly the way she is in my last memory of her.

I'd bribed her with a shopping trip in the city if she'd come to me because I hadn't wanted to drive to Rock Harbor that weekend. September in Boston was cool but sunny, and we ate at a table on the sidewalk outside a bistro I don't remember the name of. We had quiche and she squealed over an obese

pug at the next table. We went into stores we could never af-
ford and ended up at a small dimly lit bookstore with stacks
and stacks of books piled on the floor and pushed into corners.
She picked up a copy of *War and Peace* and asked if anyone
has ever actually read the whole thing, and I almost spit out
my coffee, stifling a scoff. But before I could chide her school
for not teaching basic literature, the man behind the ancient
oak counter gave us a sideways look over his glasses, and so
she bought a Ruth Bader Ginsburg bookmark and we went
to find the patisserie down the block for her favorite black-
and-white cookie. She was happy, I thought. She seemed so…
normal. I think about how her fingerprints are probably still
imprinted in the layer of dust on the book jacket of *War and
Peace* in that little bookshop.

I force myself through the double glass doors and I'm ush-
ered back to where Hendricks is, but not to his office. Instead,
it's a sterile room with items laid out on a stainless steel table.
The items are inside clear plastic, and have tag and number
on them. I can see a plain white strappy tank top in one plastic bag, and it looks like every other tank top in the world.
How would I know if it's hers? The other though has a ban-
deau bra inside of it, lacy and hot pink. I recognize instantly
that it's hers. She wears it often in the summer under loose
fitting yoga tanks and her baggy garden overalls. She loved it
so much she bought it in four colors.

I touch the bag and run my fingers down the length of it,
a flame of anxiety igniting inside my chest.

"Where did you find this?" I ask.

"Please, Kira, have a seat," he says, gesturing to a couple
of chairs across the small room. I sit numbly and stare up at
him, waiting for answers—waiting for my mind to wrap itself
around what this means. He sits opposite me and arranges his
features in a way that reads sympathy and discomfort.

"We found these a few weeks ago, about fifteen miles north of town in a wooded area next to Fog Creek. There was no reason for us to suspect that it belonged to Brooke at the time—no connection there. A couple of campers saw it, and then one of them decided to call in a few days after they returned home because it was nagging at her that there was blood on it and it was out in such a remote area."

"Blood," I say, my voice breaking.

"Not a large amount," he reassures and continues. "But we did send officers to go and find it, and when we ran the DNA, the spots of blood we sampled came back as a match. To Brooke." I bury my face in my hands and I feel my heart pounding through my shirt, my pulse in my throat. My hands are trembling, and yet at the same time, a numbness washes over me—a feeling of shock maybe that doesn't allow me to wail and pound the walls with my fists. I know I need to keep my head so I can think—so I can work to find her. I cannot get hysterical.

"What does this mean, then?" I ask in a hoarse whisper.

"Well, it doesn't give us a lot of information, honestly. We did test another spot on the item and it came back as semen, from an unknown source." I gasp and clutch my chest.

"What?"

"We know she has a boyfriend, Ryan Lambros. We've talked to him, as you know, a number of times. He willingly gave us a swab, and we ruled him out as a match. The sample we tested was weeks old. It could have been from—it doesn't mean the worst, is all I'm trying to say," Hendricks says, leaning back in his chair and crossing an ankle over one knee, his face ashen as he continues, treading gently.

"Did she have any other partners that you know of, sexually?" he asks.

"No," I say quickly. "She would have told me. She tells me

everything," and even as the words come out, I wonder what else she was keeping a secret, besides the drugs. What wild thing was she going to do that night? Why did she never tell me how she felt about Matt? It's like I didn't know her at all. I look at the floor, heat flaming my cheeks.

"The good thing is that it gives us at least somewhere to refocus our efforts. We know she was there, and that's better than nothing right now." Hedricks moves to the edge of his seat, as if he's going to get up and the meeting is over.

"The other girls, Amelia and Heather, they were killed weeks after they were reported missing. The bands match, officially. They're related. And Harry too, the bands match him even though he was killed right away. None of it makes sense, but it does mean that there is an actual serial killer out there," I say, and I make out a slight tilt of his head, a flicker in his eye that he's shocked I know this.

"We haven't made that public yet. How do you know that?"

"It's the rumor going around. Someone overheard it. So it's true?" I say, and his Adam's apple bobs as he swallows. A failure of the police department I suppose—an embarrassment that someone overheard such sensitive information. Jenny's first husband in New York used to be a cop, and he'd tell stories about him and his cop friends talking too loud about a lot of things at bars and diners. It's a miracle more information doesn't leak that way, he'd said, but that's a big city. What are the odds the right person who gives two shits about the case being discussed would be in earshot there? Not here though.

"Listen," he says, leaning his elbows on his knees and looking me right in the eye, his voice soft. "We have not made an official link between Brooke and these other cases. There simply isn't enough concrete evidence. I know there are some parallels, and of course we are looking into that, but that doesn't mean it couldn't be a thousand other scenarios, and if it is the same person responsible—if they are linked, then this information is a good thing. It means we still have time." I feel an overwhelming desire to rest my head on Wes's chest and feel the warmth of his V-neck sweater against my cheek, breathing in the citrusy aftershave and feeling his huge arms wrap around me, protecting me—just to have a solitary moment of comfort, of trust. I wouldn't be greedy; I would just take a moment. He sees my face crumple, and he moves his hand as if he might reach out to touch my knee or my shoulder to comfort me, and I want him to so desperately, but I quickly stand.

"You need to look at Matt Rivers," I say instead. He opens his mouth and tilts his head again, a crease between his eyebrows expressing confusion.

"Your husband?"

"Yeah."

"He was in New York, we confirmed his…"

"That's what fucking worries me," I say, "is that all his alibi was is some college friend of his who says he was there. And he's cleared. Really?"

"There was nothing that was pointing to him as a suspect, and you also vouched that he was in New York."

"Well it turns out he's a liar. He was here in Rock Harbor that weekend—the day she…" I stop because I'm so absolutely exhausted hearing the words again and again. *Missing. Vanished.*

"You know this for a fact," he says more like a statement than a question.

"He admitted it."

"I see."

"And you know it's all connected even if you won't tell me. The Vanishing Hour on Hemlock Lane. I've heard about it— the similarity to the other girls, the age, the time of night. They were found in the middle of nowhere and now you're telling me her things—her… They were found in the woods by a creek. In the middle of nowhere. There is a psychopath just getting away with it. You have to find out if Matt was here when those other girls went missing. I can't figure out where we were—where he was on an exact date years ago when Amelia and Heather were taken. But maybe you can."

Thinking of how much time I wasted scrolling through the calendar on my phone from 2016 when Amelia was taken, looking at the meaningless dermatologist appointments and volleyball practice that week and trying to recall if we were at the cabin on the weekend—if the times line up, but I don't know. It's impossible to remember.

I put the thought aside—the very idea that Matt had anything to do with this. But how well can you really know anyone? The thought of Brooke seeing him as creepy makes bile rise in my throat every time I think about it.

But I can trust Wes. He's maybe the only person I can trust. He sees my whole body trembling, betraying the hard, defiant look I'm trying to keep on my face. He moves in close to me and touches my shoulder. His touch feels like electricity—like the only real thing I have felt in days. I let him pull me in and hold me. I stifle the sobs creeping up my throat and cling to him for a few silent minutes, then I pull away and pick up my bag, making my way to the door.

"You can arrest him for lying to the police, at the very least, can't you?" I say, paused at the open door.

"I'll look into it and then pay him a visit," he says, and I nod and close the door behind me as I go, longing so desperately to stay in the safety of his presence as wisps of his citrus aftershave linger on my skin.

When I get to the car, I sit in the passenger's seat and breathe. I look across the street and into the windows of Dogwood's Alehouse and Giovanni's Italian Eatery next to one another. I can see the shapes of happy people through the front glass windows. A man, his spine hunched into the shape of a question mark, laughing at something on his phone; a couple gesticulating and pointing out things to one another on an oversize menu; a booby blond woman, arms slumped over the people on both sides of her, forcing shots on everyone at the bar. All these people living normal lives, completely unaware that one small tug at the thread holding together, their very existence, and their lives will unravel. Unaware that Brooke is gone. My baby.

23

I don't know how many days it's been. I tried counting them at first, and lost track somewhere around ten or eleven, so it's been a lot longer than that. Weeks, probably.

The figure didn't come this morning. There's no food. I don't know why, because I've stopped screaming when the figure does come now. I've stopped fighting. My family must be looking for me. They have to find me here eventually. There must be tons of people looking. Will they believe me when I tell them what happened? That it's not my fault? Or will they hate me for all my shitty decisions?

I have prayed over and over since being trapped down here, and promised that if God lets me get out of here alive, I'll change. Maybe cameras caught me so they know where I was—on that stupid strip where I shouldn't have been. Will they give up looking when they realize who I've become?

I run a hand through my greasy hair and try to stand on wobbly knees, weak from lack of use for so long. I feel in the darkness for the metal base of the utility sink and pull myself painfully to standing. I fumble for the faucet handle and turn on the tap, dipping my head down into the sink to drink from the trickle of water it produces.

I hold my arms in front of me and try to walk a few steps, just to make sure I still can. I feel for the wall and use it as a guide. I crash into a tall metal shelf and wail in pain. Is it time to give up? They must think I'm dead. They must at some point have to stop looking.

I'm glad the figure didn't bring the food today. I can't do this much longer anyway.

24

ADEN

When Aden finally leaves the hospital, assured that Grace is stable and will be fine to go home in the morning, he promises her he'll come back to pick her up first thing and then drives back to his parent's house. He's not sure if he should be worried that Brady isn't there. He's a grown man with his own life after all, albeit one unknowable and distant from Aden's understanding. He's used to seeing Brady in basketball shorts, Dr. Pepper in hand, draped over furniture and smoking up the house, but he doesn't know where he spends his time when he's not doing that since he stopped going to bars.

Aden sits in the dark of the kitchen and tries not to let the shadowy thought push in—that all the evidence is pointing to his father being dead. He reminds himself instead that the medications his father didn't take with him look bad, but the heart medication is really just a blood thinner and none of them are something he'd die without taking. The car looks even worse, but if he got in an accident, what if he got out of the car before it went over the bluff? What if he's out there waiting for help? It's possible, isn't it?

He feels like he's hit a wall, unsure where else to look, unsure what else he could possibly do. He sighs, then stands and goes out the side kitchen door to the fridge in the garage where his mother keeps the beer out of sight from Brady and plucks out a can of Coors Light. He opens the garage door and pulls down a plastic deck chair from a nail on the wall and sits. He looks out into the black bones of the naked trees, the vast expanse of woods that seem to go on forever. His father could be goddamn anywhere.

And his mother. Poor Penny seems to be slipping away into an impenetrable place, somewhere he can't reach into and pull her from. He's seen her go through grief—through all Brady has put her through. The wall punching and screaming when he was tweaked out of his mind, stealing her brooch and the TV in the basement to sell for drugs, the two wrecked cars, the multiple bouts in rehab. The tears she's shed over Brady are countless, but she did that in private. Blots of black mascara beneath her eyes or an "I'm fine" that rolled too quickly from her lips are the sorts of things that betrayed her. She told the world everything would be fine, and she believed it. And Aden supposed it *was* fine now, with Brady being clean anyway.

But he's never seen her crack like she had the other night. He didn't quite know what to make of it—the dark flash across her eyes, the level of delusion evident in her words and strange demeanor. He hears the howl of a distant coyote, and an unexplainable loneliness taps at his spine—an indecipherable sensation that makes him want to jump up and move, do something, stay in motion and not sit in the quiet with this dull ache.

He doesn't jump up though. There's nowhere left to go, so he thinks of all the things he knows for sure and runs the details through his mind. He thinks about all the facts he and Kira shared with each other in the hospital waiting room, swapping stories, comparing any evidence or clues they had—all the shocking blindsides down to the smallest nuances of their own stories so far. He told her what he's told nobody else—the stripper who saw Martin on that corner. The one where the men go.

And she told him about her daughter's boyfriend and the drugs and all the time she wasted not knowing Brooke had gone down that road and had been lying and hiding things. There were no expressions of surprise or judgment on either of their faces, of course. They understood one another and vowed to work together. Still, when he saw her name pop up on his ringing phone, it startled him. They'd just left the hospital. What could have happened so soon?

"Aden," she says. Her voice sounded breathless.

"Hi, are you okay?"

"Yeah, just—I saw my missed calls after I left the hospital. One of them was Wes, and—"

"Sorry. Who?"

"Detective Hendricks. He wanted to let me know that Ryan Lambros—the boyfriend I told you about—was arrested."

"Okay?"

"For soliciting sex…on that corner you were talking about. He said specifically Abbott and Fifth. That's the same place you mentioned," she says, speaking quickly.

"Oh. Okay, but what does that have—"

"I'm just thinking that maybe he'd have info about your dad. Wes said his parents are horrified and refuse to bail him out—just thought maybe that could be leverage and he'd maybe know something."

"Yeah. Yes," Aden says, dumping his beer out in the grass and moving into the house to look for his shoes.

"Any information will help all of us, and he won't talk to me. Honestly, I don't know if there is anything else I could get out of him anyway, but your case is different, and I guess he hangs out down there, dealing drugs or whatever the fuck the little psychopath does. So maybe he knows something."

"I'm—yeah, I'm on my way," he says.

"No. They won't let someone visit this late. You have to go in the morning," she says. "I'll pick up Grace and meet you at the inn so you can go."

"Okay. Just send me the details. Where he's being held, anything else you think I should know, I guess. I'll go first thing. Thanks. At least it's something," he says.

"And write this down. I don't want it over text," she says, and he's already in the back screen door, rifling through a junk drawer for a pen. He finds one and pulls out a Chinese take-out menu to write on.

"Ready," he says.

"8902 Pine Road, apartment 201. I think you could go and bond him out. I don't think they'll let you visit, so once you get him out, you'll need leverage for him to talk. That's his apartment. It's a drug den. All you have to do is threaten to expose it. If he's somehow cleaned it up—and I don't know how he could get all evidence out of there, you should have seen the place—there's another apartment. 104. One of his druggy friends lives there and I have seen him go in and out when I watch the place, so keep that in your back pocket," she says, and he's equal parts impressed by her tenacity and a little taken aback by how extreme it is.

"Got it. Thank you," he says. They hang up, and he's buzzing with electricity to have any thread of hope for a lead, but there is also a crushing come down after being ready for action. His nerve endings tingle and his heart pounds at the thought of a task, and now the quiet again. Leah far away at school. His mother losing her mind, Brady off somewhere, Grace in the hospital, his father vanished. He's never known this kind of loneliness before and it rattles something deep within him. He goes inside, pushes an ashtray shaped like a walrus to the other side of the coffee table so he can't smell it. He takes a brown afghan that's been folded over the back of the couch for thirty years and pulls it over his shoulders as he curls up into the fetal position on the ugly floral couch and waits for morning.

The next morning, all Aden can think about is Grace as he impatiently waits for Ryan's arraignment hearing to finish so he can post the bond and surprise him in the courthouse lobby as his ride home. He'd never really seen anyone have a panic attack like that before, and he didn't have a clue it could hospitalize someone. He wanted to be the one to pick her up and take her home, but he needs to be here and talk to this kid, no matter how anxiety-inducing it feels.

"Who the fuck are you?" he hears, and turns to see a scruffy-haired skinny kid walking toward him, being watched by the security officer handing him some papers and gesturing to Aden.

"Your best friend today, it looks like," he says, trying to put on a tough exterior that feels very incongruous to the way he would naturally respond to such aggression.

"You bailed me out?"

"Bonded," Aden corrects, implying it's not over yet, and very impressed with himself.

"But who the fuck are you?"

"A friend of a friend. Got any money?" Aden asks.

"No," Ryan says, staring him up and down.

"Well, then I'll drive you home. Or wherever." Ryan looks back to the security guard as if asking if this is for real—if it's safe—but the guard is already deep in conversation with someone standing at the information counter and no longer looking in Ryan's direction.

"We'll stop at Burger Crown. Hungry?" Aden asks, starting to feel a little nervous this kid will just bolt. Instead, he looks around one more time and runs his hand over his face, then looks to Aden who makes a casual come-this-way gesture with his arm, and Ryan follows.

Aden's car is parked at a meter just across the street. He beeps his Range Rover unlocked and says, "This is me."

Ryan climbs in and Aden feels a sense of relief, but also a little trepidation knowing the kid's a meth addict and could blow a gasket for any reason at any time, but surely he's sober and unarmed since he's just walked out of jail. Aden consoles himself with that, and nervously moves forward with his plan.

Ryan is staring at him wordlessly.

"I thought if I did you a favor, you'd help me out," he says and doesn't realize how it sounds until Ryan's reaction comes.

"That's some balls," he says. "You pick me up from getting arrested, and now you don't wait five seconds before asking for a favor? How do I know you're not a setup? You could have a camera in here. I'm not doin' that shit here."

"Oh, Jesus. No. What?" Aden stumbles in his words, realizing Ryan thinks he's asking for a sexual favor. He shudders at the thought.

"Then what the fuck?" Ryan says again. "Who are you then?"

"I heard you were arrested near where my...family member was known to…spend time, so I thought if I helped you out, you could maybe give me some information."

"Kira Everett sent you. Jesus Christ. That crazy bitch—I told her all I know. I got nothin' else to say. I swear to God. Drop me at the fuckin' Burger Crown, I'll get home on my own."

"This your address?" Aden asks, quickly changing tactics and sliding the corner of the Chinese menu he wrote it down on across the console.

"Jesus. Really?"

"Listen, I don't want to cause you any trouble," Aden says, pulling over now, feeling like he played his card and it will either work or it won't. Ryan looks around like Aden is going to hurt him or something.

"I really don't. I don't even know you. But I can turn right around and give this address to the discharge officer and tell them what's there, and you'll be in a lot longer than one night."

"I don't know anything! I don't have more to tell you people!"

"This man," Aden says, pulling a sheet of paper from a manila folder pushed down the side of the seat. "I'm not asking about Brooke. I'm asking about him." Ryan takes the missing poster and looks at Martin Coleman in his church suit.

"Pastor Marty. Yeah, okay, how do you know Pastor Marty? What am I supposed to tell you about him?"

"Pastor Marty?" Aden repeats, over-enunciating the words.

"He's always preaching, so that's what they call him. I don't know."

"So you know him?"

"Kinda," Ryan says, shifting in his seat, folding his arms and then unfolding them.

"Is he…" Aden doesn't know how to ask this. "Is he involved in…your line of work?" He does realize how ridiculous it sounds when he says it, but Ryan's cackling laughter makes him defensive.

"Line of work!" he repeats, snorting. "It's a quick buck. I'm not proud of it, okay. I don't have a ton of other choices."

"Okay," Aden says, trying to be patient and appear sympathetic.

"So, you're asking if he's down there suckin' dicks? Or… what? The other way around?" he says, and Aden bristles, tensing his shoulders at the sound of the words.

"Something like that. He was seen on Abbot and Fifth. I guess that means something."

"Well, the short answer is no. I offered it to him once. Thought he was there pretending to hand out Bibles and shit but was really looking for something else. He swung at me when I asked him, but he's old and kinda fat, so he missed by a mile." Aden blows out all the air he's been holding in at hearing this. But then again, as much as he didn't want his father to be living a double life, it's the end of his only lead.

"I did see him a couple weeks later though. Took a Bible from him." Ryan chuckles. "A Bible. What a weirdo."

"So he really was just…witnessing," Aden asks.

"Witnessing what? I told you nothin' happened."

"No. It means…witnessing the gospel. Trying to bring people to the Lord. Never mind. So he wasn't there for…" He finds he can't say the word.

"Blow jobs, butt sex? Naw, I don't think so. As I was saying, when I saw him a couple weeks later, I asked him if he wanted to buy anything. He pretended he didn't know what I was talking about and then next time I saw him, he asked what I had. I was like, sweet. A lot better way to make money, but new clients are always risky. This guy screamed undercover cop at first with his weird Bible shit, but then, I don't know, I could just tell he wasn't, ya know? He was there for a reason. Might have just been a little bit of drugs he was after. Anyway, I gave him a sample that day and been selling to him for months. Casual-like though. No texts or orders, just when I see him. He asks what I have, and I have everything, and then he buys just a little and that's that." Aden feels like he's been punched in the gut. This can't be real life. His dad, mixed up in drugs. In a way, knowing that he had a problem—an addiction he was trying to feed—is at least an answer to all this, but it just seems so implausible.

"What did he buy, exactly?"

"I shouldn't have even told you this much, but you're a shady fucker who totally blackmailed me, right, so fuck off. Telling you more could get me killed, ya know. Your *relative* probably pissed off the wrong person and now he's gone."

Aden feels heat flood his face and anger rise in his chest. He looks around, trying to find something to anchor himself. He glances at the address on the menu, remembering he has leverage.

"Yeah, don't even think about it, dude. You rat me out, bigger guys than me will be after you—most of that shit in my apartment isn't even mine. There's people you don't want to get mixed up with, Abercrombie." Aden is suddenly painfully aware of his khaki chinos and collared shirt, his specialty coffee sitting in the cup holder, in contrast to Ryan's hoodie and black torn jeans, but he always thought he projected a certain coolness. He'd definitely never been called *Abercrombie* before. He looked at Ryan blankly, no response waiting in his arsenal.

"And I guess you probably don't want me telling anyone about Pastor Marty on dick-suck corner and all of his little transactions with me, so seriously fuck off now. I paid you back," he says, opening the Range Rover door and hopping out onto Frontage Road A6. Aden sits in stunned silence as he watches Ryan's hunched figure pull his hood over his head and walk toward a strip of chain restaurants across the narrow highway.

25

GRACE

Grace was surprised to see Kira rather than Aden parked along the curb in front of the hospital, waiting for her. The nurse insisted that it's policy to wheel her from her room to the door even though Grace had stated she was fine a dozen times over.

The crushing weight of what she now knows, and the responsibility that comes along with it—with how she handles that—is making her feel breathless again, and the hairspray wafting from the nurse's crispy perm is turning her stomach. She watches Kira force the sides of her mouth upward in an attempt at a smile, but she understands deeply that right now it feels like there will be nothing to genuinely smile about ever again.

She can help Kira, she thinks, but she can't just blurt out what she knows. She could put them all in danger that way.

The person responsible could get away with it because the evidence she needs to put in place first wouldn't be there, and Brooke could never be found if she doesn't use the leverage she has very carefully to try to get a confession and a location. She knows what she needs to do. She just needs to get back home to the solitude of her own space and start putting it all in motion. She needs to work quickly, she knows, but she needs a minute to think—to get everyone away from her.

The overstimulation from her shocking revelation, and the trip to the hospital after having not left the inn property in many months, and all these people around her—it's too much.

"Hi," she says softly as she slips into Kira's passenger's seat. She lets out a tiny squeak of pleasure when she sees she brought Hobbes along. Hobbes jumps on Grace's lap and she kisses his nose and strokes his ears.

"Hi, I know you expected Aden, but he had to do something this morning. He said he'd be back to the inn soon though," she says, and Grace finds it strange that Kira suddenly knows more about his comings and goings than she does—it's intimate in a way she somehow doesn't like.

"Thanks for getting me," she says.

"Are you feeling better?" Kira asks, and Grace nods and looks out the window, disinviting conversation. She doesn't know what she could possibly say to this woman until she can tell her the truth.

They drive the rest of the short distance from the hospital to the inn wordlessly. It isn't until she hears a sharp intake of breath from Kira that she looks at her, and then straight ahead to what she's looking at, open-mouthed.

There's a police car pulled up into the gravel clearing in front of the inn, and two officers standing on the front wraparound porch. One is on his phone. The other is peering in a window.

"Oh, God," Kira mumbles, getting out of the car. Grace does the same, and the slam of their doors make the officers turn. Hobbes jumps out and barks at them, jumping around on his hind legs and yelping. Grace picks him up.

"Wes, what's happened? Why are you here?" Kira says in a panicked voice, and Grace finds it odd that she's on a first-name basis with a police officer.

"Kira?" the officer says, surprised. "Nothing. I mean. I wasn't here for you. I didn't know you... What are you doing here, exactly?"

Kira looks to Grace, and Grace's face loses its color. Police, patrol cars, uniforms. She just wants it all to go away. She swallows hard and clutches her handbag to her chest.

"This is Grace, she runs the place. I was dropping her off. She's not feeling well," Kira says, moving to Grace, taking her elbow to help her inside.

"Ms. Holloway, we actually came to speak with you," Wes says. "I'm Detective Hendricks. This is Detective Monohan. We just have a couple of questions if you have a minute," he says, and Grace looks to Kira like she might vomit.

"Let's go in and sit down," Kira says.

Inside the lobby is ear-ringingly quiet. Sunbeams cast rectangular shapes across the wood floor and dust particles dance in the slits of light. The antique fiddleback chair protests beneath Monohan's weight as he sits. Hendricks sits on the leather sofa next to Kira, and the air is electric with nervous energy as Grace perches at the edge of an armchair and waits to hear what they have to say. The word *missing* is always bold and red when it flashes across her memory; the shouts of police officers yelling to each other in those woods that they found something; the snap of bone in the bear trap; the wailing, the running. It all swirls in nauseating loops inside her mind.

"We understand Aden Coleman is staying here at the inn,"

he begins, looking round for him to materialize. "We called him, of course, but it went to voice mail, so we thought we'd stop by."

"You're here for Aden?" Grace asks.

"We also have a couple questions for you, but if he's here…"

"He's on his way," Kira says, and again there is a twinge of irritation that Kira knows this and she doesn't. Hendricks nods.

"If Aden is staying here, you are probably aware his father is missing," he starts.

"Yeah," Grace says, wishing Aden were fielding these questions—wishing she could go upstairs with Hobbes and crawl under the covers for days, but of course she can't. She could blow their minds with the information she has, but… *Not. Yet.*

"I don't know if you've seen the posters around town, or maybe Mr. Coleman shared with you…" he begins, placing an image of Martin Coleman on the coffee table in front of him and turning the paper around to face Grace. She feels her whole body tense. She nods.

Just then the front lobby door flies open, and they all startle. Aden rushes inside.

"What happened? Grace, are you—why are the police here?"

"Mr. Coleman," Hendricks says, standing. "There's nothing urgent, just a development we wanted to discuss. We tried reaching you." Aden pats his pants pocket and jacket with his hands, then his back pockets, feeling for his phone with no luck.

"Oh, I didn't—I was tied up. What development? Did you find something?" he asks, joining the others, sitting on the arm of the sofa. He peers at an image of his father on the coffee table, then looks to Hendricks.

"We finally received your father's phone records, and the last signal before the phone was turned off pinged off the cell tower at the end of Shiloh Road. It's pretty rural out here, so there aren't too many places he could have been."

"What?" Aden says, standing again, chewing his thumb and looking to the ceiling as if thinking hard about it. "There would be no reason for him to be over on this part of town," he says, flustered.

"Here's the list we made of businesses and residents in the area the tower services," he says, handing a manila folder to Aden. "Maybe looking at it will spark something?"

"Grace, do you recognize Mr. Coleman or remember seeing him in this area at all a few weeks back? Or ever, for that matter?" Monohan asks. Grace presses the bandage covering the place on her arm where the IV was inserted and picks at the gauze.

"I don't really leave the inn much," she says. "Sorry I'm not much help."

"Anyone else stay here over the last month or spend any time here that might be worth talking to, do you know?"

"Uh…" Grace's throat goes dry. The last time she has spoken to or even seen a cop was many years ago, and the mere proximity to one makes her stomach flip. She should feel gratitude—they saved her after all, didn't they? But all it does is bring every terrible memory back.

"Um, Vinny. Donatto. He's the delivery guy. He comes a couple times a week. Nobody else I can think of," she says, clearing her throat, and Kira must notice Grace go pale because she says she'll go and get some water and excuses herself.

"I don't—I feel like this is just more confusing," Aden says, "Besides the inn, there's a bait shop, a corner store, a liquor store, and eight cabins along Bullhead Lake. Like…" He stops and a quiet growl of frustration escapes his throat as he drops the envelope on the table.

"We talked to the corner store, and they have a security

camera that doesn't show him there. The bait shop was closed that weekend, and we will still talk to the liquor store, but since there are a dozen others nearer to his house, I don't expect much there. I did call your mother this morning. She said what you're saying—there'd be no reason for him to be on this side of town, so far into the outskirts."

Kira comes in and hands Grace a glass of water and glances down at the list in the manila envelope. Grace sees her hand fly to her mouth. Aden and the detectives continue to talk, unaware.

"Maybe he knew someone in one of the cabins, had a buddy from church or…"

"I mean, I can't really say I know his friends and his schedule anymore, obviously, so yeah, I mean, it seems weird but maybe that's… I don't know."

"We've spoken to a couple of the residents in the cabins already, but most folks don't stay off-season, so we have calls out to the rest, see if that gets us anywhere, but—"

"That's my cabin. There on Bullhead Lake, we're the third one in from the corner of the dirt road turnoff," Kira interrupts, her face blotchy and her voice shaking. Everyone has turned to look at her. The cop doesn't look surprised; clearly, he already knows this.

"We talked to Leo already," Hendricks says.

"Who's Leo?" Aden asks.

"My father," Kira replies. "He's not there. He's spending a few days up near Fog Creek where the clothes were found, searching. Or so he says."

"Right, that's what he said when we called. And again, we double-checked with the guys he was away with that weekend. He said he'd come back in and go over it all again. We'll talk to the other cabins again, of course. We did call Matt and asked him to come up for questioning and he agreed, said he'd head to Rock Harbor first thing in the morning." Kira whips a look back at the detective that makes Grace shiver and sit back in her seat, gripping the water glass in her fists.

"Why the fuck haven't you arrested him yet?" she screams, shocking everyone. "What more do you need?"

"Ms. Everett," Monohan says, and Hendricks cuts the air with his hand, a gesture that says to let him handle it.

"Kira, I wish it were that cut and dry, but we don't have enough to go on. Not even close. And you—"

"Then search my cabin. Heather. Heather Rossi had a brace-let... It was gold with little elephant charms, her mother said, and Amelia had that half of a heart locket. Oh, my God, I never—if this maniac is taking tokens off these girls, he's gotta be keeping them, right?" Before anyone can respond, she says, "Of course he would. Fuck." Then she sits and then stands and then sits again, cups her hand with her mouth. Then she stands again, her mind clearly reeling.

"Um. I'm sorry," Aden says. "I thought... We are talking about my dad's phone records, right? Did I miss something?" He looks to Grace who just raises her eyebrows back at him and watches Kira for a response.

"Matt is my dirtbag soon-to-be-ex-husband who lied about where he was the day my daughter disappeared. He was here at the cabin. Your dad was a couple weeks later and I don't know how the fuck any of this is related, but I know Matt was here two weeks ago because we were all here looking for Brooke, so this is too much. Your dad was in *this* area the night he went missing. I mean you're saying his phone pinged around here... Christ's sake, get a warrant." Then Kira freezes, and Grace thinks she might take a swing at Hendricks but she grabs her bag off the floor next to the couch and looks him dead in the eye.

"I don't need to wait around for this shit. I can do it myself," she says and heads for the door. Hendricks follows after her.

"Kira, where are you going?"

"Boston," she says, slamming the door behind her. Hendricks calls out something about not knowing if it's safe, but she's gone. Grace sees Hendricks's back tense as he stares after her. Monohan picks up his notepad and pen.

"We can't stop her," he says. "She wants to search her own house—maybe she should."

"We'll be in touch after we talk to Matt Rivers and that delivery guy you mentioned," Hendricks says stiffly, and Monohan meets him at the door.

"Anything else you can think of, give us a call," he says to Grace, handing her a card. He nods to Aden. "We'll let you know what we find out."

The silence in the lobby is back in the wake of all the chaos that tore in and out of it. Grace doesn't want Aden to make any conversation or talk through any of what just happened. She's afraid she'll say what she knows too soon, so she says she needs to lie down and disappears up to her room for the rest of the day.

Later that night, she sits at her small desk by the window and stares out into the backyard trees, boiling over with anxiety over what she's about to do. She knew the facts, but the last piece of the puzzle was put into place in that lobby conversation earlier in the day. Why hadn't she thought of it before? She knew exactly how to release the truth without herself at the center of it and with little room for failure. She thought of creating a fake email address or some social media account to send the message she needed to send anonymously, but she couldn't risk a paper trail if there was a chance this could backfire.

When she's certain Aden must be asleep, she gives Hobbes a

marrow bone to keep him occupied and turns on *The Golden Girls*, long ago deciding it's his favorite show and calms him, and hopes he doesn't whimper and wake Aden up. He would be shocked to see her willingly outside of the inn and probably call the police, thinking she'd gone missing too. It's a risk, but she takes it.

She piles on a down parka and Wellies and makes the three-mile walk toward Shiloh Road to find the third cabin in off the dirt turn on Bullhead Lake.

26

KIRA

When I violently push open the door to our Boston house, I don't know what I expect to see, but I see nothing. I don't hear Matt. There's a dish in the sink and an empty beer bottle on the counter, but other than that, the place is tidy, normal. Why wouldn't it be? It's not like I'd walk in to see him committing a crime this very minute, but that's how it felt part of the drive here.

When I fly up the stairs and down the hall, I see him in the bedroom packing a bag, a look on his face that actually resembles concern, but I know it's for himself. It's because he's been asked to come in for questioning.

"Goddamn it!" he yells, jumping back with his hand on his chest when he sees me standing in the doorway. "You scared—what are you doing here? I texted that I was coming to Rock Harbor in the morning." I don't respond. I just start pulling drawers out of his dresser and dumping the contents onto the floor. I pull out the top junk drawer and watch all of his pens and ChapSticks and earbuds and batteries and scissors and scrap paper fly across the room. I throw the drawer on the bed and pull out the bigger drawers, edging my fingers under socks and underwear before pouring it out and tossing the drawer. One of them crashes against the bedpost and cracks. Matt stands in silent awe for a moment, then...

"What in the actual fuck is the matter with you?"

I stand with furious tears rolling down my cheeks. "What did you do to her!?" I scream, and then I can't control myself. I lunge at him and pound him in the chest with my fist. "What did you do!?" I scream again, the intensity of it making my voice hoarse. He grabs my wrists and pushes me back, then puts up his hands—a surrender as long as I don't come at him again, so I go to the closet instead.

I drop to my knees and pull out everything I can reach from the floor of the closet. I push the shoes aside and start dumping shoeboxes of keepsakes and photos, diplomas, award ribbons, everything I can dump or throw.

"I'm gonna find it and you're fucked so you might as well just tell me!"

"Just—goddamn it, Kira, stop. Please. I don't know what you're doing! I don't know what the hell you're looking for, so maybe if you tell me, I can help you. Jesus!"

"You know the detective is on to you now, so you're gonna destroy evidence. I mean that's what a smart person would do, and I'm not gonna let that happen."

"Evidence. What?"

"They won't issue a search, so I will. Get out of here." Matt just blinks at me. "Get the fuck out of here!" Then, to my surprise, he walks out. I spend over an hour in the bedroom, yanking clothes from hangers, searching under the bed, in bathroom cabinets, everywhere; and find nothing. So I think about where I should have actually started—where I would have started if I hadn't found him there in the bedroom and just cracked. The attic and the garage and the basement. I'll move to the garage because I never go in there, so it's the perfect spot to hide lockets and elephant bracelets.

When I jog down the stairs, Matt is standing at the kitchen counter, beer in hand, staring up at the ceiling in an exaggerated way that infuriates me even more, which I didn't think was possible.

"I thought I told you to get out," I say, feeling nothing but more venom with each angry word.

"I know that this has to be unimaginably difficult for you, but…"

"Don't you say but! You have no fucking clue. You will *never* know. They have evidence, you know," I say.

"I was going to say, but if you want to save hours of your time searching this house, I can promise you there is nothing to find. What are you looking for? Seriously? Can you sit? Will you just sit down and talk to me and tell me what you think I did and what you're looking for, and let's just— just fucking communicate?" he says, pulling a beer out of the fridge and handing it to me. "Please, Kira." And now I have a new idea. I take the beer.

"I'll be right back," I say and go into the bathroom. I regroup and calm myself down because I need to handle this in a way where I'm in control of the information, not him.

He's sitting out on the back patio when I come back into the kitchen, as if he is the one controlling this, but he's mistaken. I acquiesce and bring my beer outside. I sit on an Adirondack chair and look down at my boots before speaking.

"The first thing you need to know is that they found bloody

clothes that they determined were Brooke's, and there was semen on them too," I say, and he chokes on his sip of beer and coughs it down.

"What? Why wouldn't you have told me that?"

"And because of that, they have DNA and they will surely ask you to give a sample to rule you out, so if you had anything to do with this, you better tell me right now, because they got ya. And it could be a murder charge if they don't find her, so if you know where she is... If you..."

"Jesus Christ. What? Why would you think I would hurt Brooke! I would never—are you out of your mind? I lied about New York and you're leaping to murder?"

"The missing guy—the old guy—his phone last pinged near the cabin. We were there that weekend too. You think all this is looking good for you? What are the odds, Matthew?"

"Near it? There's a million other places near that tower, that's why you're—"

"There aren't that many, actually. I don't think you need to pack, I'd be shocked if you weren't arrested first thing when you get there," I say, taking the upper hand. "It's DNA, Matt. You're fucked." Matt chugs his beer and fireflies blink in the distant blackness, and it doesn't seem right for beauty to exist in this moment.

"She called me asking for money, you know that, I told you that, okay...but I didn't tell you that I did give it to her," he says, not looking at me. I try to whisper the word *what?* but no sound comes out.

"I can't believe you think I would hurt her or...what...? Kill somebody? I mean, Jesus Christ, really? I mean, I could never tell you what happened, but it wasn't, like the end of the world. There's no kidnapping or murder. God, the fact that you would even..."

"She called you for money. Did you know she was doing

drugs? Did you know that? And maybe that's what got her…"
I stop, not knowing what words to even use next. He picks at
the label on his bottle and doesn't say anything.

"Oh, my God," I mutter, realizing he does know.

"I didn't know until that night. I barely talked to her since
she moved, and I did say no, for the record, but she showed
up anyway. Just showed up at the door that night." I stand,
and gasp.

"Then what? What happened? What did you do?"

"Nothing! I'm trying to tell you the truth because this *evidence* you're saying they have is painting the wrong picture. I
was trying to protect her, really."

"What happened when she came over?" I say, steadying
my trembling hands, needing the rest of the information so I
don't literally kill him yet.

"Please sit," he says, "I know you're gonna get all upset, but
I wanna tell you the truth, so you know—so you understand
that I might have made a mistake, but I'm not a freakin' killer
or psycho or whatever."

"Tell me."

"She had…coke."

"Okay?" Already knowing this terrible reality.

"And she was wearing some weird shit—like a schoolgirl
costume or something. I asked why and she just giggled at me.
She sat down at the coffee table and poured out a dime bag
and made little rows of powder like she'd done it a hundred
times." I'm frozen in my rage. I feel like if I move, he'll stop
talking and I'll never know, so I stay perfectly still, watching
him look at the ground and continue his story.

"She was saying all this shit about how we never really
bonded and how this could be fun—our little secret. It was a
guys' weekend so I'd already had a few, I know my judgment
wasn't all there, so I…did it," he says painfully.

"Did what?" I ask, still motionless.

"I did a line or two of coke with her. Then she got really chatty, talking about the clubs and stripping. I thought she worked at a coffee shop. Then she asked if I wanted to see her dance. I know. I KNOW you're gonna blame me, but I was fucking off my rocks high. I'd never done coke before. I don't know what made me, but I was gone—I had no idea what I was doing. I swear to God," he says, and I stifle a cry that's rumbling in my chest.

"THEN. WHAT?" I seethe, needing it all but knowing I can't scare him and make him stop talking by crushing his skull with a nearby loose brick, which hasn't gone unnoticed.

"She just wanted money. I mean. She asked me if I wanted to see how she usually gets a hundred and fifty bucks. I know it was fucking wrong. I'm not proud of it! I wish I could pretend it never happened, but if they think I—"

"You know the semen will match and you'll go to prison, so this is all about you now," I say, and the only reason I can form a sentence is because a numb shock is taking over. A survival mechanism, maybe.

"It's not like I had sex with her! She showed me her... *BJ skills*, and I gave her money. Okay, I did it. Like I said I'm not proud, but she was the one getting *me* high, I didn't know what I was doing. It would have never happened if it weren't for that. But I never hurt her. She laughed at me, actually, after it was done, took the money out of my wallet and left. I never saw her after that." I still can't speak so he keeps on, nervous rambling that just digs him a deeper hole.

"She was a teenager when we got married, I mean it's not like I raised her. She's never been my kid. I know it's messed up, but it was the drugs. I didn't..."

"For someone who *didn't know what they were doing*, you sure remember it pretty well," I hiss through my teeth. That's the *wild thing* she was going to do—get money from her *creepy stepfather* no matter the cost.

"Get out before I actually kill you," I say, and he starts to protest. I pull my phone from my purse and push play so he can hear the conversation we just had recorded. I know it's not much. It's not statutory rape or a confession of kidnapping, but it's something. It places him with her the night she vanished, and it shows maybe some strange motive. Just in case he decides to run or lie to the police or something, because I don't know who he is anymore. At least I have some part of the truth. He opens his mouth and gives me a look like I'm the one who's done something terrible—like I betrayed him, but he's speechless.

"And don't even think about going to the cabin. Ever again. Stay at a motel, whatever, just know that if you don't show up at the station in the morning, I'll do my best to start a national manhunt for you. There'd be no explaining away a little drug-induced tryst at that point, so be careful." He stands up and shakes his head and turns to go.

"Wait," I say and he pauses, turns to me. "Did my dad know you were there that night, or was that another lie?"

"I never said he did. I just assumed he probably might have," he says. "Jesus. You really just want to paint me as some kind of monster, don't you?"

"Goodbye, Matt," I say.

"I'm on your side, believe it or not. I wouldn't do that," is all he says. Then I hear him pick up the bag he packed, and after a moment, the garage door opens and I hear his car start and then pull away.

Probably might have, he says now. I basically accused my own father of being involved, and I doubted him even though his alibi was triple-checked and I know him and that he would never do anything even close to what my traumatized mind led me to believe.

Before I can give way to the flood of emotion threatening to suffocate me, I need to work. I need to search while I can.

I spend hours tearing apart the house. Every box in the attic is overturned, every corner in the basement searched twice. The contents of the plastic storage bins lining the garage shelves are in a pile on the floor and I don't find anything. Not even some porn mags or anything that would point to him being a complete pervert. Yet, he is.

I decide to drive back to the cabin tonight because I don't want to risk traffic or get there later than him tomorrow. They may not let me be in the room when they speak to him, but I need to be close. I need talk to Hendricks after and make him tell me all he can.

I can barely keep my eyes open on the drive that seems three times as long as the adrenaline-fueled one on the way here. And when I get back to the cabin close to midnight, I practically sleepwalk to the front door, but I'm stopped in my tracks and wide awake when I see something attached to the front doorknob.

With my heart thumping I look around to make sure I'm alone, that I'm not about to be attacked—that it's not a trap. But there's really no way of knowing that, so I rush to the front door, grab the rolled-up note, and go inside, closing and locking the door behind me.

When I open the letter, I see it's anonymous. There's a message handwritten in block letters. What I read shocks me. What I read changes everything.

27

GRACE

When Grace gets home from leaving the note on Kira's cabin door, it's time to wait. It's time to see how it all unfolds. She tiptoes up the creaky stairs and opens her bedroom door to see Hobbes asleep on his back in his little bed. He licks his lips and rolls over when he hears the door, but doesn't wake up. Sophia is telling Rose an anecdote about Sicily on the television, and Grace feels like she'll break down and cry.

After so many years living in fear, she finally knows the truth. So much still has to go right for her to be free—to really feel like she can live her life without constant panic and anxiety, but she finally knows the truth. She looks around and it's like she's seeing what she's becoming through someone else's eyes all of a sudden—holed up with her dog in a tiny room, inside an empty inn in the middle of nowhere, so afraid of the world that she's permanently paralyzed and stopped living completely the day she was taken from the laundromat bench.

Her thoughts are reeling and adrenaline is still pulsing through her veins; she can't stay in this room anymore. The anticipation of what will happen next is buzzing between her ears and she needs to try to calm down. She pads quietly down the hall to make sure Aden didn't wake up and is where he's supposed to be, but when she reaches his room, the door is cracked. And when she pushes it slightly open with one finger and peers in, he's not there. Her heart speeds up, but she tells herself it could be anything. He has a missing father. He could have gotten a call. His mother might not be well.

Still, she walks the shadowy halls of each floor and opens every guest room door, peering under beds and behind shower curtains because now she's alone, and what she's set into motion is dangerous, and she suddenly feels like she needs to leave. To run. But where could she go? It's almost 2:00 a.m., and even if it were morning, she has no one really, does she?

She puts her shoes back on instinctually, because what if she needs to run? She has always kept shoes next to her bed for that reason, just in case. She keeps a rope tied to the bed frame too, long enough to toss out the window and climb down to safety if there was danger and she was trapped on the second floor. A baseball bat is tucked behind her bedroom door. She picks it up before walking downstairs.

She clicks on a lamp in the lobby, and looks out the front windows. She scans for any movement, anything odd. Nothing. After a few minutes, she goes to the kitchen. It's quiet. Nothing is out of place. She decides to pour herself a glass of wine to calm her nerves.

Then she walks the perimeters of the lobby, poking at the oversize drapes to make sure nothing lurks behind them, opening closet doors. Her heart flutters when she sees the glowing blue light of the lobby desk computer turned on. She hasn't had reason to touch it for days.

When she gets closer, she sees Aden Coleman's name pulled up in a Google search. What the hell? He is the only one here, so why would he look himself up? There is no conceivable reason she can come up with. It's just his name blinking in the Google tab, but below are stories and stories about his missing father, and as she scrolls down, she sees the name Shannon Coleman. The wife Vinny said died mysteriously.

She clicks on one of the links about Shannon and sees the face of a lovely woman with high cheekbones and bright eyes bloom onto the screen. She reads: *Wife and mother of one killed in tragic hiking accident. Ms. Coleman was hiking alone with her dog on Ridgecrest Bluff when it's thought that she lost her footing on loose rock. She was rushed to Mercy Hospital, Portland, but didn't survive her injuries.*

She was alone. Why would Vinny say they never figured out what happened and that Aden was there? And why the hell is this up on the computer? Who was here? Could it really just be the jealousy Aden pointed out—that Vinny might have a little crush and didn't like another man around? Or is there something else behind this? All the stories about Martin and the girls are connected to the search, and she can't look at any of that right now. She shuts down the screen.

In the still quiet of the inn, she sits at the kitchen table and takes a few deep breaths. Her plan will work, and everything is fine. Nobody is here. She savors the smoky, rich flavors of the wine and closes her eyes, counting a breath in for four, out for seven.

Then she jumps to her feet when she hears something. It sounds like car tires on gravel. She freezes for a few moments and listens. Then she puts her wine down and picks up the bat and moves through the kitchen into the lobby. She looks out the front window again, and again sees nothing. Her heart pounds in her throat as she stands in the middle of the lobby holding a bat like a lunatic, not knowing what to do next.

When she hears the sound of the back kitchen door click open, she screams and blood whooshes between her ears and she expects to be attacked again. She swings the bat in the air, her grip so tight it sends pulses of pain through her fingertips. The brief moment feels like an eternity until she sees Vinny walk through the kitchen into the lobby with his hands up.

"Whoa, who, whoa, what the hell?"

"Vinny! What are you doing!?" She drops the bat and rests her hands on her knees for a minute, an unsettling mix of fear and relief confusing her thoughts.

"Sorry, I didn't mean to scare you. Jesus. I was checking in on you like I said I'd do…"

"Checking in on me doesn't mean giving me a heart attack. It's the middle of the freaking night!"

"No, I mean, sorry, but like an hour ago I drove by and I saw headlights turning off the property and I wanted to see if you were okay, so I knocked but no one answered. So I gave it an hour and came back to make sure you was safe and everything." Grace stares at him, catching her breath, then walks past him back into the kitchen, where she picks up her wine and takes a gulp.

"Well, thank you, but you almost put me back in the hospital."

"Oh, hey that's the Malbec I brought ya. How is it?" Grace sits, trying to shake off the shock, and works to keep herself calm even though he is unnerving her.

"What?" she asks.

"The Malbec. Can I try it? I should stick around a while, make sure nobody's out there. Too much weird shit going on for you to be by yourself right now, have you thought of that?" he says, selecting a glass from open shelves above the sink.

"It must have just been Aden leaving," I say.

"Where's he goin' in the middle of the night?"

"I don't know."

"That fuckin' guy," he says and sits across from her with his glass of wine.

"What did you have against him, again?"

"Nothin'. I feel bad for him actually, who wouldn't? What a mess he's got goin' on. I just don't like him creepin' around here."

"You said his wife died and they didn't know what happened—that he might have been involved," she says, trying to make eye contact, searching his face.

"Well, that's what I always heard—that's the rumor."

"Well. I saw his name up on the computer in the lobby, so I clicked on it and the story is all there. She was by herself when it happened," she says.

"No shit? Huh. Well, you know how rumors are."

"Did you look him up on that computer? Is that why that's there?"

"Yeah. I told ya I was here looking for ya. I tried to look for his contact info in the guest book and didn't see it, so I tried the computer—thought I could call him, see if he saw you or where the hell either of you was. Couldn't find his number, you were nowhere to be found. You're literally always here. I was worried sick. I was just trying to look out for you."

"Vinny, you can't just—"

"You know the cops called to talk to me again, asking where I was the night that guy went missin'—his dad. They should be askin' him. Why are they askin' me? They can't get enough of me, can they? Blame ole Vinny for everything. Joke's on them. I got time-stamped deliveries the whole night. What a bunch a' punks, huh?"

"I didn't see your car out front," she says uneasily. "Where's your car?"

"Oh, I parked on the side. I was trying to get a look at the backyard, see if anything was funny. I worry about ya with a Nutter Butter on the loose like this, ya know?"

"Did you…see anything?" Grace asks, wishing he would leave—wishing she could just fast-forward until tomorrow when her note will be found and things will be uncovered.

"Naw, but listen. You don't have to worry. Actually. Hold on. Wait there a sec," he says, standing and opening the back door.

"Where are you going? Vinny, I—"

"I got something for ya," he says and disappears with the back door standing open. Grace doesn't know if she should lock him out and run upstairs, and she doesn't make a decision quick enough because he's back in the doorframe, a shadow against the glare of the kitchen light, a figure holding a shotgun.

"Vinny, Vinny, what are you doing?"

"I thought you could use something to make you feel a little more protected. I mean what would you do if someone broke in?"

"I—I don't…" Grace starts to move away, unsure what he's going to really do. She can't trust anyone.

"I took lessons—like at the range, so I could help teach you how to use it and everything," he says, smiling. And then he quickly cocks his head to one side and puts his finger over his lips.

"What?"

"Shhh. Did you hear that?" he says, making a face like he's sniffing the air, then cupping his hand over his ear.

"No. I don't know. Just close the door. Please. Just…"

"Grace, for real. I heard something out there. Sorry. I don't want you to—last thing I wanna do is upset you, it's probably an animal, but I should check it out."

"No. No, you don't have to do that. It's not safe," she says, "Just shut the door. Vinny!"

"Okay," he says, closing it and standing there with his gun slung over his shoulder on a decorative strap.

"That doesn't look new," she says.

"Oh no, I've had it for years but never learned how to use it. Thought you'd get more use out of it, so I polished her up."

"Can you just—can we put that down? Here. Why don't you finish your wine, and we don't need that." She attempts a smile and pushes his glass across the table.

"At least call the police then. Get them to make sure it's all clear, so you—"

"No," she says too quickly. Her plan will unravel if he interferes and the wrong people get information.

"Listen, I know you're on edge, so we'll both feel better if I make sure everything is okay," he says, standing and pushing open the back door before she can utter another word.

Grace closes the door in a flurry and rushes to the kitchen window with wobbly knees and trembling hands. She tries to see if there is anything moving—any sound. She watches Vinny's back until the deck light no longer illuminates him and the darkness of the backyard swallows him.

It was probably just an animal, she tells herself. He's probably right. A deer. She has seen many of them this fall. She shakes her leg nervously and chews the edge of her pinky nail, praying it's just an animal.

But when she sees Vinny's pale face reappear under a cone of the deck light, she knows it's more than that.

"Grace," he says in a pinched voice. "Oh, my God. It's not an animal. Someone's there."

28
KIRA

When I called Aden last night after I got the note, his phone went to voice mail three times before he groggily answered with a confused-sounding, "Hello?"

"I need to see you. I have something. I have information."

"Okay. Now?"

"Yes. Now!" I yell, because of course *now*. Look how much time we've already wasted.

"Okay, where?"

"Your house. It's in the note. We have to go to your house," I say, impatient that he doesn't understand, even though there is no reason that he could.

"What note?"

"I got a note—a letter left at my cabin with a tip—with a promise that if we follow the instructions, we'll find who's responsible for this. Please, I'll show it to you. Just, we need to meet at your house."

"My brother's there."

"Shit. Really? He can't be there. We need to search the place. Nobody can be there. There's something stashed in your house that we need to find," I say, breathless, walking out to the end of the dock in the inky black darkness.

"Kira, that sounds—are you sure it's not a hoax? One of the crazies out there trying to take advantage of a terrible situation? People are sick, ya know."

"I'm not sure of anything, but I need to look—I need to follow it up anyway, 'cause what if it's not?"

"Why would someone who has information like that send it to you anonymously?"

"You're asking me things I don't know. I don't know! Maybe they're scared. Maybe…"

"Just tell me what it says," he says, and I sigh and look up to the sky. I don't have time to waste, but I need his cooperation. I don't need to flash a light on the paper. I have it memorized.

"All the evidence is in Aden's house. Search it and you'll find your daughter." My voice breaks, and I sit cross-legged on the wood of the dock floor, slippery with frost.

"Jesus. What?" Aden says, and I hear rustling like he's up and getting dressed.

"I don't know! We have to do it though."

"Yeah, but you're right. You don't know my brother, but if I bring a stranger to the house and start a police-style ransack of the place, that's not gonna go over well. Give me a few hours. Just—I'll go over there, I'll figure out a way to get him out of the house first thing. I'll text you when to come."

"I can't wait that long," I say, holding back tears, knowing he's right though. It's the middle of the night. I need to give him time to get the brother out. I thought it's his mother's house. Thank God she doesn't seem to be there. I don't want him to look for whatever it is without me, but I also don't want to lose my only lead—my only hope.

"A few hours," I say.

Inside, I lie down on the small plaid couch, still in my coat and boots, and look at the clock on the wall. The only sound in the silent room is the ticking of the hands.

I say Brooke's name and whisper mumbled prayers until I finally must have fallen asleep for an hour or so. Daybreak through the window curtains wakes me up, and I leap to my feet and look at my phone. Nothing yet. It's almost 6:00 a.m.

I go to the stove and heat up water in a pot for the instant coffee my dad keeps in the cupboard. I pour myself a mug and go outside to sit by the firepit. The gray ash against a dull sky and skeleton trees makes the place sadder than I even thought possible, but I still see Brooke's face. I see it lit by the glowing red of the fire on summer nights, twirling a sparkler or roasting her marshmallow until it's black and on fire, always chewing grape bubblegum and twirling it around a finger, mosquito-bitten legs and fireflies in a jar.

I think of my father explaining to her when she was little that they're bioluminescent and it's how they talk to each other, so it's important we set them free, and she agreed. She named him Roger and said goodbye and opened the lid so he could fly away. I slip my phone from my pocket and look to see if I missed anything from Aden. Nothing yet. I try to call my father, but there's no answer.

I'm still sitting at the ghostly firepit, three cups of coffee in at 9:54 a.m. I've called Aden three times, and he's responded that he's working on it but needs more time. If he had ignored me, I'd have gone over there and broken in. He gave me his address, but if I did just show up, would I ruin the whole operation? Is his brother still there? Is he…involved?

I'll give him thirty more minutes, I decide, and then I'll go find him. I call my father again.

"Hey," he answers after two rings.

"We have a lead, maybe," I say and I tell him about the note and that I'm waiting to go to the house.

"You shouldn't go there alone, Kir. You don't know this guy. With this Martin missing too, you don't know what you're getting yourself caught up in."

"I have to try. I don't care. I have to do it."

"I should be there—someone should go with you."

"No," I say, cutting him off. "I appreciate it. I need to tread lightly. It's Aden's house—his childhood house. Frankly, I'm surprised he's willing to help me, but I can't show up with a team. I just—listen. That's not even why I called," I say, my cheeks flush with shame and my words sound hollow. "I'm sorry for what I said."

"Stop. Honey, this is the hardest thing you'll ever have to go through. You'd be an idiot not to suspect everyone and everything you know."

"Thank you," I say. "I just feel crazy and I don't know what to believe, but…" I stop mid-sentence, and stop dead as I hear a car pull up to the cabin, quiet as a whisper, but the middle of nowhere is quieter.

"Shit, I gotta go," I say, hanging up. Then…

"What the fuck!?" He gets out of the vehicle and lunges toward me.

29

ADEN

When Aden arrived back at his mother's house in the small hours of the morning, he had no earthly idea what he was really doing. Was this letter for real or the most ridiculous spoke-and-the-wheel tactic he'd ever seen? It didn't really matter much because neither he nor Kira was in a position to ignore it if it was a remote possibility.

He needed to get Brady out for the day—that is, if he was even home, which he tended not to be late at night these days, but certainly *did* tend to be when it came to eating Hot Pockets and watching *Dr. Phil* on the sofa sleeper all day.

He worked out a story in his mind on the sleepy drive over, and he couldn't alarm Brady in the middle of the night. But he would try to work his angle to get him out for the day once he either woke up or rolled in with last night's clothes on in the morning.

As he slowly turned the key in the lock, he listened for sounds of life, but the house was quiet, as you'd expect at this hour. He took off his boots by the front door and called softly for Brady to see if he was up. It wouldn't be abnormal for him to be on the sofa in the garage, spread-eagled in his boxers with a smoke hanging off his lips and losing at online poker, so you never know. He didn't see Brady in the garage. He wasn't in the kitchen or on the back deck.

When Aden starts to head upstairs and hears a strange noise, he stops in his tracks and sits on the brown-carpeted steps a moment just to listen. He can't place what he's hearing, but Brady is definitely home. Is it crying? It's definitely moaning and...yelling. He knows he hears a female voice now, in small staccato cries.

Aden stands and runs down the stairs two at a time and stops outside Brady's basement room. He flings open the door and immediately cups his hand over his mouth and steps out. He sees legs in the air, then his brother's bare white ass accosting his vision. A woman screaming, "Pervert," at Aden and covering up her breasts all happens in the space of three seconds.

"Sorry!" he repeats to the door he closes behind him before going back upstairs and trying to erase the images from his mind. He lies down in the living room on the ugly sofa. Great. Brady has a lady friend, and now he has two people to get out of the house in the morning.

He wonders if this letter Kira found is a prank, because, let's face it, people are sick. He wonders, if it is real, what does that mean? Did someone plant something here? Does someone in his family know something about where Martin is? Where Brooke is? It makes no sense, but of course none of this does, so he has to let Kira look, since she believes the letter means something. It could. Of course, it could. There's just no way to know. But he has to try too. Who would he be if he didn't?

He pours himself a glass of rosé from the box in the fridge, and then he stares at a water stain on the ceiling and thinks of Leah and how in the world he can protect her from all this. He thinks of how much smarter than him she usually is and there's a part of him who wishes he could tell her, because she'd surely have some wisdom to impart, some anecdote, she always does. He eventually falls asleep just before the sun rises.

By 8:00 a.m. Kira has called three times, and his brother and his lady friend have not woken up. He texts her back to say he needs more time. He makes a pot of coffee and pulls some Eggo waffles from the freezer and pops them in the toaster, thinking the smell of coffee and flaky waffles would wake anyone, especially sober people who aren't sleeping off a couple bottles of wine like he was, and he managed to get up. It's not until a quarter after nine o'clock that Brady comes into the kitchen in SpongeBob boxers with a cigarette already poised between his middle and index fingers. He's trailed by a very short twenty-something woman with blue hair and a tongue ring. She wears his Say No to Drugs T-shirt over underwear and goes directly to the fridge like she lives here and pulls out a gallon of skim milk.

"Sup?" she says to Aden, as she opens the pantry and looks through the cereal options. "Lucky Charms, babe, really? And what's this Count Chocula shit? You're a grown man," she says, and Aden looks at Brady, waiting for some sort of recognition while she makes herself at home.

"Morning, perv," he says, and Brady and the girl laugh.

"Yeah, hi. Could we have a minute, please?" Aden asks.

"For what?"

"Like, can I talk to you privately?"

"What am I? Chopped liver?" the blue-haired girl asks.

"I'm sorry, who are you exactly? What's your name?" Aden asks, taking her milk away before she can pour it over the Lucky Charms she chose.

"Brandi?" she says, like it's a question.

"Of course it is," Aden mumbles. "Look, I need to talk to you for a minute," he says.

"Give us a minute," Brady tells her, and she shrugs and takes her bowl of cereal back downstairs.

"What's up, perv?" Brady says again, chewing his waffle with his mouth open and laughing.

"I didn't know you were here, okay, and then I heard something... Never mind. Who's this chick?" he asks.

"She told ya. Brandi. My girlfriend," he says, and Aden has to sit on a stool.

"Since when do you have a girlfriend?" he asks, not remembering one since high school. "Is this where you've been going all the time?"

"What do you mean all the time?"

"Late at night when you're not here," he says, standing, flailing his arms in the air. "You don't think you showing up with a girlfriend for the first time in like fifteen years is noteworthy?"

"No," Brady says, biting off half an Eggo and shrugging.

"You've never had one before," Aden says, trying to control the volume of his voice.

"I've never been sober before," he states matter-of-factly.

"Oh," Aden says, his shoulders softening and his temper cooling. "I guess that's true."

"Pretty hot, huh? Boom-chicka-boom-boom," he says, an obnoxious bro laugh escaping his lips between waffle bites.

"Okay?" Aden says, not knowing how else to respond.

"Look, listen, I mean. I've been seeing her a while now. It's... Shit, it's no disrespect to Dad, bringing her here like this. She just kinda showed up at Rusty's last night and one thing led to another, ya know?"

"Rusty's?" Aden asks, "The bowling alley?"

"Yeah, I'm in a league." Suddenly, Aden thinks about the many reasons Brady might have to be away from the house at night that he never considered—the rich life he assumed his brother was incapable of.

"No, cool. That's great. Sorry for barging in, I just—I didn't know you were here, and…"

"And shit's creepy right now. If I didn't know you were here and I heard that shit, I'd probably have shot ya, so no hard feelings," Brady says, dipping a spoon into the Skippy jar and slapping a heavy serving onto his waffle.

"Yeah, thanks. So, listen. I wonder if you can help me today," Aden says, and Brady halts the spoon a few inches from his mouth and looks at his brother.

"Did something happen? Do you know something?" he asks, pushing his plate away.

"Actually, Ginny called, and they could really use your help," Aden says, giving Brady the gift of a task.

"What? Why?"

"She thinks the press found out where Ma was staying and they're gonna start harassing the house like they did here."

"Oh, shit," Brady says. "Ma okay?"

"Yeah, so." Aden leans in and lowers his voice as if they are in on the same secret. "Don't mention that though, 'cause Ginny was gossiping with the neighbors and she thinks it's her fault the press found out, so it's sensitive. She just needs help—someone to make sure those fuckers don't get near the house—the lawn even. Just for a day or two. Can you do that?" he asks, and he doesn't know when he became so well-versed at lying, but tragedy can make you do really unexpected things.

Brady jumps up and stands in a very awkward military-looking stance and then spits Wheaties and waffle specks at Aden from he corners of his mouth as he salutes and says, "Hell yes I can!" and then he takes his can of morning Dr. Pepper and shuffles downstairs to tell Brandi.

Aden quickly pulls out his phone to call Kira and tell her he almost has Brady out and she can head over soon, but there's no answer. He tries a second and third time, still...no answer.

30

KIRA

"Stop," I scream at him, stumbling backward and tripping over the log bench next to the firepit. "What the hell is the matter with you!?" I try to scramble to my feet but he's over me, grabbing my wrist and twisting it.

"Matt! What are you doing?" I kick at his shin with the bottom of my foot and push myself backward across the muddy grass, a searing pain in my shoulder where it hit the ground when I fell.

"You think you can just take me down with you, ruin my life too?" he says, still coming at me. He grabs my arm and yanks me up off the ground.

"What?" I try to twist away from him, but his grip is strong and his face is red and contorted. I try to pull away from him, but he's reaching into my pockets, looking for something and squeezing hard. I cry out and bite the top of his hand so he releases his grip.

"Fuck!" he yells, and he does let go, but at the same time he pulls my phone from my coat pocket. He holds it up and takes a few steps away from me, a look that almost dares me to try to get it back. Then, to my surprise, he starts to run toward the dock. I don't know whether to get in my car and get away—if he's going to hurt me or kill me, but the instinct to fight takes over. If he's switched from victim, poor Matt who has to go in for questioning and have his sins exposed, and turned into this angry, manic version of himself overnight, something has happened and there must be information he knows that I don't.

I run, breathless, down the muddy slope to the dock just in time to see him throw my phone into the glossy lake with the force of a pitcher on a baseball mound. It hits the surface with a tiny splash and then sinks to the bottom.

Now I get what he's doing. Still, I keep a little distance, standing at the head of the dock, but not moving closer. I could lunge at him maybe, push him in if I need to.

He turns to face me, something like relief washing over him, and he doesn't say anything for a moment. Now that he's destroyed my recording of him, I don't know what he plans to do next, so I take a step back, poised to run when I see a demented smile spread across his face.

"I don't know if that detective buddy of yours doesn't tell you shit because he's protecting you from details you don't need to know, or he doesn't trust you, or maybe you actually did know."

"Know what?" I ask, and he starts walking closer to me.

"They already had my DNA from weeks ago and they were processing it, and I guess when you told them I lied about being at the cabin, they fast-tracked it. It's not a match, Kira.

You probably knew that and just wanted to fuck with me anyway, ruin my life with your recording," he hisses, spit flying from the sides of his mouth.

"I didn't know that," I say, but I've stopped listening to him because I can only hear the blood rushing between my ears and feel my head becoming weightless. If that DNA wasn't from him—if it can't be explained by his fucked-up story of that night with Brooke—then someone else has hurt her. Tears prick my eyes, but I don't let them fall.

"I'd lose my job, I'd lose everything I have worked for if you decide to play games—make it public—whatever you were playing at by recording me."

"I don't care," is all I manage, because I care nothing about him anymore, and he's wasting my time now that I know this was just some self-centered tantrum.

"I know! That's the problem. I already lost you and now you're after the rest of me just because you're miserable. You're wasting your time is the worst part. Now that they know I was here, they talked to Colby and Mike like I told you to," he says, like I hadn't tried calling them seventeen times with no response.

"I'm sure they're on your list to go hunt down and harass. Jesus, you're all over the place. You know that security camera caught her after she was with me at the cabin," he says and the words *with me* are disgusting. They sound intimate now that I know what he did, and bile rises in my throat.

"Colby has photos on his phone of the trip. With the date. They cleared me. 'Cause guess what? I'm not a psychopath."

"That doesn't matter. You could have seen her after the security camera and before you went to meet your friends," I say, but with less certainty, because I'm not ready to let go of the idea—the possibility—even if it's starting to look like I'm wrong about his involvement. I don't know what I was expecting to find at Aden's—how Matt could have any connection to the family, or why he'd hurt an old man, but since, of course none of any of this makes sense, I still thought I'd find that connection back to Matt. Somehow. I thought this note left for me would answer the question and lead me to her. Now, I'm not so sure.

"You could have hurt her so she wouldn't tell what you did to her," I say, still holding on to this theory.

Matt just shakes his head and walks the length of the dock, pushing past me. He stops at the top of the slope, standing with outstretched arms.

"I'm not proud of this. I didn't want to do that, but you've lost it, Kir. You're not thinking straight anymore. You need help. Ya got the wrong frickin' guy," he says, turning and walking to his car, and he drives away.

And maybe I do.

31

ADEN

By half past ten o'clock, Brady had packed an overnight bag to bring to Ginny's, told Brandi he'd drop her off for her shift at Super Saver and gave Aden a strong pat on the back and another salute, signaling he was ready and willing to take on his assigned mission. After he'd gone, Aden tried to call Kira again.

When he didn't get an answer, he stood in the quiet of his childhood home and felt an emptiness he couldn't name. The letter said they'd find an answer here, and so he had to try to find that answer, but he didn't know where he would even start. He had no idea what he was looking for.

Every surface of this house was covered in photo frames and Precious Moments figurines, dog-eared paperbacks, misshapen ashtrays, and knickknacks. Every drawer crammed with paperclips and screwdrivers, batteries, pencils, take-out menus. There was no closet you could open that wouldn't drop a pile of folded sheets or shoeboxes onto your head. It was overwhelming, but he had to give it his best attempt.

He figured if some outside person—a stranger—left this note, that there was a clue here, a huge case-blown-wide-open piece of evidence to find, then maybe it had been planted here. Why would anyone do that though? But he has nothing else to go on. He decided the garage and the back shed are the places to start because it would be easier for someone outside the family to access those.

Inside the garage, he stands looking up at the rafters full of old bikes, Christmas decor, canoe paddles, and fishing rods, and he's already completely overwhelmed. Why did this phantom tipster not offer any sort of direction? It makes him think that maybe this is a sick prank. He walks out of the garage and goes into the kitchen. He picks a limp Eggo and chews the edge of it, his mind trying to wrap around a strategy to begin when he hears a car pull up in the driveway.

Before he can even get back outside, he sees a shock of blond hair pass the front door and then Kira appears in front of the open garage door. She stands, taking it in, when he comes out and looks at it next to her.

"Shit," she says.

"Yeah. I tried calling. Sorry, I just—it took time to get Brady out."

"No, my phone—well, I don't have it, so…let's just—God, where the hell do we start?" From this angle, Aden sees a dozen creepy ceramic dolls in Victorian dresses lining the shelves on one side of the garage, a couple box fans, a transistor radio, empty Pringles containers, piles and piles of old newspapers, and a couple broken television trays.

"I don't know. I mean how do I know one of those newspapers from 1982 isn't a clue? What the hell?"

"Maybe we don't dissect a whole room at a time yet, maybe we go to each room and look at what's right in front of us first. I can't even…" She makes an arm gesture to the whole mess and shakes her head. "With this," she says.

"Yeah, it's a lot. Why here? Like, why is there a clue here? If I believed that and I could figure out any possible reason, maybe I'd know where to start," Aden says, sitting on an overturned apple crate and blowing air through his cheeks.

"We just start," she says, and so they stare at the walls of the garage until the frustration of nothing meaning anything brings them to the kitchen where they open each cabinet and drawer and see nothing but regular dusty clutter. After three more hours of looking superficially in each room, feeling for loose floorboards or wall panels, scooping sticky Q-tips and old makeup out of bathroom drawers, and searching nightstand drawers and under beds, they regroup in the kitchen. Aden feels defeated, but after picking through his mother's underwear drawer and his brother's Hustler collection, he also feels like he's betraying his family's privacy, and it doesn't sit well.

He pours lukewarm coffee into two mugs and sits across from Kira at the kitchen table. "There's probably only leftover tuna casserole and Pizza Pockets if you need to eat something. We can order out."

"No, I'm fine," she says, taking the coffee and looking down at her hands.

"Do you feel like this is a joke? Someone trying to throw us off?" he asks, pushing aside Brady's gloves left on the table that smell like an ashtray.

"Maybe. But it seems like a pointless way to do it. What would anyone gain?"

"Well, we've established people are fucking crazy and generally terrible, I think, so maybe there is no reason," he says.

"There has to be. They knew where I lived, they avoided a paper trail or they could have emailed or posted it on one of the blogs. They knew about you and our connection—that you'd show that note to me. This was very intentional. It can't be meaningless."

Aden presses his lips together and spreads his hands out on the table and stands. "Then let's get back to work." She nods, and they decide to start in the garage and shed, then basement and attic, then main house. They create zones in the garage—a section to place small bins and boxes that have been searched, and a small length of red tape on the bigger items that have been looked over. Kira starts on one side, Aden on the other, and they work in anxious silence until every inch of the garage has been investigated and four more hours have gone by.

Finally, Kira stops and sits down on a five-gallon paint bucket and buries her face in her hands. For a fleeting second he thought she found something upsetting, but he realizes she's just feeling the same way he is. Infuriated and exhausted at this futile, bullshit task.

He moves to her and places his hand on her back, but she doesn't look up. She flicks away tears and takes a deep breath. Aden opens the refrigerator in the garage and hands her a Coors Light. She takes it, and they both just sit a while, staring out at the strip of orange sun beginning to fade below the horizon.

Once they decide to move on from the garage, it's pitch-black outside and they'd barely finished one area. They spent almost three hours out in the back shed before moving to the basement.

Aden feels a chill when they both stand at the bottom of the stairs and look the place up and down. Now they need a new zone strategy for a bigger space, and his body aches with the thought of the effort. Half the basement is Brady's, but that was really just a flimsy drywall job with an area rug closing it off from the rest of the basement. The other half has a concrete floor, washer and dryer, and metal shelves piled with more shit—lamps, board games, a baby rocking chair, coolers with broken wheels, a fax machine, and an uncountable number of plastic storage bins stuffed with even more useless garbage. Aden actually feels for a moment like he might just start crying himself. Kira's face looks ghostly and weary, but she asks him where to start and he gives her the north facing shelves to begin with. He'd start on Brady's side of the basement. It's only right that he did that himself.

By midnight, they've come up with absolutely nothing. Or maybe they did find the ridiculous, elusive clue and had no idea what they were looking at. Aden finally orders a pizza and they sit side by side on a futon next to the water heater and eat.

Finally, Kira says she just needs to close her eyes for a few minutes, and Aden is surprised she's lasted this long. The woman looked like she hadn't slept in weeks and they'd been performing physical labor for over thirteen hours. After she lays down, Aden pages through crates of old records and a plastic bin of Legos for another hour before he curls up on Brady's bed just for a minute, but he falls into a sweaty, dreamless sleep himself.

When he wakes up, the digital alarm clock on the bedside table blinks 5:09 a.m. He doesn't know if Brady will be coming back today, although he'd try to persuade him to stay on another day or two. He might argue that there is no press anywhere around the house and he's coming back for Brandi or who knows what, because Brady is very unpredictable. But in case he just shows up, the house could not look like this, especially the basement—Brady's space.

Aden sleepily moves his body off the bed and wills himself to finish the basement search. He looks in the wardrobe, every dresser drawer, and scours the storage bins under the bed. Nothing.

But as he's lying on his stomach feeling around under the bed for the last box just out of reach, his eye catches something. Across the room is a woodworking bench his father used to use in the garage to varnish an old chest of drawers or fix their bicycles on. He moved it to the basement years ago, and now Brady says it's his drafting table, although he has nothing to draft.

Aden notices something that's very out of place. There's a small lockbox duct-taped to the underside of the workbench. He feels his stomach flip over.

"Kira. Kira!" he yells to her, still not daring to move from his spot on the floor, thinking maybe if he takes his eyes off it, he'll find he was seeing things through the fog of his exhaustion and that it's not really there.

Kira blinks like she's remembering where she is and then she flies to her feet.

"What!? What, what, what? Did you find something?" she asks. "Where are you?" she says, looking around until she spots him on the ground. He sits up and points to the workbench. She looks at it, then back to him.

"What?" she asks again, hands out and shoulders shrugged. He crawls over to the workbench and reaches underneath. He tries to pull it free, but the tape is too strong.

"Hand me that," he says, and she picks up the Phillips-head on the side of the bench he's pointing to and gives it to him. He stabs at the tape a few times, grunting, and then the box comes loose and makes a loud crash as it falls onto the cement floor.

32

KIRA

I look at the box, slack-jawed, and then back to Aden, who mirrors my expression.

I kneel on the floor beside him and touch it, then shake it and hear what sounds like maybe coins or jewelry—bits and bobs inside. I jiggle the small padlock, but of course it's locked. Without a word between us, I jump up and start to feel through the drawers of the workbench to find something to open the lock. Aden runs to a giant red toolbox sitting near the washing machine and opens it, clinking and clanging, dropping tools on the floor until he returns with a hammer and flat-head chisel.

I was going to try to pick the lock with a paper clip, but before I even suggest it, he's on the ground, the flathead wedged against the U-shaped hook of the padlock, the hammer smashing down against it violently until a piece breaks off and flies across the floor, skittering under the bed.

"Fuck," he says as we both look at it as if it could hurt us, or even worse, could be nothing more than passports or nudie photos or some stupid thing this Brady guy wanted to keep hidden. I slide the box closer to me and sit cross-legged in front of it, and when I open it, a moan of utter torment escapes me. I cup both hands over my mouth and rock, tears pouring down my face.

"What is it? I don't know what any of this is! What?" Aden says raising his voice in frustration, picking up a small bracelet with elephant charms hanging from it and half a heart-shaped locket, which has the photo of a young girl the spitting image of Amelia, inside—her sister. And there's a ring—the ring I bought Brooke on her sixteenth birthday—silver with a tiny amethyst moon and star on either side.

I pick up her ring and hold it to my heart. Aden is rambling, asking what it all means until he stops, and I look up through blurry eyes, still unable to speak—to explain it—to think what to do next, and he picks up a driver's license and stares at it. Grace Holloway's sixteen-year-old face looks back at him.

I see him register what it all means. His face is ashen, and his Adam's apple bobs as he audibly swallows.

"I don't understand," he whispers even though he does, or if he doesn't fully, the pieces are coming together, that his brother kept trophies from all the girls he took.

"When is he coming back, your brother?" I say, now springing back into action, newly fueled by the fact that knowing who took her means he could tell us where Brooke is. Just because he has this ring doesn't mean she's... It could mean she's still out there.

"I don't know, anywhere between any minute and two days from now. He didn't specify. Shit."

"We need to go," I say, putting all the items back in the box and tucking it under my arm.

"Where?"

"Somewhere not here. If he finds us—all this—Jesus. Let's get out of here, for one. We need to go somewhere safe and call the cops, tell them where he is. But not from here," I say, already halfway up the stairs now, looking for my bag and boots. Aden follows right behind.

"We should go to the inn. We owe it to Grace to tell her what we found too," he says and I nod, pulling on my UGGs and racing out the front door into the pouring rain.

33

GRACE

Vinny watches protectively from the kitchen window the next morning, after he'd discovered what I'd been hiding. He stands with his shotgun by his side as I take a plastic bowl of rice and fruit outside, the way I have done nearly every day for weeks now.

I open the root cellar door and place the bowl on the top stair. There's no fighting today. No screaming either. He saw the shotgun last night when Vinny discovered him in the cellar, so he's probably scared now. When I close the doors behind me and lock the chain, there is the rush of relief there always is when I come away unscathed—knowing he wasn't able to get me again.

When Vinny heard a man screaming from the cellar last night he told me there was someone out there, and I had to explain it to him, but all I told him is that it was the man who hurt me and hurt those other girls and I had him trapped and didn't know what to do…until now.

When I told him I needed to wait until I had the right evidence in hand before I said more, he stayed with me through the night. I had to talk him down from going out and killing the man, but he didn't make me explain further. He just held me and let me cry and stayed up by the back door with his gun all night, chewing sunflower seeds and spitting them angrily at the back screen door.

Today, we move quietly and strangely around one another, waiting to get a call from Kira so I know it's all going to be okay—that it might finally be over—that he'll be forced to tell us where Brooke is when he knows we have the evidence to put him away forever if he doesn't.

34

There's a man now. The figure that wears a hood and leaves the food has always looked too small to be a man, but now there's a guy with a shotgun. The hooded figure opened the door last night and he aimed a flashlight down the stairs, right in my eyes and I screamed for help, hoping he was the police or someone who discovered me and was there to help.

I yelled at the guy, "Help me! I'm Martin Coleman. People are looking for me! Please, tell my wife, call the police. Please." But the guy just looked at me wide-eyed, then to the figure, and then closed the doors again.

35

GRACE

When Aden and Kira come through the front lobby doors with gray faces and rain-soaked clothes, I know this is it. I rush from where Vinny and I have been sitting solemnly at the kitchen table into the lobby, and when Aden sees me, his face falls. He's holding something in his hand.

"Grace, we need to call the police and have them come here right now," Kira says, pushing past Aden and setting a metal box on the coffee table in front of the leather sofa.

"No, wait. Did you find it?" I ask, and they both jerk their heads to look at me. Then Vinny comes into the room, still with his shotgun slung over his chest on its strap. Kira stands and takes a step back.

"What's going on?" Aden asks.

"It's okay. Vinny knows everything. He's fine. I left you

the note." Silence. "You found it, didn't you?" I say, sitting next to her, looking down at the dented metal lockbox. Kira exchanges a look with Aden who closes his eyes and shakes his head in confusion, then sits across from me.

"Okay. Wait—what? Back up. You left a note for us to search MY house. You knew we'd find what? How could you know what we'd find?" he says angrily, accusatorily. He places the object in his hand on the table, and it's my old ID. I look at him and pick it up. My breath catches but I go on.

"Because when Kira said that he was taking tokens from the girls, I knew he'd keep them. He's the same man who took me." Kira's mouth opens and then closes and Aden just stares at me.

"My brother...he did that to you?" Aden asks, his face drained of all color.

"Your brother? No..."

"Then what are we talking about here? We found this in his room." He flips the box open with a finger, exposing the sparkly jewelry.

"No. What? Martin Coleman. I'm talking about your father."

"Is this some sort of game, like you planted that shit in my house and then tipped us off to it? My father is missing. What the hell are you talking about?" he seethes.

"Please just let me tell you what happened."

Aden stands and runs his hands over his face, looking like he's gonna punch something. "I'm so goddamned confused right now," he says.

"Let her explain then!" Kira raises her voice impatiently.

"I'm so sorry, Aden. I left the note because I was positive he kept the things he took, but I could never prove that if you didn't find it. If I just told the police it was him, why would they believe me? He leaves no evidence or they would have caught him. He doesn't show his face, he wears gloves, he uses different places to keep women. It would be my word against his."

"If he doesn't show his face, then how do you know it's him? How have you just not said anything this whole time? And where is he then, huh? This is insane," he says, walking toward the windows, looking up at the ceiling, then back to all of us sitting on the couches. "I don't even..."

"I didn't put it together until the other night when I saw his photo. I didn't know that was the same man in my cellar, I swear to you. I heard you say your dad's name. I knew he was missing, but I didn't see a face to match it to the man I attacked!" My tears start, but everyone is now completely silent and Aden and Kira just stare blankly at me.

"What?" Aden says. He looks like he will say more, but he just stands there with white shock across his face. Kira pulls his arm to make him sit down—to make him listen and he reluctantly does so.

"A few weeks ago, I heard a car pull up outside late at night, and nobody comes here off season. Well, you know that, except you of course, but so, I was scared and I have this bat in my room, you know, and I carry it with me if I hear something 'cause I'm here all alone and everything. I come down and it was kind of misty out, and I see this car sitting right out front, I think it's a traveler maybe looking for a room. Who else could it be? But it's a man and he's on the side of the property, trying to jiggle the lock on the old barn out there..." I stop to breathe and everyone, even Vinny who I didn't tell the whole story to, has their mouths agape, holding perfectly still, listening to what will come next.

"I say *who are you?* and he whips around, I can tell he's shocked. He comes over to the front door and he's nervous, asking if we have a room, and I can tell though, I surprised him. He wasn't there for a room. He got caught," I say and then the sobs climb up my throat and I don't think I can go on.

"You're saying this was my father? That's the man?"

"I know that now, but when he asked me for a room, I said we're closed. He looked relieved, he didn't want a room." I try to stop the hiccupped cries. Kira comes and sits next to me and puts her arm around my shoulder, rubbing my forearm with her free hand.

"It's okay. Hey, it's okay. What happened?"

"There was a girl, I think?"

"What? You think?" Aden says, and Kira shoots him a look to stop and hear me out.

"Someone ran from his car and I heard a scream and a figure flashed through the woods behind the inn in bare feet and not much, like, clothes on... I could tell. I just saw skin. I didn't see who it was, but I think someone got away from him."

"Jesus Mother of Mary," Vinny says, standing and punching his palm with his fist.

"I still don't know how you think this is the man who hurt you? Like...you can't know that it was my father."

"I didn't know at first," I say, controlling myself better now. I breathe in and steady myself. "There was something about his voice and the smell of his cologne that hit me right away. Familiar and unsettling, but it took me a second, and then I saw his wedding ring. He wore gloves almost all the time back then, but once, one day, he took them off just for a moment and wiped his face with the back of his hand, and I saw it and it's unusual—it has a diamond-shaped blue stone on a gold band. I never forgot it," I say, and the tears come again. Aden buries his head in his hands, and I don't know what he's thinking.

"I froze. He thanked me and started to leave...and when he was halfway to his car, I snapped. I just..." I'm sobbing now.

I'm embarrassed I can't hold it together. I know time is still a factor for Kira, but I'm baring my soul, and out of all people, it's to the man's son, who probably hates me right now but has to believe me.

"It's okay, Grace. It's okay," Kira says, pulling me in.

"I just. I hit him once, and he fell, and I didn't know what to do," I say, remembering the drizzle that started to fall and how it took all my strength to pull him by his feet to the cellar before morning so I could think and figure out a plan.

"I thought I killed him, but he woke up. I was going to call the police. And then the next day, you came, and I was still gonna call the police, because I didn't know he was Martin. He still had no name to me, but I know if I told them what he'd done, why would they believe me with no evidence? I'm sorry. I needed this evidence. There was a moment I thought I'd just open the cellar door in the middle of the night and he'd go free because he probably didn't know I was the one who hit him—it came out of nowhere from behind. He didn't even know who I was either. It was dark, it's been years, there was no flicker of recognition in his eyes when he saw me, so I thought that was a way out. I almost did it, but how I could just let him go?! And then you told me about the other girls, and how could I let him hurt more people? I couldn't tell anyone."

Aden wipes his hand heavily across his mouth and lets out a small noise from his throat. Kira's eyes are wide open and she's looking at the floor, paralyzed by all of this.

"You have the wrong guy, that's all there is to it," Aden says suddenly. "Brady... I mean, that—I was...stunned when we found this. But at least that makes sense! But...no. I don't accept this, I—"

"He took me while I was sleeping in a laundromat on the same strip the other girls were taken from," I say as composed as I can force my voice to be. "He has what I would assume is a pretty big scar on his right side. Right? Because that's how they found me. He put bear traps around the property in case I escaped, and I did. I got free one day when he was gone, probably home with you having dinner or something, and when he came back, I had a kitchen knife. I got one good swipe in before I ran and the only reason they found me before he did is because he was bleeding too bad to run after me. That scar is the reason I'm alive. You know what I'm talking about, don't you?"

The room is silent except for the rumble of radiator heat switching on. Then, the sound of soft weeping as Aden holds his head in his arms, his back shaking, and nobody knowing what to do now.

"I'm sorry. I really am."

"You don't have to be sorry, Jesus," Kira says, "I can't believe you went through that all alone."

"I thought if you found that," I say, nodding to the box, "and we show it to him, he might tell us where Brooke is, in exchange for letting him out." Kira holds her heart, and her eyes well up. She nods vigorously. But we all just stay there a moment, all of the bombshells that have been dropped on them sinking in.

I drove his car into the river that night, when I thought he was dead. I'm, I don't know—hardwired I guess now to deal with trauma so I just acted quickly, but that small fact of the bigger picture isn't on anyone's mind right now and nobody has asked about it. I can't imagine what they all think of me in this moment.

"We can't call the cops," Kira says, looking to Aden. "My only chance is using calling the cops as leverage. She's right. We need to get him to tell me where she is." Then she looks at me.

"What does he say to you? Has he told you anything? At all?" Kira asks.

"I've never spoken to him," I say, and Aden again looks at me with utter bewilderment.

"Where is he?" Aden says, an eerie shadow across his eyes. He stands and everyone else copies him. Vinny slings the shotgun back over his shoulder and leads the way to the backyard.

36

ADEN

Aden hovers over the hole in the ground when Grace unlocks the chains and opens the metal cellar doors. The wasted-away man he scarcely recognizes blocks his eyes from the light and moans, and then he looks up and sees him.

"Oh, my God," Martin whispers. "Son, you found me. I knew you'd find me," he says, crawling up the stairs.

Aden covers his mouth and gags at the smell of urine and unwashed body and rotten food that hits him like a punch in the gut. Then the sight of his father in the soiled elastic-band Levi's he's had for twenty years and the filth on his face makes Aden run to the bushes nearby and throw up.

"Aden!" his father yells, "Help me!" He's crawled to the top of the stairs and is met by Vinny's shotgun aimed at his chest. "Aden," he cries, but Aden has to look away. "What's happening? Call the police! What—what are you doing?" But Aden won't look at him.

Vinny leads Martin inside the back door where Grace stands with a box of zip ties from the pantry. She secures his wrists together, then connects the zip ties, binding him to the slat in the back of a kitchen chair they put him in.

"Where's my daughter!?" Kira screams at him. This wasn't the plan, but she lunges at him, almost toppling his chair, and she claws at his face, screaming, "Where's my daughter!?" Vinny has to restrain her and pull her across the kitchen. Her hair has come loose and falls across her face, and her eyes are wild.

"What is she talking about?" Martin says, cowering, "What's happening? Why aren't you helping me?"

"Dad," Aden says, barely able to look at his father. "We know everything, so you can stop pretending you don't know what this is about. Please. We know." He stops and tries to repair the break in his voice.

"Know what? Aden, I was attacked! I was held against my will. You need to…"

"This is Grace Holloway, Dad. It's all over. I know what you did," he says, and looks to Grace who is in front of the sink across the kitchen, holding Kira's hand.

"I don't know who that is! What are you talking about?" Martin says, but Aden sees it—the glint of recognition, of panic in his father's eyes.

"She says you hurt her…a long time ago, you took her."

"She's crazy! I have no idea who that is. You have the wrong person, don't you see that? Who the hell are all these people who somehow have you turned against me? I've never seen her before, not in my whole life!" And it's a small thing in the midst of all this, but there is also a flash of something behind his eyes, and he sees the first flicker of a different man under the facade—he starts to see the man Grace sees in that moment.

Aden picks up the metal box and opens it for his father to see, but keeps it out of reach. He sees Martin's face change. He sees panic. His eyes shift, his mouth twists.

"What's that?" he finally says, and Vinny mumbles something behind him he can't fully hear.

"Goddamn it, Dad. Do you understand what's happening? It's over. I found this on your workbench myself—saw it with my own two eyes. In our house."

"That's nonsense. I don't even know what that is. If that were true, you would have called the police by now," he says, and Aden sees him twist his hands and shift in his chair, testing the tightness of the ties, ready to make an escape.

"If you tell me where my daughter is, maybe we won't call them," Kira says in a tight, forced, incredibly desperate voice.

"Who's your daughter?" he says again, and Aden is losing patience. He slams his fist into a cabinet and makes a guttural noise. Grace was absolutely right thinking he would deny it until the end and probably get away with it.

"If you found that in the house, then you should be calling the cops on your brother. I always knew he was capable of something like this," Martin says, and he can hear Grace's sharp intake of breath. "If you turn in the box, the only fingerprints that show up will be Brady's," he says with a self-congratulating smirk.

"What? What do you…" he starts to ask, thinking for a moment that Brady is in on this and then realizing. "You set him up?"

"He's dumb as shit, Aden, come on. I told him I was trying to pick a gift for your mother, so he handled all of the pieces in the box. Picked the ring, you'd be happy to know," he says, looking to Kira, and Aden sees her frozen in shock, and still has Grace's hand clasps around her arm so she doesn't lunge at him. "I even borrowed his phone at night when I went to visit the girls and he was fast asleep, left my phone at home…just in case they checked records. I'm not an idiot," he says, but before Aden can say anything else, Vinny has his gun raised against Martin's head.

"Amelia was my friend, you sick fuck. Brooke is *her* daughter—" he makes a head tilt to Kira "—and you're gonna tell us where she is before I splatter the inside of your skull all over the walls." Martin holds his breath, then continues to push the game he's playing further.

"You wouldn't do that…"

"Vinny," Aden starts to say, but Vinny talks over him and pushes the barrel of the gun right up against Martin's face.

"Try me, motherfucker. What do I have to lose? I'll be the hero who killed the sicko everyone is looking for. Without you here to deny it, we have all the evidence to justify blowing your head off," he spits. Then he cocks the gun, and there are gasps all around and then silence. In the quiet, only breathing and swallows are faintly heard as everyone tries to figure out what to do next.

"Okay," Martin finally says. Kira clutches her chest and holds herself steady against the counter. Aden is frozen in disbelief and Grace looks ready to faint. Nobody speaks still, until Martin finally starts to tell the truth.

"I never meant to hurt anyone, son. Please, you have to believe me. I just… I have a sickness."

"Jesus," Aden whispers. He swallows a bit of his own vomit and sits down in the kitchen chair on the other side of the table.

"I know it's my mind that's not right and I need help, but I went a long time without giving into the urge—years… until those junkie kids hanging around down there started offering me… I was trying to stay on the right path, I was really trying. I was down in that area—The Strip—but I was doing the Lord's work, until those guys offered me… Rohypnol one night, and it was like a sign. A gift. I felt like I was getting permission from God to fulfill my needs."

"What's that? What's that mean?" Kira asks.

"It's a roofie drug," Vinny says with disgust, pushing the barrel of the gun harder into the side of Martin's head.

"I just wanted to be with them. I needed to touch them, it's a sickness," he whimpers. "I had to—I didn't want to hurt them. They would tell. If I didn't… They left me no choice, I had no choice."

"God. This can't actually be happening," Aden says, standing, moving away from Martin, his back turned to him now, his face numb with grief.

"So…" Aden says slowly, still trying to make all the pieces fit. "Harry isn't connected to this after all," he says, just trying to understand.

"He just showed up at the wrong time," Martin says, and Aden grips the edge of the counter until his knuckles go white but he doesn't look back to face him. "I promise, I didn't want to hurt him either—anyone. He saw me with Brooke in the car. I was driving out to…" He stops, realizing he can't betray the location. "Harry was coming back from fishing out on Maypole Road and I was pulled over with the girl, and he stopped. I never heard him coming and she yelled to him for help. I had no choice."

"Brooke!" Kira cried. "You took her where!? Tell me where she is. Is she still there? What did you do to her? Please. Is she still alive?" she pleads. Martin shifts his eyes up to Vinny and the gun on the side of his head and then to Kira.

"Maybe," he says, and she lets out a sound like Aden has

never heard a human make. Kira falls to her knees in front of Martin—too close for anyone's comfort—and begs.

"If you tell me where she is, we will let you go," she says, looking behind her for comradery as if they'd all agreed, but nobody speaks. She just keeps pleading.

"It's a sickness, you're right, and if you tell me where she is, Aden will get you the help you need instead of turning you in. We'll all agree that he'll keep an eye on you and you won't ever do anything like this again, and we'll let you go. Just go… All you have to do is lead me to her. Please. Please," she implores. Grace exchanges glances with Vinny, and Kira looks up at Aden with pleading eyes. He gives her an almost indiscernible nod.

"I don't want to turn you in, Dad. If you're sick then…we'll get you help, Kira's right. You tell us where she is and we'll promise to leave the police out of it." The air buzzes and nobody breathes.

"I can't tell you. I wouldn't know how. There's no street signs for miles. I have to show you."

37

KIRA

A long and lonely tangle of back roads stretch out in front of us as Aden drives his car with Vinny and his gun in the passenger's seat, keeping Martin in his place in the back. Grace and I follow in my car behind. Time is elastic, and it feels like we've been driving for days, but the clock tells me it's just under an hour.

Grace and I don't speak. We just stay wide-eyed and white-knuckled as we bump over the increasingly rocky terrain the farther away we get from civilization. I know it's crazy and maybe reckless to not involve the police, but it's the absolute only way I could have gotten this far. What if she's here? What if she's really here?

I notice myself mumbling prayers under my breath as I notice Aden's car in front of us start to slow. I see his window lower and his hand gesturing—not like he's motioning to me, but that he's looking for something he's being told to find and gesticulating, asking this way or that with his hands. I try to see in the back windshield, but it's too tinted. Then, my breath catches when his car pulls over slightly and stops.

We're deep in the woods. This path is at least eight or nine miles off of paved road. The bony trees sway against a misty gray sky. Even though most of the leaves have fallen, the density of the woods is still remarkable and disorienting. You'd never find your way out of here if you didn't know there was a road, and it's not easy to spot unless you're on it.

Aden steps out, followed by Vinny who takes a few steps away from the car clutching his gun at his side, letting Aden open the door to let Martin out. His hands are still tied, and his head hangs low.

I slam the car door and look around, thinking we've been tricked. There's nothing here—no place someone could be hidden, surviving.

"Where is she?" I say, moving too close to Martin, so Aden has to put his arm up to stop me attacking.

"It's not drivable. There's a place down the hill—an abandoned house," he says, and nods northeast. "We have to walk." And so we begin our descent down the wooded incline, with Martin leading the way and Vinny's gun just behind. As we walk, I begin doubting that any of this is true. How could a man his age make this sort of trek? I feel panicked that we are being messed with, but why? What's his angle? What does he have to gain?

After several minutes of walking, I see something twisted up in a low tree branch—a swath of yellow. A sweater with polka dots on the wrists. Brooke's. I call out, screaming, and in that moment Vinny turns instinctually, maybe thinking I'm hurt, needing to help. He runs a few steps back to me, looking in the direction I'm staring for a moment, before Aden bellows back at us.

"He's gone!" And when we turn to look, Martin has made a run for it and is weaving through the trees with a head start that's not immense, but the thickness of the forest swallows him up. My heart thumps hard against my rib cage as I sprint into the trees in the direction I thought he'd go, but I can't see anything. Aden is on my heels, breathless, running as directionless as me.

"Oh, God," I say, bolting now in the other direction. "Where is he?" We run back to the clearing where we started and Grace is standing, hugging herself, looking like she's afraid to move in case he materializes out of the trees and captures her again. Vinny is pointing his gun in one direction and then the next, equally afraid to get ambushed.

"Nobody saw which way he went?" he asks in futility, because everyone was looking at me. And then a howl echoes through the treetops—an animal-like wail coming from somewhere deep inside the woods. I run as hard as I can, my arms pumping, my chest burning, in the direction of the sound. Footsteps follow behind me, I hear more cries, and I run and run until I see it.

I stop, still and disbelieving. Aden and Vinny appear at my side, and we all stare in horror at what we're looking at. After a few moments of stunned silence, Grace appears, her leg slowing her down, but she catches up and stops dead in her tracks along with us.

Martin Coleman is caught in his own bear trap.

38

KIRA

He lays there with his leg twisted up in metal teeth, writhing in unimaginable pain, but it is imaginable to one of us.

Before anyone can make a move to help him, I see something in a small clearing of trees just ahead. I squint at it, and Grace follows my gaze.

"That's the house," she says in an astonished whisper.

"Oh, my God," I think I say out loud, but I'm not sure. I'm already running toward it, chopping my hands through hanging vines and invisible threads of spiderwebs until I make it to the clearing. The others leave Martin and follow. Aden slings Grace's arm over his shoulder to help her, and they run.

When I stand in front of the structure, I see it's an old Tudor-style with cross cables and peeling paint. There is no glass in the windows that look like black dead eyes staring back at me. It looks like it's been sitting empty for decades. When I push at the front door, it opens easily, and I'm standing in a room with a crumbling staircase and walls that look like they're bleeding.

"Brooooooke!" I scream. "Baby!" My voice is raw and strangled. "Where are you!?" Aden and Grace appear inside the front door, followed by Vinny.

"Find a door. She'll be in the basement. Check all the doors!" Grace says, and she limps to the door to her left, which is a closet. Aden and I run and begin flinging open doors while Vinny stands guard at the front door.

"Brooke!" I scream again and again. My hands shake so violently I can barely grasp hold of the doorknobs, and then I come across a door that's locked.

"Oh, God. Oh, God," I cry.

"Vinny!" Aden yells and Vinny comes rushing to find us. "Vinny! There, next to the kitchen," he says. Vinny appears and Aden backs up and takes a running start, slamming his body against the door to break the lock, but nothing happens. Vinny understands, and helps. He kicks the door as hard as he can with the bottom of his foot. Grace cups her mouth behind us and tells them to be careful. Vinny and Aden both kick the door with all their might at the same time, and the wood in the middle of it snaps and it swings open.

"Brooke," I call, feeling my way down the steep cement staircase in the darkness. Aden turns on the flashlight on his phone and shines it down, which I didn't have the wherewithal to do. And, my God. My God, I see something.

There's a small shape hunched on a pile of soiled sheets on the floor, tucked up into the corner of the room. "No!" I cry. The figure doesn't move. "Please, God, please, God." I move closer and kneel down and reach my hand out. I feel breath.

I feel an arm that's still warm. I shake it. I turn her over and see her face.

"Mom," she says in a tiny rasp of a voice, and she can barely move, but I see a tear roll down her face. "Mom," she says, and then she sits up just a little and collapses into my lap in weak sobs.

Aden runs down the stairs two at a time and keeps repeating, "It's okay, it's okay."

"Let's get her outside. Vinny saw a road leading right up to the house on the other side. He's gone to get the car," he says, carrying Brooke up the stairs with me behind, still gripping her hand.

"You're gonna be okay now," I say again and again.

"We have to call an ambulance," Grace says once we are upstairs and I'm sitting on the floor of the crumbling front room with Brooke in my arms, rocking her gently, whispering to her. There was a utility sink in the basement and old jars and cans of food on rusted-out shelves—just like what Aden explained Grace's experience was like from what he read about her, and I can't believe it. I can't believe Brooke survived—that she's here, barely conscious in my arms, but breathing. She said my name. She's here.

"We're not calling an ambulance," Aden says, hovering above us. "No one is calling anybody."

39

ADEN

Aden kneels down and looks Grace and Kira in the eye.

"No cops, no ambulance," he says. "It's faster if Kira drives, medics will never find this place."

"He's right," she says, "but we still need to call a medic for…" She stops and gestures vaguely outside.

"No we don't. And no cops," he says again.

"What are you talking about?" Grace snaps.

"He's gonna pin this on Brady. He's a church deacon, Brady's a recovering addict…and weird. Nobody will ever believe Martin Coleman did this. No one. The only evidence we have is that box, and we found it in Brady's room. I know we have our own testimony, but what proof—besides something he can blame Brady for—do we have? We were just mistaken, *mislead, had the wrong Coleman*—that's what he'll say. Brady's phone and fingerprints will put him away. Martin will say we were confused—conspired against him, and we were wrong. Brady had a head injury—he's...he can't defend himself. He'll be eaten alive by the system when my father throws him under the bus," he says, thinking about his own daughter when he looks at the frail skin-and-bones girl in Kira's arms. "What if there is even a fraction of a chance he goes free?" he says, not knowing which of them would be more terrified by that possibility.

"You're saying...leave him here?" Grace asks, as Vinny comes back through the door.

"Come on, the car's running," he says and helps Kira carry Brooke outside and down the rickety porch stairs.

"It would kill my mother, literally. And send Brady back to rehab, for sure, but more than that...just what if," he says as he and Grace follow them outside.

"I vote leave him," Vinny says, only hearing half the story.

"What about the other victims?" Kira says, tears coming again as she watches Vinny gently lower her daughter into the back seat. "They deserve to know. They need closure."

"You told me that Heather's mom died, and Amelia's mom's a monster," Aden says, "Harry has no family. I've already thought about all this, all day—about what we do with him in general. There may be other victims we'll never know about, but it's just us now. This is the only way for any real justice."

Each of them looks at one another. Kira nods.

"We never tell anyone," Aden continues. "Just go, and say you found her on one of your searches somewhere else. Say you don't know—you don't remember exactly, because you were in shock. There are a million miles of nothing out here. They'll never know," he says. "I have a daughter too." Aden's voice wobbles and coughs, keeping the tears at bay.

"Then let's go," Kira says, and looks to Grace who nods, and so does Vinny, who repeats Kira's words, "let's go."

And then Kira speeds away, leaving curls of dust in her wake.

40

ADEN

SIX WEEKS LATER

Deer hunters came across Martin Coleman's remains almost a month to the day they walked away and left him in those woods. Now, just days before Christmas, Aden sits on a folding chair across from his daughter, eating a square of cake off a small paper plate at his father's wake.

The celebration of his father's life takes place at a local Irish pub he used to play cards at with his church friends, and is well attended. Strings of colored lights are strung across the ceiling, and a wall-mounted plastic elf sings "Joy To The World" from behind the bar, as if on queue, making people laugh and touch each other's arm, saying how fitting it is because he was so Christlike and loved the holidays to boot.

Leah nibbles at the frosting on her carrot cake and twists her ponytail with her finger, looking around at all the people she's never met and scooting closer to Aden, which makes his heart swell.

"Doing okay?" he asks. "We can go whenever you want," he says.

"Wouldn't that be rude?" she asks, and he shrugs.

"I just don't want it to upset you," he says.

"I'm okay," she says. They watch the crowd together. Pints are raised and an Irish folk song is sung by a group of drunk men swaying together in the middle of the room.

"Weird funeral," she says.

"He requested this… I guess. So your grandma says. It is a little weird," he says, and she smiles and shoves him with her shoulder.

"If we did leave, where would we go?" he asks her.

"Uhhh. Home?"

"That's not very imaginative," he says, and she sits up and understands the game.

"Oh! Ice cream. Wait, no… Humane Society. There was a pug on the website today. His name is Cheddar, and I already love him, so…" She claps and then becomes self-conscious, realizing again where she is and that a few people have looked her way. She rearranges her features and leans back in her chair.

"I mean, that's okay, but that's all ya got?" he says, and she giggles at him quietly.

"What's better than a pug?"

"Do you really want me to answer that?" he asks, and she slaps him playfully.

"What about Florida?" he says, knowing her obsession with all things beachy will get her attention. She stops mid-finger-scoop of cream cheese frosting and cocks her head at him. Then she looks around like she's being pranked.

"Uh, yeah. Okay?" She smiles skeptically.

"For real," he says. "You wanna go?" he asks, and her eyes

look wet and shy all of a sudden, and he hates that she's deciding whether or not she's being tricked or that she ever questioned if he wanted her, or how much he loves her. He hates that there are people in the world like his father, and that nobody will ever know who he really was—and that they are here at this complete sham of a wake. But he hates most of all that she was hurt by a boy she trusted, just like every other woman he knows, and he hates that she will be hurt again no matter what he does to protect her, and he hates how wrong he handled everything with her.

And right now, he knows it won't solve the lifetime of trauma she's experienced, and maybe it's totally overboard, but he wants to love her even harder. For Amelia, and Brooke, and Grace, and even Shannon. For right now, he just wants to give her the world.

"Like you're really taking me to Florida, Dad. Sure. You said we'd go on vacation there like every year since I was ten. *Someday.* I stopped believing you," she says, refocusing on poking at her piece of cake.

"Well now it's someday," he says, and she bites her plastic fork and looks at him with expectant eyes.

"Not for vacation though," he says, and she punches him in the arm.

"Yeah, ha-ha," she says.

"For good."

"Seriously. What are you talking about? Are we playing a game I don't know the rules of?" she says, looking around as if other people are in on it.

"Lee," he says, taking her plate out of her hand and turning his chair toward her. "You hate that school?"

"Yes," she says a little too quickly.

"I'm sorry. I didn't know what else to do and that's on me. I am really sorry, I thought it would help you. All I wanted to do was help," he says, and she must register some uncomfortable intensity in his tone because she becomes very agreeable.

"I know," she mumbles, turning away, but he turns her face back gently with his hand.

"You and me. We go. We move to... What's the one you like?" he asks, smiling, and she lets a little burst of laughter loose and then covers her mouth.

"Tampa?"

"Yes, Tampa. I'm serious. Let's find a little place on the beach and find a school you like. I can't promise a pug," he says, and her eyes fill up and she looks away and then back to him.

"Are you serious?"

"Yeah. I am," he says, and she flings her arm around his neck and hugs him tighter than he ever remembers her doing before.

He's interrupted by Brady and his mother coming over and sitting in the empty folding chairs next to them.

"Go call your friends," he tells her with an insider smirk, giving her a nudge, and she squeaks and runs off.

"Tell them what?" his mother asks.

"Nothin', Ma. Just teenage stuff," Aden says. Brady sips on his O'Douls. His eyes are red and puffy.

"God, all these people loved Dad," Brady says, sniffling. "He was such a good guy, I'm so glad everyone came out like this." Brandi comes over and hands him a plate of miniature sausages that he refuses, but she sits down next to him and hugs him, wiping under his eyes with her thumb and kissing his head, which makes Aden smile.

"Wanna scotch, Ma?" Aden asks, taking her hand to lead her to the bar. She dots her eyes with a handkerchief and follows. He orders the drinks and hands her one. He nods and clinks her glass. She holds her glass to his a moment.

"'Justice is like a train that's nearly always late,'" she says, and he coughs so he doesn't choke on his drink.

"I'm sorry, what was that?" he asks.

"Your father's favorite quote. I'm sure you knew that," she says. "I thought it an appropriate occasion for it." And then she drinks, and Aden sees a darkness in her eye he's never seen before and he's sure it's just grief, but he wonders, for just a moment, if she knew who he really was.

41
GRACE

SIX WEEKS LATER

I stay with Kira and Brooke in their Boston home while Brooke recovers. The press covered her miraculous discovery in the woods from a basement she escaped from that she can't locate. It was just like my story, and then the media moved on to new missing girls all around the country and every other wisp of celebrity gossip or political scandal that's happened since, and Brooke was forgotten, which suits all of them very well.

And it makes me wonder about that figure I saw—I'm sure I saw it—the flash of pale skin in the moonlight between the stretches of shadowy trees. Did Martin have another victim? Was he at the inn to access the cellar with that girl? Did I save her life? There was never a report of the incident, but that doesn't surprise me. So many girls disappear after dark—during the vanishing hour, and some make it back. Most don't. If there was a girl, I hope she's safe now.

I've been able to sit with Brooke and be someone who can truly understand what she's going through and it's changed me. Now I sit on the sofa in Kira's living room with Brooke curled up in a fleece blanket and a Hallmark Christmas movie playing on the television. She scrolls through her phone and smiles at something she's looking at. She's been out of the hospital a month and has most of her strength back now, and she'll have help—the way I never did—to handle it all emotionally, mentally. She has me and the fiercest mother I've ever met, so I feel like she really might be okay and not end up like me.

"Mom," she says, leaning back over the arm of the couch dramatically, just like a silly teenager should, as Kira makes popcorn in the kitchen behind us.

"What?" Kira asks, a beaming smile across her face that I haven't seen leave her face in weeks.

"Grace has literally never played a video game. Like ever," she says, and Kira comes in, placing a bowl of popcorn in the space between us.

"Well that's impressive if you ask me," Kira says.

"And she's never seen *Bridesmaids*. *Bridesmaids*!" she exaggerates and pushes my knee because we had conspired together when Kira was in the kitchen, since she'd suggested a documentary tonight, that we'd come up with a plan.

"You haven't seen *Bridesmaids*?" Kira then asks very seriously. "Everyone's seen *Bridesmaids*."

I shrug and push Brooke's knee back and Kira picks up the remote and starts scrolling all of her subscription channels until she finds the movie. Then she winks at me five minutes in, knowing she's been had.

The next morning, I have a train ticket back to Rock Harbor, and Kira makes me a travel mug of coffee and asks me to sit down a minute before I go.

We sit at the fancy marble kitchen island and she takes my hands in hers. She blinks back tears and squeezes my fingers.

"I can never repay you." She hangs her head a moment and regroups because we both promised no more tears.

"You don't have to keep saying that," I say softly.

"Listen, listen," she says, waving the air in front of her face, dismissing all her emotion. "Matt picks up the rest of his crap next week. Come and stay. Get the hell out of there. Stay as long as you need until you find… I don't know, college, a job you like, or stay forever. But just come back. You don't need to be there," she says, and I think my heart will burst, and there is a moment I hesitate to make sure she's really serious, because I've never in my life had a choice before—an option. Money. A place to go. And I do want out, so desperately.

"Yes, okay, if you think so," I say, circling my coffee mug with my finger because if I don't, I'll scream, *Yes, please, God. There's nothing I want more*, but she probably already knows that.

"Call me when you get things sorted out there and I'll pick you up. You can't fit all your stuff on a train. And shut up, it's no bother," she says, and I hug her tight.

And then I walk to the front door and see her bring Brooke a mug of coffee too, and they sit under the couch blankets together, knee to knee, and my heart is filled with a sort of joy I didn't know was possible.

42

KIRA

I didn't want to lie to Wes, but what choice did I have? I see it all play out the way Aden said it would—Martin blames Brady, says Grace was mistaken—she saw something familiar in him because he's Brady's father, but that his son is the real perpetrator here. Grace snapped and attacked him, and kept him against his will, a prisoner for days in a cellar. We all ganged up on him and we threatened to kill him if he didn't confess, so he had no choice. And then he'll find a way to make sure Brady's fingerprints and phone records seal the deal, and it's just our word against his with no evidence.

I think we'd win. I think all of us with the same story would certainly be enough, but Aden's right. What if? The deacon versus the drug addict. Our hysterical account against his calculated victim act he's been setting up for years. I can't take that chance—for Brooke and Grace, for Brady, for future girls out there, and so I have to come to peace with the fact that the police will continue to use resources to search for the still unknown monster. Is it more or less than they'd used for a long drawn-out trial we could potentially lose? At some point, Brooke's tragedy will be in a cold case file, and one day I'll tell her the truth, but right now, Wes Hendricks searching for weeks or months more, vowing to find the guy who did this, can't be my concern. They'll dead-end eventually.

I slip into a booth in the front window of a crowded café in Beacon Hill and blow on a cappuccino while I wait for Wes to arrive. When he does, he looks very different from the uniformed man without a smile. He's in jeans and a wool coat, and his face lights up when he comes in the front door and sees me waving at him.

I stand and hug him when he reaches the table. The hug lasts a long time, and I take in the feel of his cold skin and scent of spicy cologne clinging to his shirt collar, until I pull away and we sit across from one another.

"How is she?" he asks immediately, and I notice the waitress approach and then hesitate, somehow sensing she's interrupting something important. Wes looks at my coffee.

"Bourbon for me," he says. "Woodford Reserve if you have it." She nods and disappears into the crowded café, and I smirk at him.

"What? I'm never off duty it feels like, and Boston. Well, it's kind of like a vacation."

"I was just reacting to how fancy that sounded. I didn't know that about you."

"Lot you don't know about me," he says, and the shyness in his voice and his flushed cheeks makes it seem like an attempt at flirting.

"She's doing okay," I say, changing the subject. "She has

great doctors and she's getting the best therapy." I don't go into detail about the topic of whether rehab is necessary at this point, since she hasn't been on a drug in weeks, and had a short-lived relationship with them over the space of a summer, and that we are just taking healing a step at a time and monitoring it all. "She's being closely watched and she's still thinking about college next year, but she just needs time right now…and all the help I can throw at her, but she's strong as hell, so I mean, I'm hopeful."

"Well, I'm glad to hear it. When we spoke to her last, she didn't remember much."

"I don't blame her," I say.

"And I know you are tired of talking to us, but I have a couple more questions."

"I thought this was pleasure, not business," I say, beginning to feel cold sweat forming under my sweater.

"It is, it is. It's just one thing. You said you found her in the woods, east of Fog Creek, and you drove to the hospital. Mercy…which is west of the creek."

"Okay."

"But people—the nurses who were waiting out front after you called in, saw you rush in from the west. Eastbound to the front of the hospital."

"Wes, we've covered this. I was—I searched every inch of the freakin' state for weeks. It's dense woods. I might have been mistaken. I don't even remember what I said."

"No, I get that. You didn't call 911 though, and I know…"

"That it was faster for me to go, they never would have found us."

"Right," he says. "It's just that, and hear me out, Kira, I'm on your side. I'm just trying to get the story straight. The medical records—the doctors from the hospital, say it would be impossible for her to have been running through the woods.

She would have been too weak, dehydrated, she was only half-conscious when…"

"Did I say running?"

"You did."

"You understand I was out of my mind with relief and panic and…shock when I found her. I know it being a blur isn't convenient for you, but that's what it is. The woods are blinding—it all looks the same. I just don't remember."

"Okay," he says, softly reaching across the table and placing his hand on top of mine for a brief moment.

"It's just that we have disturbingly little to go on at this point, and I hate to tell you that. No DNA, no real suspects. Thousands of these sorts of cases go unsolved every year. We'll keep looking, but I just don't want you to be… I want you to be able to move on if we can't find the guy," he says. "If it turns cold like the other cases did." But there is something about the tilt of his head and the pitch of his chin, and the look in his eye that I can't decipher that makes me, just for a moment, wonder if he knows. Not the whole story, that's impossible, but if he has some kind of sense that I'm hiding something—that I know more.

"All I care about right now is that she's home."

"Of course," he says. "Just…at some point in the next couple weeks, you'll have to come in and answer some more questions for the record, now that we have more information. I know you hate Rock Harbor but we need the whole picture. And I know you want to help."

"Yeah. Okay," I say.

"Okay," he says, as if ending the business portion of the meeting, and when his drink is set in front of him, I order the same. And we talk about that summer years ago, and I always want to remember him that way—a blanket in the bed of his pickup by the river, ice-cream cones in the Dairy Queen parking lot, getting caught in the sprinklers on the football field after dark, June bugs and good-night kisses, burned CDs and wine coolers.

And when he kisses my cheek next to my car on the street and the snow starts to fall, he asks if he can come and see me again sometime. I say, "Of course," but I know I won't really let that happen even though I very much want it to because my lies would grow like a cancer between us. Then I marvel at the ripple effects of destruction that one man can cause.

I pull over for a moment on my way home when the tears begin to blur my vision, and I let myself finally really cry— for all of it. For lost love, for trust I'll never feel again, for the life that was robbed from us, for my damaged child, for all the things I haven't begun to process yet—the tough road in front of us, and what will happen if somehow we get found out.

And when there are no tears left, all I can hear is the low hum of traffic moving past and the murmur of a love song on a country radio station, and then my phone buzzes, and Brooke's face appears—something I feared I'd never see again, and my heart swells. And then plans for me to pick up brownie mix on the way home and take Hobbes to the dog park together is really all that matters in the world.

43

GRACE

It's a bitter January morning just after New Year's when my two weeks' notice is up and I'm all packed to leave. Vinny calls while I'm sitting in the lobby on top of three suitcases, waiting for Aden to stop in and say goodbye the way he insisted on doing before Kira picks me up.

"I've been thinking about you," I tell him, and he laughs a little.

"Me? Grace Holloway was sittin' there thinkin' about me. I'll never believe it," he says and chuckles.

"I just know you always liked this place, and... I don't know. You wanted something quiet...peaceful, so now that I gave my notice, what if you took over? I already told the owner you might call. Ya gotta write that book, right?" I say.

"You serious? You did that for me?" he says.

"Of course. I mean, if you want it."

"Grace Holloway, I'm sure gonna miss ya. Thank you. That's probably the nicest thing anyone's ever done for me, but I gotta stay put. It's my family business, even though it sucks a bag of dicks. Plus, there's lots of girls I still need to try to persuade to go home. Maybe not Amelia, but I gotta still try while I'm here," he says.

"Well if you change your mind," I say, and then I sip my tea and we talk for a little while about how he's ordering pickle chips for his shop and some customer who tried to pay with seventy-five rolls of quarters. Then I tell him Brooke is doing well and yes I know the snow forecast, and he tells me he's gotta go 'cause someone put a diaper in the slushy machine, and before we say goodbye, I tell him...

"You should come and visit when I'm settled somewhere," and I mean it.

I drag my suitcases near the front lobby door and watch as the snow lightly falls outside. When Aden pulls up, he has his daughter in the car and he only has a minute, and that's okay with me. I'm surprised when he pulls me inside the door into the lobby and we stand there one last time, away from his teenager's gaze. Our eyes meet.

"Hi," I say, shyly.

"Hi. I'm so glad I could see you before we leave." We stare at one another, and I don't know what to say.

"Florida, huh?"

"Yeah, yes. And...you. You're gonna go stay with Kira," he says. "That's—that's so great, I'm so glad you're getting out of here."

"Yeah. New start and all that." I look at the floor, not knowing how to act for some reason. There's a sharp pang of grief I can't explain at the thought of saying goodbye to him.

"Well, I'm happy for you," he says and gives a nervous

glance back outside, then back to me, hurriedly. "And, Grace," he says, and I meet his eyes, "I wish all the time that we met under different circumstances, I really do."

"Me too," I say, and then he cups the sides of my face with his hands and kisses me, and I kiss him back, the sudden bliss of it exploding into my heart and leaving me breathless, and something else… Happy. This is what happiness feels like. I don't want him to go, but of course he has to. He walks away. He pauses at the door and holds up one hand, a goodbye. I do the same, and then he's gone.

And even though I have to hold back the flood of tears as he drives away, I know it's better this way.

I got to have a first love, and a heartbreak…and a friend just like I always wished for.

When I notice, on top of my suitcase, a small blue collar with a silver tag reading "Hobbes." My cry turns into a sharp, sudden laugh and my heart is full. I latch the collar around Hobbes' little neck and he follows me as I step outside into the world, and I'm ready.

★ ★ ★ ★ ★